Dee Williams was born and brought up in Rotherhithe in East London, where her father worked as a stevedore in Surrey Docks. Dee left school at fourteen, met her husband at sixteen and was married at twenty. After living abroad for some years, Dee moved to Hampshire to be close to her family. She has written sixteen previous sagas including *Sunshine After Rain* and *Love and War*.

AFTER THE DANCE

It's late 1935 and Sue Reed is living with her parents in Rotherhithe, working in the office of local car dealer Fred Hunt. Pretty and vivacious, Sue has many admirers, including her best friend Jane's brother, Ron. But her main love is dancing, and Sue and Jane are always to be found at the local dance hall. When one night the band has a new singer, Cy Taylor, Sue can't help falling for him. Handsome Cy invites her to visit him in his hotel room . . . Afterwards, however, reality hits hard. For Cy has neglected to tell Sue he is married. And, just when she thinks life couldn't be worse, tragedy strikes. Will Sue ever find the love and happiness she craves?

Books by Dee Williams
Published by The House of Ulverscroft:

KATIE'S KITCHEN
FORGIVE AND FORGET
A RARE RUBY
LOVE AND WAR
SUNSHINE AFTER RAIN

DEE WILLIAMS

AFTER THE DANCE

Complete and Unabridged

CHARNWOOD
Leicester

First published in Great Britain in 2007 by
Headline Publishing Group, London

First Charnwood Edition
published 2008
by arrangement with
Headline Publishing Group
a division of Hachette Livre UK Limited, London

British Library CIP Data

Williams, Dee
    After the dance.—Large print ed.—
    Charnwood library series
    1. Pregnancy, Unwanted—Fiction 2. Unmarried
    mothers—Fiction 3. Great Britain—Social life
    and customs—*1918 – 1945*—Fiction 4. Rother-
    hithe (London, England)—Fiction 5. Domestic
    fiction 6. Large type books
    I. Title
    823.9'14 [F]

    ISBN 978–1–84782–087–7

Published by
F. A. Thorpe (Publishing)
Anstey, Leicestershire

Set by Words & Graphics Ltd.
Anstey, Leicestershire
Printed and bound in Great Britain by
T. J. International Ltd., Padstow, Cornwall

This book is printed on acid-free paper

I would like to dedicate this book to all lovers of the big-band era. It was a great time to go dancing.

Also especially for Colin, who provided me with the list of the hit parade in the 1930s. Many thanks, Colin.

I would also like to say a big thank you to Marion, who was my editor for many years, and now how much I am looking forward to working with Sherise.

I wish to thank the DVLA, who gave me all the information about driving tests, L-plates and licences. You really did need them in 1936.

1935

Sue Reed walked slowly along Rotherhithe New Road and waited at the bus stop, knowing that her best friend, Jane Brent, would be getting off the next bus. They lived next door to each other, so every evening when they finished work they would walk home together discussing what they had done and who they had seen at work. A slight breeze made Sue pull her cardigan tighter round her and she touched her navy beret, hoping that it would stay in place on her nondescript dark hair, which she now wore in a bob. Her parents had been upset when they saw what she'd had done to her long and naturally curly locks, but she was fed up with looking like a schoolgirl.

It was late September and summer was almost over; soon it would be autumn and with that came the dark nights. Sue, who was almost eighteen, a few months younger than Jane, who had had her birthday at the beginning of the month, smiled to herself. She and Jane didn't mind the dark nights, as when they went dancing on Saturdays or to their evening classes for ballroom dancing lessons, it was nice to walk home in the dark with a handsome young man. Although not all of them were that handsome,

1

with their spots and the cuts where they had tried to shave. And they had to make sure their parents didn't catch them giving the lads a goodnight kiss.

The girls had been friends all their lives. As children they'd squabbled and had fights but always made it up. To Sue, who was an only child, Jane was more like a sister than a friend, and she was very fond of her. They had both left school at fourteen. Jane had gone to work in the millinery department of the Co-op in Rye Lane. Sue had gone on to secretarial college; it was something her father had insisted on. He had said she needed a proper skill. At the time she had hated it, but now in many ways she was pleased she'd learned to type and do shorthand, as she had a good job working for Mr Hunt at Hunt's prestigious car showrooms in Rother-hithe New Road.

When the bus came in sight, Jane was standing on the platform. As usual she gave Sue a little wave and a huge grin. Last week Jane had also had her dark hair cut into a bob. Sue was a little envious of her friend's dead straight hair, not like hers, which had a mind of its own. Jane could have a Marcel wave and it would stay in place for days.

They walked along arm in arm, and although Jane was taller and rounder, they made an attractive pair, with their ready smiles and laughing eyes that often brought forth many admiring glances.

'Guess what?' said Jane after she'd returned a huge smile that one young man had given them.

'When I passed the town hall today the notice outside said that that band's going to be there again on Saturday the twelfth of October — you know, the one with that singer that makes you go all silly.'

'He don't make me go all silly,' said Sue.

Jane stopped and looked at her friend. 'Then why are you blushing just thinking about him?'

'I ain't blushing, it's just that I feel a bit warm.' She slipped her arms out of her cardigan, hoping to emphasise that point. But she did feel a warm glow just thinking about Cy Taylor. He reminded her of Tyrone Power; like her screen idol, he was tall, dark and very good looking. When he sang 'Sweet Sue', she thought it was for her alone, even though he didn't know her name. She had never spoken to him, but he still made her go weak at the knees. He had been to the town hall twice before, and each time, along with many other girls, she had stood in front of the bandstand drooling over him.

'You ain't listened to a word I've just said,' said Jane.

'Sorry, what did you say?'

'I said can we go to the pictures tomorrow night? They've got that film *Top Hat* on at the Astoria.'

'Why not? I love Fred Astaire and Ginger Rogers. Now, they *do* make me go all gooey.'

'Let's face it, anything with music in is wonderful.'

They continued walking, talking about their favourite films. Films and dancing were the two most important things in their lives. Soon they turned into Lily Road and walked along the row of terraced houses towards their gates. Sue lived at number twenty-four and Jane at twenty-six. Sue gave a little shudder when she saw Jane's brother Ron leaning on the gate and knew she would have to pass him.

''Allo, little Sue. You gonner come out with me?' When he grinned, his piggy eyes almost disappeared into his round podgy face.

'I've told you before, Ron, no I'm not.' She jumped back as his stubby fingers reached out to touch her.

'Why don't you like me?' He said it in a creepy way.

Ron was five years older than Jane. He had never been very bright at school, and had now grown into a big, lumbering, clumsy-looking man. Although Sue felt sorry for him, she had been frightened of him ever since she was small. She had never forgotten the evening when she was about four years old and had gone to the lav, and he'd held on to the door and wouldn't let her out. He'd kept telling her spiders and creepy-crawlies would come and jump on her. Everybody in Lily Road had an outside lav, and as there weren't any windows or a light in there it was very dark when you closed the door. Ron had stood outside laughing, while Sue cried and begged him to let her out. It was only when her screams and his laughter brought his mother out and she gave him a whack round the head that he let go of the door. The next day her father had put some wooden planks between the back yards to stop him coming through.

4

'I'll see you later, Jane,' said Sue, going to her front door and pulling out the key that hung on a string through the letterbox.

'All right,' said Jane as she too disappeared inside her house, leaving her brother standing at the gate grinning.

★   ★   ★

'Hello, love,' said Granny Potts, who was sitting in front of the fire. A large mirror hung over the ornate fireplace. Sue stood in front of it and took off her beret, watching as her hair sprang back into its natural waves. There was an oven at the side of the fire that her mother black-leaded daily, as well as whitening the hearth and polishing the brass fender. They didn't use that oven now, as they had one of the new gas stoves. Although it was Gran who did most of the cooking, it was her mother's pride and joy. She was very proud of being one of the first in the street to have one of the modern contraptions. Despite working as a cleaner at the school, Doris Reed was very houseproud and always seemed to be bustling about.

'Had a good day at work?' asked Gran.

Sue took off her cardigan and smiled. She loved her gran; she was there whenever she wanted someone to talk to. Her mother had always gone out to work, and when Sue was little Granny Potts had looked after her. She was a real old-fashioned Victorian-looking granny, with her almost white hair scragged back into a bun. She wore long black frocks and a flowery

5

wraparound overall over the top.

'I should say so. We had two new cars delivered today. Talk about posh. They're black Fords and ever so shiny.'

'Will that boss of yours take you out in one?'

'Dunno. He does sometimes, just to get the feel of 'em, so he says. But I reckon he just likes driving around showing everybody how well off he is.'

'And that he's got a pretty young lady sitting next to him. I reckon he likes you.'

'Oh Gran. He's an old man and I'm just the dogsbody who types his letters and makes the tea.'

'Well your dad reckons he's got a good business there, so he's got a lot to be proud of.'

'S'pose so. That dinner smells nice. What is it?'

'Shepherd's pie, and there's a rice pudding for afters.'

'Sounds good.'

Granny Potts smiled. She loved her grand-daughter, and would always be grateful that Charlie, her son-in-law, had let her come and live with them after her husband was killed. She did the cooking, which she enjoyed, and it made her feel wanted.

'Where's Mum?'

'Out the back, bringing in the washing.'

'I'll go and give her a hand.'

'There's a good girl. Your poor mum does work hard and those kids don't help; she said they'd spilt ink all over a couple of desks and she had to scrub 'em.'

'I'm sure she don't have to do that school

6

cleaning now I'm bringing in some decent money, and Dad always seems to be in work.'

'I know. But your dad could be off for days if no ships can get up the river. You know what your mother's like. She's a bit of a worrier.'

Sue knew all about the work in the docks. Her father had sometimes taken her there when she was home from school, and told her very proudly that being a stevedore was a better and more responsible job than just a docker. He had to make sure the ships were unloaded and loaded properly, otherwise they would turn over.

'I think she's scared that one day you'll get married and leave home.'

Sue laughed. 'I don't think so; well, not for years yet. I've got to find Mister Right first.'

Outside in the tiny yard, Doris Reed, her back to her daughter, was busy putting the clothes through the big mangle.

'All right, Mum?' asked Sue, taking one end of the sheet she was folding.

Her mother was thin and wiry and hardly ever sat down. 'Is that the time already? I'll have your father home soon; I'd better go and see to the dinner.' Although her mother did the cooking, Doris always liked to dish it up and put it on the table. 'Look, you can put this sheet through the mangle, then I won't have to iron it. I've done all the others.'

As Sue watched her mother go indoors, she took the folded sheet and, placing it on the heavy wooden rollers, began to turn the huge handle.

'You're too little to be doing a heavy job like that,' said Ron. He was standing behind the plank that served as a gate between the two houses. 'You look like a proper little housewife.'

'I like to help me mum,' said Sue, drawing herself up to her full five foot two inches. 'What about you? Do you help your mum?'

'Na, that's women's work.'

'But you're home all day.'

'Yer, I know.'

'No luck with a job, then?'

'Na.'

Sue knew Ron didn't stand much chance of getting work. Over the years he had had many jobs, mostly sweeping and other menial tasks, but had always walked out after a day or two, saying he wasn't going to be bossed about. Jane and her mother had given up on him.

Sue put the folded sheet in the basket and picked it up. 'See you later,' she called over her shoulder and made her way back into the house.

Her mother was looking out of the window. 'That boy will be the death of Maud, for all her going to church and praying for him,' she said as Sue walked in.

Sue laughed. 'I feel sorry for poor old Mrs Brent, but does she reckon the Good Lord will make him better?'

'Sue, don't blaspheme. The poor woman ain't been the same since Harry had that heart attack.'

'I'm sorry. I know.' Sue had been very upset when Jane's dad had died very suddenly two years ago. She knew how much her friend missed him. So far the family had managed on the pittance they'd got from selling their shoe repairing business, but they knew it wouldn't last for ever, and what if Jane wanted to get married and leave home? Sue didn't know how she'd feel if anything like that happened to her own dad. And what about Mrs Brent? Jane had been very worried about her mother when she started attending church sometimes twice a day. She helped the vicar and did the flowers, and said she was too busy with that to go out to work. She said the Lord would provide. Jane was used to the situation now, and accepted that as well as doing most of the cooking and housework, it was also down to her to provide. But she wasn't happy about the pictures of Jesus that hung from every wall, and the shrines dotted around everywhere. She was also concerned about the money her mother gave the vicar, who always seemed to be round at the house. Sue felt very sorry for her friend.

★   ★   ★

When Charlie Reed walked in, he didn't have his usual big smile that lit up his weatherbeaten face. He looked troubled as he took off his cloth cap, and his shock of dark hair sprinkled with grey sprang up. He put his cap in his jacket pocket, then slowly took off his jacket and hung it on the nail behind the kitchen door. Although not over tall, he was a broad, well-built man. He kissed his wife's cheek before she disappeared into the scullery, then turned and kissed his daughter.

'All right, Ma?' he said to his mother-in-law.

'Not bad, son,' she replied with a smile. 'Had a good day?'

With his foot on the shiny brass fender, he put his pipe on the mantelpiece next to the clock. Along with a selection of china knick-knacks, the mantelpiece was covered with a green cloth that had matching tassels hanging from it. Then he sat in the chair opposite Granny Potts and silently began to unlace his heavy black working boots.

'There's been a bad accident today,' he said at last.

Doris came back into the room carrying a dish. 'What happened?' She put the dish in the middle of the table.

'One of the tall cranes toppled over and the bloke in it got killed. Nasty business; had to have the big chiefs down to go over the situation.'

'How did it happen?' asked Granny Potts.

'Must have been picking up the load at the wrong angle.'

'Has the family been told?' asked Doris.

'Would think so. Can't keep that out the papers for long.'

Granny Potts looked at her daughter. 'Did you know him?' she asked her son-in-law.

'No, not really. Seen him around and knew he worked the cranes, but don't have a lot to do with them. Sorry about this, Ma.'

''S all right.' She gave him a weak smile.

Sue knew that her grandad had been killed at the docks, crushed by wood falling from a crane. She'd only been a baby when he'd died, and didn't remember anything about him.

Although she didn't know them, she felt very

sorry for the family of the man who'd been killed today. She looked round her own family; she loved them so much, and never wanted anything to change.

2

The following day as Sue entered the office, Mr Hunt came through the door that led to his flat above the showroom.

'Good morning, Susan, could you see to the post first.' He always called her Susan, as he said that Miss Reed made her sound old. 'I'm expecting an important invitation. It's the motor show next month and I've been invited to the Ford stand for a drink.'

'That's nice.' Before taking off her hat and coat, Sue began to look through the letters she'd picked up off the floor as she came in. Mr Hunt trusted her with a key to the office and she could let herself in, as he would sometimes be out with a client before she arrived.

'Have you been to the show before?' she asked.

Fred Hunt drew himself up to his full six foot. He was a powerful-looking man with darting dark eyes that never missed a thing. His small pencil moustache and almost black slicked-down hair all added to his swarthy good looks. He was a bit like Clark Gable, Sue thought; she always associated people with film stars. He wore expensive-looking suits with matching waistcoats and a gold watch and chain dangling across the front, and with two gold rings on his fingers it all smelt of money. He smiled. 'Been to the show, but never been invited to the stand before. Must be selling enough of those to keep the big boys happy.' He pointed at the cars sitting on the forecourt.

To Sue, her boss seemed like an old man, but her father said he thought he was in his early thirties. He was full of admiration for Fred Hunt. Hunt had taken his late father's little workshop, which had also sold spare parts for cars, and turned it into a thriving and prosperous business. Over the years he had bought the adjoining property, and now he sold new cars as well as second hand. He also had a workshop in the next street.

'I think this could be it,' said Sue as she handed him an expensive-looking envelope.

Smiling, he went over to his desk just as his phone rang.

As Sue got on with her work, she could hear her boss talking to a customer, sorting out a problem. To her he appeared to be a fair man, but he didn't stand for people who tried to get the better of him. More than once she'd seen him lose his temper, and a few times she had overheard him saying: 'Don't you try and get smart with Fred Hunt. Remember, I've been round the block a few times.' He had told Sue he was a Londoner born and bred. He was an only child, but he hadn't been spoilt and was brought up to be tough in a tough neighbourhood. He'd worked for his dad, helping with his coal round when he was still a schoolboy. He'd also told Sue that when his mother was a baby and her parents had come to England from Italy, life had been very hard for them.

All morning Sue checked invoices and hire purchase agreements and answered the phone when Mr Hunt left the office to see to a client. After lunch she was busy typing when her boss came up to her.

'What are you doing in two Saturdays' time? Not sure what the date is.'

'That's the twelfth of October.' Sue knew the date; she had been counting down the days. 'I'll be going dancing with me mate.'

'That's a pity.'

'Why?'

'I'm going to a Freemasons' do. It's a ladies' night, and I was wondering if you'd like to come along?'

Sue giggled. 'What, me? I ain't no lady.'

Fred gave her a beaming smile. 'And I certainly ain't no gent. Anyway, think about it.'

Sue thought about it. That was the night the Jeff Owen Band with Cy Taylor was going to be at the town hall. What should she do? Should she go out with her boss, or should she go and gaze at Cy Taylor? Suddenly she asked: 'Would I have to wear a long frock?'

Fred looked up from what he was doing. 'Yes. Would that be a problem?'

'Well, yes. You see, I ain't got one.'

'We can soon get over that. I'll give you an early Christmas box.'

'I can't take money from you. Besides, Christmas is months away.'

'I'd be very honoured if you would come with me, Susan.'

Sue blushed and looked away. She wanted to

ask why wasn't he taking one of the lady friends she'd seen around from time to time, though she knew they didn't usually last that long. What should she do? It was very tempting; she would be mixing with all those posh people and seeing how the other half lived.

'Can I think about it?'

'Certainly.'

★ ★ ★

Sue was still thinking about it when Jane got off the bus. She began telling her friend all about the invite she'd had.

'So, what you gonner do?'

'I don't know.'

'I thought we was going dancing. That's the night Cy Taylor's gonner be there.'

'I know, but this is really too much to turn down. He said we'll have a posh meal as well.'

'Why ain't he got a girlfriend his own age to take with him?'

'I don't know. He does have some but they don't seem to be around for long. Might just be after his money.'

'If you ask me, I reckon he's just a dirty old man who only wants to get you back to his flat and get inside your knickers.'

Sue giggled. 'Course he don't.'

'How do you know? You've only seen him at work; you don't know what these blokes are like when they've had a few drinks. Look at what's-his-name from the Co-op. He turned out to be a right bugger when I went out with him, hands like a bloody octopus.'

Sue laughed. 'D'you know, I reckon you're jealous.'

'No I'm not. It's just that I thought we'd be going dancing. And what about lover boy? I reckon he'll miss you.'

'Don't talk daft. He don't even know I exist.' Sue was still turning things over in her mind. She wanted to go to both. Why did they have to be on the same night? 'I've got to have a long frock.'

'Who's gonner pay for that?'

'He said he will; it's me Christmas bonus.'

'Sounds very fishy if you ask me. A bloke buying his secretary a frock.'

'Why?'

'Blokes of his age don't need to take young girls out or buy 'em frocks.'

'It's a ladies' night, and I think taking a lady is the proper thing to do.'

'Well I wouldn't go.'

Sue was upset. She wanted her friend to be more supportive. 'I'll see what me dad has to say about it.'

★   ★   ★

After they'd finished their meal that evening, Sue tried to sound casual as she said: 'Mr Hunt's asked me to go to a Masons' do with him Saturday after next.'

'What?' asked her father, looking up from his newspaper.

16

'You heard, Charlie,' said Gran. 'What did you say, love?'

'I said I'd think about it.'

'What a nice man,' said her mother, putting her sewing to one side. 'Wanting to take his secretary with him. I hope you're gonner say yes.'

'I dunno. I've got to wear a long frock.'

'That could be a bit of a problem,' said Doris. 'S'pose I could knock one up in time.'

Although her mother was a good dressmaker, Sue certainly didn't want a home-made frock. 'I couldn't let you do that, you've got too much to do as it is. Besides, Mr Hunt did say he'd give me the money for one.'

'What?' yelled Charlie, folding up his paper. 'I hope you turned his offer down. We ain't taking no charity.'

'He said it would be my Christmas bonus.'

'I bet. Christmas is bloody months away yet. I don't want any bloke buying my daughter frocks, do or no do.'

'Don't be so silly, Charlie,' said Doris. 'I think Mr Hunt must be a very lonely man not to have a lady friend to take with him. We should be flattered that he thinks our little girl's good enough to take to a posh do.'

'Hark at you two,' said Granny Potts. 'You'd think to hear you, Charlie, that he was gonner whisk her orf to the white slave market.'

'He could well have that in mind,' joked Charlie.

'Will you stop it. I ain't gonner be whisked off anywhere. If you don't want me to go with him, then I won't.'

17

'Well I think you should go,' said her mother. 'It will be nice for you to see how some people live, and if you turn him down you might not get another chance.'

Sue didn't answer.

'Could be really grand, love,' said her gran.

Sue looked at her father.

'Don't look at me, I'm only the dogsbody round here.'

Doris Reed stood up. 'I reckon we can afford to give you some money for a frock if you don't think I'll have enough time to make you one. That way you're not beholden to Mr Hunt. What d'you say, Charlie?'

'Could do, I suppose.'

'Good, that's settled. Saturday you can go shopping. D'you want me to come with you?'

It seemed to Sue that her mind had been made up for her. 'I'd rather go with Jane if you don't mind, Mum. Her half day's on Thursday, so I'll ask Mr Hunt if I can have extra lunchtime. I can meet her at the Co-op and we can go up West.' Sue knew that Jane wasn't happy that she had to work all day Saturday, and some evenings until nine o'clock.

'Please yourself.'

'I'll just pop next door and tell her.' With that she was out of the door. Was she doing the right thing?

* * *

'Hello, Sue love,' said Mrs Brent. 'Come on in. Jane's in the back room. I've got the vicar in here

18

just offering up a little prayer for me.'

She opened the front-room door and Sue could see the vicar sitting in an armchair drinking tea. He gave her a nod.

Sue made her way down the passage to the kitchen and found Ron there.

'Well if it ain't little Susan from next door. You come to take me out?'

'No I ain't, Ron. Where's Jane?'

'I'm here.' Jane walked in behind her. 'I was upstairs. And Ron, behave, otherwise I'll send the Reverend in here to talk to you.'

Ron blanched. 'No, Jane, don't do that. I'll behave.' With that he sat at the table.

In many ways Sue felt sorry for Ron. One minute he was full of bravado, the next he behaved like a little boy.

'I've decided. I'm going to that do with Mr Hunt and I was wondering if you'd come up West with me to get a new frock.'

'When you thinking of going?'

'Could you come on Thursday?'

'You gonner take time off?'

'No, but I think he might let me have a longer lunch hour. I could meet you outside the Co-op.'

'You gonner let him pay for it?'

'No. Me mum and dad said they'd give me the money.'

'Bloody lucky, ain't you?' Sue could see her friend wasn't happy about that. 'All right, I'll come.'

'Will you go to the dance?' Sue asked tentatively.

19

'No. I ain't going to a place like that on me own.'

'Won't someone at work go with you?'

'Dunno.'

Sue could see that she had upset Jane. But there would be other times when Jeff Owen's band and Cy Taylor would come to the town hall.

★ ★ ★

Fred sat back in his chair and tried to concentrate on the book in front of him. He did so hope that Susan would come with him to the Masons' do.

He'd never realised when he first employed Susan that he would fall in love with her. She was just a slip of a girl, but over the last couple of years she had blossomed into a beauty. She was always smiling and nothing seemed to upset her; even when a customer came in ranting and raving, she could always calm them down.

Sometimes it took him all his will power to stop himself from thumping the blokes who came in and started to throw their weight about. He had been brought up the hard way and was a tough nut. Fighting had always come easy to him.

From a young age Fred used to help his dad delivering heavy sacks of coal on his horse and cart. He'd always admired his dad; he was a clever man who wanted to go far. When cars began to come on the scene, he taught himself to do repairs and passed his skills on to his son.

Between them they expanded the business and when Fred's father died, his mother went to live with her sister Rosa in Surrey, and Fred used the few bob his father had left him to employ people to work for him. When he turned thirty, he bought this showroom with the flat above. He'd had to do a bit of wheeling and dealing in his time and pay for a few favours, but he also had contacts who would help if need be.

Just as he settled down again the phone rang. Fred looked at the clock; he knew that would be his mother checking on him.

3

On Thursday lunchtime Sue was waiting outside the Co-op for Jane to finish work. She was excited; she was going up West to buy a long frock. She'd seen what she fancied in the magazines that she and Jane were always poring over. It was one with a petal hem that had caught her eye; she'd never had a long frock before and knew that was the style she wanted.

'You took your time,' she said when she saw Jane.

'I can't go gallivanting off whenever I fancy it.'

Sue wasn't sure if she'd done the right thing asking Jane along; she had been a bit offhand since she'd first heard about the do. Sue knew she had to keep this as light-hearted as she could. 'Right, let's be off,' she said.

As they began looking in the big store windows, Sue was astonished at the prices. She pressed her nose against the glass and drooled over a flimsy green petal dress that had a little gold bolero over. 'I'd love that, but look at the price.'

'Three guineas,' said Jane. 'Who'd spend that much on one frock? That's twice as much as I get in a week.'

'Me dad only gave me two pounds. I can't afford any of those, let alone shoes to go with it.'

'You're gonner get shoes as well?'

'Well I can't go in me ordinary dance shoes,

they might not match.'

'If you ask me, you're making too much of this do. When you gonner wear a frock like that again?'

'Dunno.' Even Sue was beginning to have doubts. It was a lot of money just for one night.

'Should have stayed in Peckham; you don't pay all these fancy prices there.'

'What's the Co-op got?' Sue asked, tearing herself away from the window.

'Dunno, ain't never had to look at long frocks,' said Jane irritably.

Sue knew that it had been a mistake asking Jane along. They had always been such close friends and she'd wanted to involve her, but it wasn't to be. 'I think we'd better go home. I'll see what's around Peckham on Saturday.'

★　★　★

'Did you get something pretty?' asked Fred Hunt later that day when Sue walked into the office.

She shook her head. 'The ones I liked cost a lot more than I had.'

Fred Hunt didn't reply. He looked over at his slim, pretty dark-haired secretary. He would happily give Susan Reed anything she wanted. He had been fond of her for a very long while, but knew because of the age difference that he had to keep his feelings under control. He would bide his time, give her a chance to mature and flourish. Taking her to the Masons' do was the first step to many outings he had planned.

Sue sat at her desk. She was very disappointed

that Mr Hunt hadn't bothered to comment. Had he changed his mind about taking her?

All afternoon she worked, but her heart wasn't in it and she was pleased when it was time to cover her typewriter and go home.

★　★　★

'Did you get anything nice?' asked Gran as soon as Sue walked in.

Sue shook her head.

'That's a pity.'

She gave her gran a big smile. 'Everything was a bit too posh for me. I'm going to Peckham on Saturday.' She wasn't going to tell the family that the things she had liked were too expensive; that would have upset her dad.

'I still reckon I've got time to make you one,' said her mother.

Sue smiled. 'Let's see what happens on Sat'-day.'

★　★　★

When Sue finished work on Saturday she went to Peckham and wandered around the department stores there, finishing up at the Co-op. She gave Jane a smile as she went through the millinery department, where a lady was trying on a lovely big black floppy hat, but didn't stop to speak to her as she didn't want to get her into trouble. Jane had told her that one girl had got the sack through talking to a friend.

When she walked into the dress department

24

she saw the frock of her dreams. It was pale blue and floaty, with a petal hem, and the label said it was only one and a half guineas. She could easily afford that, and it would leave her enough for some shoes and maybe a handbag. She held the dress up against her as the sales assistant came over.

'Would you like to try it on?'

'Yes please.'

'Follow me.'

Sue suddenly felt very grown up, and when she put the dress on and twirled round, it was as if her world had changed. She wasn't a little girl wearing a home-made frock; this was a proper shop-bought one, and with its back cut almost to her waist, she knew she looked like a film star.

'I'll take it,' she said, coming out of the changing room.

'Do you know your Co-op number?'

Sue smiled. Not only was she buying a dress she loved, but her mum would be over the moon at getting her divi on it.

She almost skipped from that department to get new shoes and a handbag.

★　★　★

'Well, did you have any luck this time?' asked Gran as soon as she walked in.

'I should say so.' Even before taking off her hat and coat, Sue brought out her treasure. 'Mum, Mum, come and look at this.'

Doris Reed came into the kitchen wiping her hands on the bottom of her pinny just as Sue

25

held up her dress. 'Oh my. That's a bit flimsy.'

Sue tried not to register her disappointment. 'It's the very latest, and I got it in the Co-op, so you'll get your divi on it as well as on me shoes and handbag.'

'You bought shoes and a handbag?'

Sue nodded with a big grin.

'Go and try it on, love,' said her gran.

In her bedroom she stood and looked at herself in the full-length mirror on the front of her wardrobe. If only I could wear this to see Cy Taylor, he would certainly notice me then, she thought As she walked down the stairs she tried to move like she'd seen the models do, holding her frock up carefully and trying to be sophisticated and graceful.

She pushed open the kitchen door.

'Oh love. You look like a princess,' said Granny Potts.

'It's a bit daring,' said her mother. 'Turn round.'

Sue did as she was told.

Her gran laughed. 'I'll tell yer something, girl, you won't be able to wear your vest under that.'

'I think you should have a cardi or something,' said her mother.

'I can't wear a cardi,' said Sue in alarm. 'It would ruin the whole effect.'

'Well I don't know what your father's gonner say when he sees it.'

'I hope he likes it.'

'I'm sure he will, love,' said her gran. 'Doris, you've got to realise your little girl's growing up.'

'I know that, Mum, don't I?' said Doris Reed,

adding under her breath as she went back into the scullery, 'And I don't like it.'

* * *

Sue brought out her dress when her father came in. 'Well, Dad. What d'you think? D'you like it?'

He looked a bit taken aback. 'I dunno. It ain't gonner keep you very warm.'

Sue laughed. 'It ain't supposed to keep me warm.'

'I told her she couldn't wear her vest,' chuckled her gran.

'I still think she should have a cardi or something to wear over.'

'I agree with your mother. You're going out with your boss, and, well, you don't want to be showing yourself off too much.'

Suddenly Sue felt deflated. They didn't know anything about fashion. She was going to be mixing with some posh people and she didn't want to appear like some country bumpkin. She suddenly had an idea. 'I'll tell you what. One frock I saw had this little gold bolero over. What if you made me something like that? Would you have time, Mum?'

'I should think so. Go back to Rye Lane and get a pattern and the material and I reckon I could knock one up tomorrow.'

Sue ran and kissed her mother's cheek. She knew now that they would be happy, and she could always take it off when she got to the hall.

* * *

As Sue was preparing to leave the office on Saturday lunchtime, Fred Hunt said, 'I'll pick you up about seven.'

Sue smiled. 'D'you know Lily Road?'

'Course. Now be off with you.'

Sue hurried home. Tonight she was going to be dressed up and going in a posh car to a grand do.

At seven o'clock, her mother called from the front room: 'He's here.'

Sue came from the kitchen clasping her new gold clutch bag. 'Do I look all right?' she asked.

'You look a picture.'

'Just told her that,' said her gran, who was right behind her. 'That little jacket just finishes it off a treat.'

'Knew it would,' said Doris.

'You're very clever, Mum. Now I'd better be off.'

Her father came out of the front room. 'He's got one of these new Fords. Looks a real nice car.'

Sue left the house. She didn't want to turn round in case Jane was looking out of her window. She still felt very guilty at not going to the dance with her.

But it wasn't Jane who was standing watching Sue; it was Ron, and he was cursing under his breath: 'You wait. I'll show him. Taking my girl out in a posh car.'

4

As her boss was driving her home he asked, 'Did you enjoy yourself tonight?'

When they had first entered the large hall, Sue had felt intimidated, but Fred Hunt had gently taken her elbow and steered her through the throng, nodding now and again at various people and exchanging a few words with others. When he found their table, he very quickly put her at ease and made her feel grown up, and she wasn't going to let him down.

'It was wonderful. I've never been to a do like that. All that lovely food, and the music.' Sue lay back against the car's soft leather upholstery.

'By the way, you looked very nice tonight. I admire your taste. That's a lovely frock.'

'Thank you.' She suddenly sat up. 'I didn't know you could dance so well, Mr Hunt.'

'As far as being able to dance, that was 'cos I had lessons from me ma. And Susan, please, call me Fred.'

'I can't do that. You're me boss. It wouldn't be proper.'

He laughed. 'That's one of the things I like about you: you don't take advantage. Some women I've been out with would be throwing drinks down their throats all evening, but you, you only had one.'

'I know. Remember, I've never tasted wine before.'

'Did you like it?'

'Not that much.'

'Nor me, I'm a beer man meself.'

All evening he had watched the way she glowed. Her slim figure and the very fashionable dress even had one or two ladies giving her the once-over. And the innocent excitement in her eyes was something he would always remember. When he was dancing with her, he could see some of the blokes were giving her the eye, and he knew if they hadn't been with their own partners they would have been vying for a dance. She was young and refreshing and he'd had a few comments about her when he was in the Gents. There had been a couple of remarks from one bloke who at any other time he would have willingly punched on the nose, but he didn't want to cause a fuss, not here, not tonight.

'Besides, I'm more interested in dancing and listening to the music, and me dad told me not to drink too much,' she said, breaking into Fred's thoughts.

'Sensible man, your father.'

He turned the car into Lily Road. The lights were still on in number twenty-four.

'Looks like someone's waiting up for you,' said Fred, stopping the car and going round to her side.

'I expect it's Dad.'

'Well, he can see that I've delivered you home safe and sound.' He held the car door open for her and helped her out.

'Thank you, Mr Hunt, for a really nice evening. I had a lovely time and I shall remember this for a long, long while.'

He grinned. 'So will I. And if you ain't married by this time next year, perhaps we could do it again.'

'I'd like that. Good night.'

'Good night, Susan.' As she walked away he would have loved to have taken her in his arms and kissed her long and hard, but he knew she would never mix business with pleasure, so there was no way he was going to rush things. As far as he had gathered from their conversations, there wasn't any spotty youth on the scene; after all, she was still very young. He gave her a wave as he drove away.

Sue glanced at next door's window. It was very late and she knew Jane would be home from the dance by now; if she had gone at all, that is. When they'd last spoken, Jane still hadn't known if one of the girls from work was going with her or not. Sue knew her friend's bedroom was at the back, but would she be in the front room looking out for her?

Someone was indeed watching her from the dark room, but it wasn't Jane. Ron stood back from the window when Sue stepped out of the car. He'd been there all evening waiting for his girl. When he'd seen the car draw up, he'd clenched his fist in anger. One day when he, Ron Brent, was married to Sue, she wouldn't have to work for that flash bloke any more. 'Good night, my darling,' he whispered softly and blew her a kiss as she went into her house.

As Sue opened the front door, her father was standing at the kitchen door.

31

'Don't make a noise. Your mum and gran's in bed,' he whispered. 'Did you have a nice time?'

She nodded, and when she'd closed the kitchen door behind her said, 'Oh Dad. It was wonderful. It was like being in a different world. I've brought the menu home so you can see what we had to eat, and look at me present. Every lady got one.' She opened her bag and brought out a gold-coloured powder compact.

Her father smiled. 'That's nice. Must have cost someone a pretty penny. I'll look at it in the morning, and you can tell us all about it then. I'm off now.' He kissed the top of her head. 'And Sue, you looked very nice. I was very proud of you.'

'Thanks, Dad. Good night.'

Charlie Reed left his daughter with her thoughts. She was turning into a very beautiful young lady, he reflected. How long would it be before they had blokes banging on the door for her? At first he hadn't been worried about her going out with her boss, but after seeing how grown up she looked, doubts began creeping in. As he climbed the stairs, the thought that filled his mind was: I don't want her to leave us, but he knew that it would happen one day.

Sue sat in the armchair and went over the evening. It had been almost magical. It was something she would never forget. And her frock . . . She knew she looked good, as she noticed one or two ladies looking at her and nodding their approval. She took off her little gold bolero; it had matched her shoes and bag perfectly. Holding it up, she smiled. Her mother had made a wonderful job of it. In the Ladies Sue had even been asked where she'd bought it. That comment would really please her mum.

★ ★ ★

The following morning over breakfast, Sue told the family all about her evening.

'I must go and tell Jane about it,' she said as she helped her mother with the washing-up.

'Don't be too long. I know what you two are like when you start chattering.'

Sue hung the tea towel on the nail behind the back door and made her way to her friend's.

'Hello, little Sue,' said Ron, opening the door as soon as she knocked.

'Hello, Ron. You was quick. Was you waiting behind the door?'

'Course not.' But he'd heard Sue call out to her mother that she wouldn't be long, so he had waited behind the door for her.

'Is Jane up yet?'

'Course I am,' said Jane, coming slowly down the stairs. She looked sleepy and dishevelled. 'Do you have to be so cheerful first thing?'

'I'm very happy.'

'So I see. Can't understand why, after staying out half the night.'

'I wasn't out half the night.'

Ron touched his nose and grinned. He knew better. He knew exactly what time she had got home.

Sue ignored his gesture. 'Your mum gone to church?'

'What do you think?'

'Could we go up to your bedroom?' Sue asked her friend. She didn't want to talk to Jane in front of Ron.

'S'pose so.' Jane turned and mounted the stairs, with Sue following close behind.

'Did you go to the dance last night?' asked Sue, closing the door.

Jane nodded.

'And?'

'And what?'

'What was Cy like?'

'Good as always.'

'Did he sing 'Sweet Sue'?'

'Yes.'

'And did he look round for me?'

'No. I don't think so.'

Sue sat on the crumpled bed. 'I had a nice time last night.'

'That's good.'

Sue was disappointed that Jane wasn't enthusiastic about her evening. 'D'you want to hear about it?'

Jane shrugged. 'If you want.'

Sue stood up. 'I know you're jealous of me going, but I would have thought you'd have shown a bit more enthusiasm. I would have done if it had been the other way round.' She moved over to the door. 'Ain't no point in me staying if we've got nothing to talk about.' She flung open the door to find Ron outside. 'And what d'you want, creep?' She was very angry with Jane and her brother, and as she ran down stairs the tears began to fall.

'I'm sorry, Sue,' called Jane. 'Come back.'

At the bottom of the stairs Sue turned. 'I only wanted to share it with you.'

'Come on back up. I'm sorry.'

Slowly Sue went to her friend.

Jane put her arm round her. 'It's just that I don't want that dirty old man getting his hands on you.'

'He ain't a dirty old man,' sniffed Sue. 'He was very polite.'

'Did he kiss you?' asked Ron, who was now in the bedroom with them.

'No he didn't, and besides, what I do is none of your business.'

'It will be my business when I marry you.'

Both Jane and Sue laughed.

'I don't think so,' said Sue as she wiped her nose.

'You just wait and see, little Miss Sue Reed.'

It was said slowly and very menacingly, and Sue looked quickly at Jane, who said to her brother, 'You know what, Ron, you can talk a right load of rot sometimes.'

'We shall see.' He left the bedroom and went downstairs.

Jane turned to Sue. 'Now tell me about last night.'

Sue settled herself on the bed and began telling Jane about her wonderful evening. After she had finished, and had shown Jane her gift, she stood up. 'I'd better go. Mum'll want me to help her.'

'I'm sorry I was a bit of a cow earlier on. I am really glad you had a nice time. And I bet your frock looked really good.'

'Thanks.' Sue wasn't sure if Jane meant it. Would this be the beginning of them falling out?

As Sue went down the stairs, Ron was standing with his back to the front door. His dark eyes were like slits in his podgy face. 'I mean it, little Sue. I am gonner marry you,' he hissed.

Sue smiled, but she was irritated that he was blocking her way. 'Can I come past, please?'

'Not till I get a kiss.'

'Come off it, Ron. Get out the way.'

He grabbed her shoulders and held her tight, his fingers digging into her flesh. Then he forced his lips on hers, hard and demanding.

Sue began raining punches on his broad shoulders. When at last he let her go, she ran the back of her hand across her mouth and shouted, 'Get out me way, you bloody animal.'

'What's going on down there?' asked Jane from the top of the stairs.

'Ask him.' Sue opened the front door and ran.

Next door she went straight out to the lav. She wanted to be sick. Ron's bad breath had made her feel ill.

'What's wrong with her?' asked her mother.

'Might have an upset stomach. All that rich food last night, she ain't used to it,' said her gran.

When Sue came in, she agreed that Gran might be right. There was no way she would tell her parents what had really happened. Suddenly she was frightened of Ron. He was a big, strong man and was capable of anything. She would have to be very, very careful of him from now on.

5

It was a cold, dark Friday evening in November. As the girls walked home, the icy wind whipped round their legs. Sue wasn't worried about the weather; she had so much to look forward to this weekend. On Sunday she would be eighteen, but the best present she could have would be tomorrow evening, when Jeff Owen's band was coming to the town hall. Sue and Jane were busy discussing what they were going to wear to the dance.

'Wish I could wear me long frock.'

'It'll look a bit out of place there.'

'Might be able to wear it at a Christmas Eve do.'

'I said all along you'd only get to wear it once, didn't I?'

'He might ask me to go again next year.'

'If he does, you can't wear that frock again, not to the same do. Besides, he might have a girlfriend by then.'

'Could be. But I ain't seen one around.'

'Would you go with him if he asked?'

'I should say so. Best night of me life.' Although they hadn't spoken of it since the day after, Sue knew that even a month later it still niggled her friend. She hadn't told Jane how disappointed she'd been when Fred Hunt hadn't invited her to the motor show last month. Had she let him down?

37

'What's your mum and dad getting you for your birthday?' Jane asked.

'Dunno. Dad was saying it ain't easy now he can't buy toys. I expect they'll give me money, though I told them I was more than happy with having my frock and that'll do for me birthday.'

'I wish I had a dad to give me money.'

Sue suddenly felt very guilty. She had it all: a mum, a dad and a gran who loved her.

'Would be a help if Ron could hold down a job, especially with Christmas coming,' Jane continued. 'Mum was having a go at him last night. She reckons he could get a sweeping job somewhere. We was wondering about Fred Hunt; does he want a cleaner?'

Sue took a breath. The last thing she wanted was to have Ron around her all day. Since he'd kissed her, she had made sure to keep well away from him. She still cringed at the thought of it. 'Dunno. We have a lady in to sweep the office.'

'What about cleaning the cars?'

'Dunno,' she repeated, trying to think of the right thing to say. 'He mostly does that himself. Now and again he has a kid in on Sat'day morning and sometimes in the school holidays, but he don't reckon anyone polishes 'em like he does.'

'Now that winter's here he might need someone to do it, and as you get on so well with him, you could ask.'

'Suppose so.' What could she say? She knew Mrs Brent was desperate to get her son out to work, but the thought of having Ron near her all day made her feel sick.

Jane tucked her hand through Sue's arm. 'Thanks. That'll be the best Christmas present me mum could have, our Ron in a proper job.'

★　★　★

At work the following morning, what Jane had asked her to do was still turning over in Sue's mind. She hadn't mentioned it to her parents, as she didn't want them to know how Ron had behaved towards her. She looked out of the window and was pleased to see that her boss was busy with clients; hopefully he wouldn't have a chance to chat. She was worried about asking him about a job for Ron. Apart from her own fears, Ron was also very unreliable.

Fred Hunt came into the office rubbing his hands together. He went over to the paraffin heater that stood next to Sue's desk and held his hands above it. 'It's a bit parky out there. Still, we've had a good morning. Sold two new ones; that'll help push the money up for Christmas. You can go off now, Susan. Shouldn't get too many wandering in now, as it looks as if we're in for some snow. If I get any sales I'll sort the hire purchase agreements out and you can type them up on Monday.'

'Thank you.'

Fred glanced anxiously through the window. He was waiting for an acquaintance who had got hold of a stolen car and was selling it cheap, and he didn't want Susan to be around as this one wasn't going through the books.

She turned and gave him one of her dazzling

smiles. 'Do you go anywhere for Christmas?' she asked casually as she covered her typewriter.

'Only to me ma's.'

Sue knew his mother lived in Surrey with her sister. 'That's nice. I expect she's always pleased to see you.'

'S'pose she is, although her and Aunt Rosa can be a bit much at times. Thank goodness I get on all right with her husband. Now be off with you before the weather turns and you have a job to get home.'

'Thanks. Bye.'

As she walked home, Sue felt guilty about not mentioning Ron. She would tell Jane that they had been too busy and she would do it on Monday morning. With her head down against the sleet that was now beginning to fall, she began to worry about the weather. What if Cy Taylor and the band couldn't get to the dance? What a letdown that would be.

Her thoughts went to last night and the extra trouble she'd taken with her bath and hair-washing. The tin bath was always brought into the scullery on Friday nights. The heat from the fire under the big copper warmed the room, but stepping out on to the cold flagstones wasn't so good. It didn't take her long to dry herself and put on her winceyette pyjamas and warm dressing gown. Friday nights in the winter were nice and snug, as she sat drying her hair in front of the fire, drinking cocoa and listening to the wireless with her family round her.

★　★　★

When she got in, she could see that her mother had propped her slippers in front of the fire so they would be nice and cosy.

'Come into the warm before you catch your death,' Doris said, hovering round her.

'It's freezing out there. Hello, Dad. What you doing home this early?'

'Been waiting for a ship to dock, but it won't be in till tomorrow. I hope you ain't thinking of going out tonight?' said her father.

'Dunno. I'll have to wait and see what Jane wants to do.'

'You'll both want your heads examined if you go out in that lot,' said her gran. 'This could end up being a blizzard and you'd soon get lost.'

Sue laughed. 'I don't think so. Besides, we'll be on a bus.'

'No you won't. Not if they stop running,' said her father.

Sue began to get worried. She desperately wanted to see Cy Taylor again. 'It might all blow over before we go out.' She knew that sounded pathetic.

For the rest of the afternoon she watched as the snow-drifts began to build up. 'I hope Jane manages to get home all right,' she said as she came in from the lav.

Doris Reed wiped the condensation off the inside of the scullery window with her hand. 'It really is bad out there. I don't want you risking life and limb just to go to a dance.'

Sue knew that her hopes of seeing Cy Taylor tonight were diminishing by the minute, but she would willingly go through hail, fire and storm if

41

she thought he would notice her and kiss her and . . .

'Did you just hear what I said?'

'Yes, Mum.'

That evening, when Jane finally got home, her mother popped in to tell Sue that she was too tired to go out.

'She had to walk all the way home. She said she could hardly see her hand in front of her. When it started to get late, I just got down on my knees and prayed.' She smiled. 'I knew the good Lord would look after my little girl.'

After Mrs Brent had left, Sue sat and gazed into the fire. She felt very sorry for Jane having to walk home in this weather. She started to think about Cy. Why was everything so against her? How long would it be before she saw the love of her life again? She knew that the next time she saw him, she would certainly make sure he knew she existed.

★ ★ ★

On Sunday, Jane came in for tea.

'That's a lovely birthday cake you've made,' she said to Mrs Reed as she admired its blazing candles. 'You're very lucky,' she said to Sue.

'I know,' said Sue.

'I'll cut you a piece to take in to your mum,' said Mrs Reed.

'Thank you. She'll like that. Now come on, Sue, blow out your candles and don't forget to make a wish.'

Sue did as she was told.

'So what did you wish for?' asked her gran.

'I ain't telling, or else it won't come true.' Sue looked at Jane and grinned.

After they'd finished tea, they played cards, and all the while Sue was thinking of what she'd wished for.

'If you ask me, you're making too much of that bloke,' whispered Jane when they were alone, for she had guessed her friend's wish.

'I can't help it.'

'What if he's married? Why waste your time thinking about him?'

'I'll let you know when I find out more about him.'

'By the way, did you ask your boss about a job for Ron?'

'No, I didn't get a chance as we was too busy, but don't worry, I'll do it first thing in the morning. It'll be a lot quieter then.'

Jane looked at her suspiciously.

★   ★   ★

On Monday when Sue got to work, she knew she had to ask Mr Hunt about Ron. To her surprise, he told her to send Ron along to see him.

That night, when she met Jane and they walked home together, she said, 'By the way, can you tell Ron to come and see Mr Hunt tomorrow.'

'Thanks. Mum will be ever so pleased. I've got some good news for you as well. Your dreamboat is going to be at the town hall on Christmas Eve.'

Sue was almost jumping for joy. 'Please don't

let there be any snow that night. You'll have to ask your mum to pray for us.'

'Don't talk daft.'

'Well it's weeks away yet, so it should be all right.'

'That snow was awful. I never thought I'd get home. It was all right for you; you were home before it really came down. It was ankle deep in places; me feet were like blocks of ice.'

'Thank goodness most of it's gone by this morning.'

'Don't forget I don't finish till late on Christmas Eve.'

'I know, but don't worry, we'll get there.'

'Just hope I ain't too tired after being run off me feet all day.'

'You'll be fine when you hear that music.'

'Hope so.'

★   ★   ★

Ron had been working at Hunt's garage for three weeks, and Jane was telling Sue how much he enjoyed it. 'He ain't stopped talking about it. He reckons your boss is gonner teach him to drive.'

'Heaven help us all if and when that happens.' Sue still couldn't believe that Mr Hunt had taken him on. She had started dreading going to work, as Ron insisted on walking with her and walking her home again at night, though only as far as the bus stop, as he didn't like to hang around waiting for Jane.

'Do you see much of him during the day?' asked Jane.

'No. I'm busy in the office.' She wasn't going to tell Jane that she made sure she was always doing something so she didn't have to talk to him. But she was surprised at how well he got on with Mr Hunt.

'He was saying what a nice bloke your boss is.'

'I know. Now, about Christmas Eve.'

'What about it?'

'What time d'you reckon we'll get there?'

'I dunno. As I said, I have to work till late. The store don't close till nine, then we have to cover everything up, so I won't be home till after ten.'

'Wouldn't have thought many people would want a new hat for Christmas.'

'You never know.'

Sue would have loved to tell Jane she would go ahead and meet her at the town hall, but she didn't think that would go down very well.

★   ★   ★

The build-up to Christmas was always exciting, and when her father brought home the Christmas tree and it stood in pride of place in the front room, Sue happily decorated it while her father was busy putting up colourful paper chains.

Mr Hunt put a small tree in the showroom and gave Sue the job of hanging the baubles and tinsel on it. He stood at the window and watched the joy on her face.

'She's like a little girl, ain't she?' said Ron, coming up to him. 'I always call her my little Sue, 'cos she's small and cuddly.'

Fred Hunt turned quickly and looked at him. He had noticed that Sue avoided Ron whenever she could. Did she dislike him? But she had got him the job. Should he ask her what she thought of him? Did she feel sorry for him? He knew Ron was a bit slow, but he did his job well enough. What could he say?

On Christmas Eve, business was very slow. Fred came into the office and sat at his desk. 'Could you make up Ron's wages?'

Sue was shocked. 'Why? What's he done?'

'Nothing. I said when I took him on that I'd only need him for a couple of weeks, and as there's not a lot doing, I'm letting him go today. Are you worried about it?'

'No.' Sue looked out of the window. Ron was carefully polishing the windscreen of a new car and grinning at everybody who walked past. 'He didn't tell me it was only for a few weeks.'

'No point in keeping him on, not at this time of the year. I told him to come back in the spring if he ain't settled in a permanent job.'

'Does he know he's going today?'

'Yes.'

Sue couldn't believe it. What would Jane and her mother say? They had been over the moon at Ron getting a job. She got the wages ledger out and began writing down how many hours Ron had done this week.

'Oh, and Susan, put an extra pound in his pay packet as a Christmas box.'

'That's very generous of you.'

'Well, the spirit of Christmas and all that.'

'He'll be very pleased with the extra pound.'

'And we might as well call it a day. There's not a lot going on now and it's beginning to get dark.' He gave her a beaming smile.

Sue counted out two pounds ten shillings from the petty cash tin and put it in a brown envelope. Although she didn't want to, she asked, 'Shall I take this out to him?'

'No. I'll do it.'

Sue was pleased about that, although she would still have to face him and the family. Why hadn't Ron told them the job was only temporary? She was dreading going home with him. Today Jane was working late, so they would be walking all the way home together.

When it was time to go, Ron came into the office. 'I think you've made a mistake,' he said, coming up close to her.

'What d'you mean?'

'I've got too much money here.' He looked over his shoulder at Mr Hunt, who was still outside. 'I know you like me, little Sue, but you might get into trouble if the boss finds out.'

'No, Ron, you've got it wrong. I didn't do it. It was Mr Hunt, he said to give you a pound as a Christmas present.'

Ron touched his nose. 'I understand. Don't worry, I can keep quiet. And I'll be extra nice to you.'

Sue cringed. 'I'll get Mr Hunt to tell you himself.'

'Na. Don't bother him. Anyway, you ready? He said we can go now.'

'I'll just say goodbye to Mr Hunt.'

Ron took her arm. 'Come on, let's get home.'

She shook his hand off. 'Leave me alone. I ain't going anywhere till I've said goodbye.'

'If that's the way it is, I'll be off.'

He walked away, and Sue gave out a sigh of relief. As she tidied her desk and covered her typewriter, Fred Hunt walked in. She stood up and began to put on her coat.

'Ron went off in a huff. He all right?'

'Yes. I'll be off now too. Have a nice Christmas.'

'And you, Susan. By the way, I've got a little something for you.' Sue sat back down, and Fred Hunt went to his desk and took out a small package.

'Merry Christmas,' he said, handing it to her. 'Don't open it till Christmas.'

'Thank you. Thank you so much. But you've already given me a bonus.'

'That's because you work hard.'

'I enjoy my work.'

'That's good.'

Sue turned the packet over. It was wrapped in pretty Christmas paper and had a lovely red bow on the top. 'I ain't got you anything.'

'And I don't expect anything. Now off you go and I'll see you on Friday.'

'Bye. Have a nice Christmas. And thank you.'

'Bye, Susan.'

He stood and watched her as she walked across the forecourt. She turned and waved, and as he waved back, he thought about what he would have liked to be doing over Christmas. Not driving to Surrey to be with his mother and aunt, but going off somewhere with Susan Reed.

She didn't realise what a beautiful young woman she was. One of these days he would tell her.

* * *

Sue had a spring in her step as she walked home. She smiled to herself. That parcel felt like a bottle of scent, and she guessed by the packaging that it was probably very expensive, not like the Evening in Paris she usually wore. She knew she wouldn't be able to wait till tomorrow to open it, and if it was scent she would wear it tonight to help make Cy notice her.

As she turned the corner, she was aware of footsteps behind her. She stopped and turned. She thought she recognised the figure in the gloomy gaslight. 'Ron, is that you?' she called out. Her heart began to beat fast when he didn't answer. 'Stop playing silly buggers and say something.'

6

Fred Hunt was still staring out of the showroom window long after Sue had left and it had become dark. He had stood and watched her till she was out of sight. After turning out the lights, he made his way through the door that led to his soulless flat upstairs. In the small kitchenette he filled the kettle and put it on the gas stove. He should be going to his mother's tonight, but he'd phoned her earlier and told her he'd be down in the morning. One day with Aunt Rosa and his mother was more than enough. When the two sisters, started, even if it was only an ordinary conversation, with their Italian blood it still sounded as if they were having an argument. And although Aunt Rosa's husband Ted was all right, it wasn't as if he was very interesting. Perhaps Fred was being unfair; after all, living with those two would make anyone disappear into his shell. Apart from his grandchildren, Ted was only interested in being a grocer and what his customers said and liked.

Fred grinned to himself as he switched on the wireless. Sinking into the only armchair, he took off his tie and shoes and prepared himself for a quiet night in. If only Susan was a few years older, he could have taken her out to a lovely restaurant and wined and dined her, but he knew that the age gap wouldn't be accepted. He remembered some of the comments when he'd taken her to the Masons' do, 'Cradle-snatching' was one of the remarks he had overheard. Not that that really worried him, but what about her family? How would they react? He had had plenty of girlfriends — with his money and status they were like bees round a honey pot — but they were all so shallow. Some couldn't even hold a decent conversation.

The whistling kettle took him out to the kitchenette again. Later he'd have a walk down to the Queen's Head for a pint, then on the way back he'd call in at the pie and eel shop. Maisie did a nice meat pie and mash, complete with lovely thick liquor.

★ ★ ★

Sue walked quickly on; she was beginning to get nervous. She stopped and called out again, but the only sound was the hissing of the gas lamps. She couldn't see anyone; were they hiding in a doorway? When there wasn't any reply, she broke into a run, but still the footsteps were behind her. She was frightened, and tears began to trickle down her cheeks. Where were all the people who were usually around at this time? All in the warm, she shouldn't wonder, waiting for Christmas. Should she stop and confront whoever it was, or should she keep running?

Just as she reached the railway arch, a train rumbled overhead and she felt a hand on her shoulder. She dropped her handbag and screamed, but the sound was lost in the noise from the train.

'What's wrong, little Sue?'

'You! You!' Sue pummelled Ron's chest with her fists. 'What are you doing creeping up behind me like that? Why didn't you answer when I called out?'

Under the gaslight Ron tried to hold her close. 'You're trembling. I wouldn't hurt you. I was trying to protect you.'

'Protect me from what?'

'You never know who's lurking about.'

'Let go of me. Look what you've done, you've made me drop me bag. I could kill you, Ron Brent. You're a bloody nuisance.'

'I only wonner look after you, little Sue.'

'Get out me way.' She squatted down and gathered together the contents of her bag. As she hastily replaced them she cried out; 'Oh no! You clumsy great oaf. Look what you've done. You've gone and broke me bottle of scent.' She looked at the soggy mess in her bag. The smell was overpowering.

'Cor. That smells nice.'

'That was me Christmas present.'

'Did *he* buy you that?'

She nodded. 'I ain't ever had expensive scent before.'

'I'll get you another bottle.'

'You couldn't afford this.' She began to walk on. 'And I want you to leave me alone.'

'I've got to go this way. This is where I live. Don't you remember?'

Sue ignored him. She was too angry to talk to him. Breaking that bottle had already spoilt her Christmas, and if she didn't go to the dance tonight then that would really be the last straw.

★ ★ ★

'Oh my God! What's happened? Are you all right, love?' asked her father, jumping up when she walked in.

Sue guessed her make-up was in a state and he could see she'd been crying. She couldn't tell him about Ron, though, as her father would go after him and that would spoil everybody's Christmas, so instead she wiped her eyes with the back of her hand and smiled. 'I'm just being a bit daft, that's all. Mr Hunt gave me a lovely bottle of scent for Christmas and I went and dropped it.'

'That's nothing to get upset about,' said her mother.

'It looked like it was very expensive.'

'It was only a bottle of scent,' said Granny Potts.

Sue knew she would never forgive Ron, and what would Jane have to say when she told her? Sue looked at the clock. It would be hours before Jane got home, and would she still want to go to the dance? 'If Jane ain't home be the time I'm ready to go out, tell her I've gone on without her.'

'That's not very nice,' said her mother.

'She can always come on after, and that way I'll be able to save a couple of chairs for us. Otherwise we'll have to stand all night, and she won't want that, not after being on her feet all day.'

'What if she don't want to go?'

'I'll be all right. I've been there before on me own. Besides, there's always someone I know there.' There was no way Sue was going to miss the opportunity to see Cy Taylor.

'That was back in the summer, and it was light then,' said her mother.

'I don't want you coming home in the dark with some yobbo,' said her father.

Sue laughed. 'I'll come home with Father Christmas. I think he should be around be then.'

★ ★ ★

At eight o'clock Sue looked at the clock. She was all ready and decided to go to the dance on her own. 'I was hoping Jane would have finished a bit earlier tonight.'

'Those bosses will want their pound of flesh,' said her gran.

'Are you going to tell Mrs Brent?' said Doris.

'No, she's probably gone to church. You know what she's like.' Sue certainly wasn't going to go next door, just in case Ron was there on his own.

'Well just be careful,' said her mother.

'I will.'

'I expect we'll still be up when you get home,' said her father.

Sue didn't doubt that for one moment. She picked up her handbag and dance shoes, and after kissing all the family went off out.

This was going to be the night she'd dreamed about, and she was determined to speak to Cy Taylor.

When Sue pushed open the door to the dance hall, she stood for a moment or two taking in the scene before her. The band was playing 'Pennies From Heaven', and Sue felt as though she had indeed stepped into heaven. Paper chains, huge paper bells, stars and twinkling lights hung from the high ceiling. A large silver ball sent tiny shards of light round the room, and although she had been here many times and seen this silver ball before, somehow tonight it had a magical glow. She looked at the love of her life up on the stage. In his brilliant white shirt, black evening suit and black bow tie, he was everything a girl could wish for. Sue gave out a deep sigh.

'You gonner stand in the doorway all night, gel?' said a man standing behind her.

'Sorry.' She smoothed down her frock and quickly made her way across the floor to two empty chairs she had seen near the bandstand. Sitting on one, she put her evening bag on the other. She had changed her shoes in the cloakroom after checking in the long mirror that the frock she was wearing was just right. It was a pretty blue with lacy sleeves, and her mother had made it for her last Christmas. How she wished she could have worn the frock she'd had for the Masons' do.

Very soon her foot began tapping. She looked around at all the couples and girls with their friends. She did feel a bit out of it, and wondered if she'd done the right thing; after all, it was very daring to go to a dance all on your own.

However, it wasn't long before she was asked to dance, and as she was whirled round the floor, she couldn't take her eyes off Cy. Almost every dance she was on her feet. She was in a dream as a succession of all types of men and boys spun, swirled and whisked her round the dance floor.

During the interval Sue went and got herself a ginger beer. A few blokes had asked her if she wanted a drink and each time she'd politely said no, as she was waiting for a friend. She was just coming out of the Ladies when she spotted Cy going outside. She hurried after him. He was leaning against the wall having a cigarette.

'Hello,' she said. 'I think you're wonderful.'

'Me or me singing?'

'Your singing,' said Sue, embarrassed.

'Why, thank you.'

Sue was at her wits' end. Her mouth had gone dry. She was lost for words. What could she say?

'Would you like a cigarette?' He took a silver case from his inside pocket and, opening it, offered her one.

'No thank you.'

'Have you been here before?'

'When me and me friend can make it. We were coming the last time you were here but we had all that snow.'

'Yes. Well you didn't miss much; we couldn't make it either. Is your friend here tonight?'

'No, she had to work late.'

'Oh, so it's a she. Are you on your own?'

'Yes.'

'So what's your name?'

'Sue.'

'I'm doing 'Sweet Sue' later on, so I'll sing it just for you.'

'Thank you.'

With the toe of his patent leather shoe he stubbed out his cigarette. 'I have to go now. And you'd better come in as well; you're shivering.' He took her arm.

Sue thought she'd died and gone to heaven. She wasn't shivering from the cold; it was because she was so near to him. As he left her and made his way backstage, she gazed after him.

By eleven o'clock, Sue knew that Jane wouldn't be coming, but she didn't care, and when Cy sang 'Sweet Sue' he looked straight at her and gave her a little wave. She waved back and felt smug when she saw a couple of girls whispering together and looking in her direction.

The rest of the evening flew past. When Jeff Owen, the bandleader, announced it was twelve o'clock, everybody began rushing around wishing everyone else a merry Christmas. Kisses were exchanged, and Sue found herself kissed by many men as she made her way towards the bandstand. Then, at last, she was in his arms.

7

Even though Jane was tired and didn't want to go to the dance, she was still very angry when she called on Sue before she went home, only to find that she had gone without her. She had been on her feet all day, dealing with customers who had been jostling and shoving each other in their haste to get served, some buying right up to the last minute. To find that her so-called best friend had gone to the dance without her had been the last straw. Sue should have stayed and waited for her, not gone gadding off just to try and see her fancy man.

'Mum's left your dinner on the gas,' said Ron, who was sitting at the table trying to read the paper.

'I suppose she's gone to church?'

'I got the sack today.'

'What? Why? What have you done?'

'Nothing. He don't want me any more. And,' he looked round sheepishly, 'little Sue gave me some extra money.'

'What? How much?'

'A pound. A whole pound. I think she pinched it, but don't tell Mr Hunt, I don't wonner get her into trouble.'

Jane sat in a chair. She couldn't believe what her brother was saying. 'Are you sure that's what happened? I can't see Sue doing anything like that.'

'I think it's 'cos she wants me to start saving for when we get married.'

Jane stood up and walked towards the scullery. 'Do you know, you can talk a right load of rubbish sometimes. And I'm sure you're getting worse. If you ain't careful, they'll come and take you away.'

Ron was across the room in a flash. He gripped the top of Jane's arms very tight and spoke right in her face. His breath was bad and she tried to move away, but she was pinned against the door.

'Don't you say fings like that. D'you know, I could break your arms just like twigs.' He let go of her and she reeled back, rubbing her arms.

Jane had never seen her brother act like this before. He had wild, darting eyes, but he had never been violent. She had always made fun of him. He was a big man, though, and for the first time in her life she was frightened. 'I'll just get me dinner. Have you had something to eat?'

He nodded and sat back in his chair.

'I might go along to church and walk home with Mum. Do you want to come?'

'No. She might send the devil after me.'

Jane was just about to tell him not to be so daft when she stopped. After the way he'd just acted, she knew that she had to watch her words.

★   ★   ★

Sue had collected her coat from the cloakroom but had hung about till most of the other dancers had left. The sound of laughter and

59

hooters blowing gradually faded away. When the lights went up, she blinked against the harsh light. The floor was strewn with cigarette butts, streamers and burst balloons. The band was beginning to collect their instruments and pack them away. She walked up to the bandstand, and as Cy had his back to her, she pulled on his arm.

'I'd like to wish you a merry Christmas.' The thrill of his kiss still lingered on her lips.

'And a merry Christmas to you.'

'When will you be here again?'

'Not till the end of January.'

'You're not coming for the New Year?'

'No, we've got another booking, much better pay.'

'Come on, Cy,' yelled one of the band. 'We've got a lot of drinking to catch up on.'

'See you in January,' he said as he walked away.

'Come on, gel, ain't you got no home to go to?' said a man who was pushing a large broom around the floor.

Reluctantly she left and made her way to the bus stop. She knew she would be here in January come hell or high water, and she would make a point of going up to him as soon as she arrived. He was all she had ever dreamed he would be. She touched her lips. His kiss would keep her going till she saw him again.

★   ★   ★

It was very late when she got home but her father was waiting up for her.

'Didn't think you'd be this late.'

'Sorry, but I just missed a bus and had to wait for the next one.'

'Well you're home now. Your mother went to bed ages ago, so I'll be off as well.' He stood up and folded the paper he'd been reading. 'By the way, Jane popped in when she got home from work. She wasn't very pleased to hear you'd gone out without her, so you'd better go in first thing and make your peace. I hope you've bought her something nice for Christmas.'

'Yes, I have. Good night.' She kissed his cheek. 'Merry Christmas, Dad. I hope you've got me something nice.'

He smiled. 'And merry Christmas to you, love. You'll have to wait till morning to find out. Good night. Sleep well. And I hope Father Christmas comes and visits you.'

'I didn't see him on me way home.' Sue smiled, too.

As she made her way up the stairs, she thought guiltily about her friend. Poor Jane. She had been working till late, and what sort of Christmas would she have with her mother in church all day? Sue guessed Jane would have to cook the dinner, and didn't think there would be a lot of laughter in that house today. She knew how lucky she was; she had a wonderful family and she had been kissed by the man of her dreams. What more could she ask for?

★　★　★

61

Sue opened her eyes to see her mother standing there with a cup of tea in her hand.

'I've brought you up a cuppa.'

'What time is it?'

'Eight o'clock. You was late coming in last night.'

'Yes. I missed me bus.'

'So your father said. Anyway, merry Christmas.' She kissed her daughter's cheek.

'And to you, Mum, and thanks for the tea, I'll be down in a tick.'

As her mother closed the door, Sue knew that as soon as she could, she had to go to see Jane and make her peace.

When she walked into the kitchen, she kissed her gran and dad and wished them both a merry Christmas.

'We're having the presents after dinner,' said her mother, walking in and wiping her hands on the bottom of the pretty colourful pinny she was wearing. 'That way we can sit and open them together.'

'Good idea,' said Sue. 'That's a nice pinny.'

Doris smiled and smoothed it down. 'Your father bought it for me as an extra present.'

'And very pretty it is too,' Sue said, sitting at the table. 'Is there anything you'd like me to do?'

'No, it's all under control. Your gran did all the veg last night. You can make yourself a bit of toast if you like.'

'I'll pop in to see Jane after that. Anyone else want a bit?'

'No thanks, love, we had our breakfast a while

ago. You can ask Jane if she'd like to come in this evening. We won't be doing much: just playing cards and a few games, but it's got to be better than sitting in there.'

'Thanks, Mum. I'm sure she'll jump at the chance.' Sue plonked herself in front of the fire, and with a slice of bread on the end of the toasting fork, sat and dreamed about last night.

★ ★ ★

It was late morning when Fred Hunt arrived at his aunt's house. He collected the presents from the car and made his way up the path, then let out a big sigh, for he could hear them having a friendly conversation right through the closed door.

Ted opened the door and grinned. 'Thank God you've arrived. It's been like a battlefield in here.'

'Why?' asked Fred, putting his presents on the hall stand and taking off his hat and coat.

'It's over who does what in the kitchen.'

The kitchen door burst open and the wonderful smell of cooking filled the air.

'Frederick. Frederick, my boy.' First his mother, then his aunt took hold of his face and kissed it all over.

'Why didn't you come down last night?' said his mother. 'You shouldn't be on your own on Christmas Eve.'

'Unless he was with a young lady,' said his aunt.

'Don't talk rubbish. He would tell his mother

63

if there was someone, wouldn't you, son?' She patted his cheek.

Fred looked at Ted, who raised his eyes skywards and shrugged. Fred felt about twelve.

'Don't reckon he would,' said Ted, giving him a wink.

'Now come and have a glass of whisky; you must be frozen driving all that way. You can take your things upstairs later.'

'Thanks, Mum.' Fred allowed himself to be taken into the front room. It looked very warm and inviting, with its blazing fire and a tall tree standing in the window covered with lights and baubles it.

'Get Frederick a drink while I get back in the kitchen. Can't leave Rosa on her own for too long, we don't want the dinner spoiled.'

Fred grinned as his mother left the room. She always called him by his full name. He would be forever grateful to his father that he had a good solid English name and not some Italian moniker. Apparently that had always been a bone of contention between them.

'Whisky, Fred?'

'Please. Are the kids coming today?' asked Fred.

'They'll be here for dinner. Getting to be quite a houseful now Sofia's had another one. That makes five altogether.'

'Not all Sofia's, though.'

'No. Bill's got two and Sofia's got three.'

'Quite the grandad.'

'Bloody expensive. How's business?'

'Not bad. Not bad at all. What about the retail

business?' Ted had a grocer's shop in the village.

'Mustn't grumble. This weather plays the old bones up, though.'

Fred settled down into what he knew would be a companionable silence till the family arrived, at which point all hell would be let loose with three young boys and a girl running about wild. Thank goodness he was only staying one night, although his mother would be sure to have something to say about that.

★　★　★

Sue didn't have to knock on Jane's front door, as Ron opened it as soon as she walked through the gate. Was he always looking out of the front-room window?

'Merry Christmas, little Sue.' He went to kiss her but she quickly stood back.

'Merry Christmas, Ron. Can I come in?' she asked as he was blocking the doorway.

'Course.' He stood to one side and bowed very low as she passed him.

Sue guessed Jane was in the scullery and went on through. 'Merry Christmas, Jane,' she said, going up to her friend and kissing her cheek.

'Is it?'

'Oh dear. I can see someone hasn't got the Christmas spirit.'

'Neither would you if you'd been working till ten o'clock, then found your so-called best mate had gone out without you; then on Christmas morning you'd got to cook the dinner while your mum'd gone to church for all that singing and praying.'

Sue threw her arms round her friend. 'I'm sorry. I wish there was something I could do.' She could feel Jane shaking. 'What is it?'

Jane stood back and wiped her eyes. 'I feel so unhappy.'

Sue held her tight again. 'I am so sorry. What can I do?'

'Nothing really. I'll get over it.'

'Can I help with the dinner?'

Jane shook her head. 'I've done all the veg and just put the bit of beef in the oven. We can't have our dinner till Mum gets in.'

'Well as soon as you've finished, you must come over to our place and be waited on. That's an order. And here's your Christmas present. You can open it now if you like.'

Jane gave her a weak smile. 'Thanks.' She blew her nose, then opened the small packet. It was a bracelet.

'Oh Sue, this is lovely, thank you. I ain't got you such an expensive present.'

'And I don't expect one.'

'I'll go and get it, it's in the front room.'

Jane quickly returned and handed Sue her present. 'You can open it if you like.'

Sue held up the delicate scarf. 'Jane, this is really lovely. Thank you.' She kissed her friend.

'I do get a discount on my purchases.'

'That's good. Mr Hunt gave me a bottle of expensive scent.'

'Lucky old you.'

'But I ain't got it now.'

'Why? What happened to it?'

Sue looked into the kitchen to make sure Ron wasn't there, then told Jane what had happened. 'I was so frightened.'

'I know what you mean.' Jane went on to relate what had happened to her. 'He never used to be violent. He's always been a bit simple. What's happened to make him change?'

'I don't know.'

'By the way, he said you gave him a pound out the till.'

'What? That was from Mr Hunt.'

'Ron reckons you gave it to him so that he can start saving for when you two get married.'

Sue laughed. 'Me marry him? As we just said, he seems to be getting worse.'

'I know. But d'you reckon that's what's wrong with him?'

'What?'

'Well, you know. He might want to go out with a woman.'

'Well he ain't going out with me,' said Sue.

'Just make sure you're not alone with him.'

'Shouldn't you tell your mum?'

'No, she ain't got over Dad dying yet. If she found out about this, it might send her round the bend, then I'll have two nutters to look after.' Jane laughed. 'Come on, it's Christmas. Don't let's be morbid. Did you see lover boy last night?'

Sue laughed with her friend; it was good to see her back to her old inquisitive self. She nodded.

'And?'

'He kissed me.'

'What? How? Why?'

'Give me a chance.'

Suddenly Ron was in the scullery with them. 'Who kissed you?'

'A bloke.'

'You can't let another bloke kiss you. You belong to me.'

'I don't, Ron. I don't belong to anyone.'

'We shall see about that. Where does he live?'

'I don't know. Stop being so daft. I can do what I like.'

Ron screwed up his eyes. 'I ain't ever gonner let anybody else have you. You're mine.'

Jane looked at Sue and shook her head. 'Ron, shut up, otherwise I'll tell Mum.'

Ron suddenly changed. 'Don't tell Mum.' He cowered away and buried his head in the towel that hung on a nail behind the door. 'I'll just go to the lav.' He went outside.

'Don't worry about him,' said Jane. 'Just make sure you keep out of his way.'

'I will.' But Sue was worried for Jane and for herself; they had both seen what Ron was capable of.

8

It was late in the evening on Boxing Day when Fred Hunt drove back home. He was glad Christmas was over. Although he was always pleased to see that his mother was well, one day was more than enough with her. And as for the kids, they were all right, but he was used to peace and quiet. He shouldn't be selfish, they all did their best to make him feel welcome, but the thought of getting back to work and seeing Susan again brought a smile to his face. He had made up his mind: he was going to ask her to go out again. A nice restaurant out of town somewhere.

The rain was steady and the swish of the wipers soothing. Fred opened his window to help clear the misty windscreen. He was taking extra care on the twisting country roads and had been keeping his speed down when a car came racing round a blind bend with its headlights blazing and on his side of the road. He pulled the wheel over and found himself going towards a hedge, then nothing.

★ ★ ★

On Friday morning when Sue got to the garage, she was surprised to see that it was shut. Most mornings Mr Hunt opened the showroom before she arrived. Perhaps he hadn't got home till late

69

and was still in bed. As she walked in, the phone was ringing.

'Hello. Hunt's Motors. Oh, it's you, Mr Field. No, Mr Hunt's not around. I'll tell him to pop round when I see him. Yes, I'm sure I ordered those parts the week before Christmas. Hold on a minute and I'll check.' Sue put the phone down and went to the filing cabinet. She pulled out a file and took it back to the desk. 'Yes, the order's here. I'll chase it up but I don't reckon we'll have any luck till next week. Bye.' She replaced the phone. She knew her boss wouldn't be very happy waiting for parts for the garage. He was fussy about getting spares quickly for the mechanical side of the business, as waiting meant that the repair was held up and he was losing money.

For the rest of the morning she was kept busy seeing to the odd customer and answering the phone, and still Mr Hunt hadn't come down. It was almost lunchtime when she ventured over to the door leading to his flat and tried to open it, but it was locked. She was getting worried. Was he ill? He would have phoned if he was staying with his mother for another day. She rapped gently on the door and called out: 'Mr Hunt!' But there was no reply.

Harry Field, the foreman from the workshop, came in. 'Tell you what, gel, it's bloody freezing out there, and lying on that cold floor ain't gonner do me rheumatics any good. His lordship showed himself yet?'

'No, he ain't. Mr Field, I'm a bit worried about him. I'm sure he would have let me know

70

if he was staying another day with his mum.'

'He's probably got himself a nice young lady up there and is spending the day in bed.'

Sue blushed and looked away.

'Sorry, love, didn't mean ter shock yer, but he is his own master. Now about this 'ere stuff, When we gonner get it?'

'They said they'll try and get it here today, but if not, it'll definitely arrive next week.'

'OK. What we'll have to do is get on with another job till then. If the customer comes in for that car, you'll have to explain it to him. All right, love?'

'Yes.'

'And don't worry about 'is nibs, he's a survivor. Remember, he was brought up in a rough neighbourhood and had to look after his mum after his dad died, so he can look after hisself.'

Despite Harry's reassurances, as the afternoon wore on Sue was beginning to get more and more concerned about Mr Hunt. At three o'clock the phone rang and when she picked up the receiver she was surprised to be told it was a hospital in Surrey that was calling.

She sat open-mouthed as the caller told her that there had been an accident and that Mr Hunt had been injured.

'Very badly?' asked Sue softly, dreading the answer.

'No, he should be out at the weekend. He said he was worried about you.'

'I'm fine. Tell him not to worry, everything is under control.'

71

'He'll be pleased to hear that.'

After she'd put the phone down, Sue sat and gazed through the window. Poor Mr Hunt. After a while she put on her coat and locked up, then went round to the workshop to tell Harry Field.

He was equally shocked. 'It must've been the other bloke's fault. Mr H. is a damn good driver. I wonder what state the car's in? Didn't say if he wants us to tow it back at all?'

'No. I didn't speak to him. I suppose I'd better tell his mum. What d'you think?'

'Dunno. I expect the hospital's already done that. After all, she's his next of kin. Anyway, love, don't you worry your pretty little head too much about it. As I said, he's a survivor. Now, you sure you can see to things here for a day or two?'

'Yes thank you.'

'Well remember, if there's any problems, just give us a bell.'

'All right. I'll be going home now. See you tomorrow.'

He gave her a wave as she left and Sue felt a little better. She knew she could rely on Mr Field if anything went wrong. She made her way to the bus stop to wait for Jane.

★ ★ ★

'The poor man. Did the hospital say how bad he was?' asked her mother.

'They wouldn't tell her that, would they?' said Granny Potts. 'Only the next of kin.'

'What about the garage?' asked her father.

'I can manage for a few days.'

72

'Well I don't like the idea of you being in that place on your own,' said her mother.

'I'm all right. Mr Field is only round the corner.'

'But what if someone comes in with a lot of money and wants to buy a car?'

'We've got a safe. Not many come in with cash; most of the business is done on hire purchase and I fill in all the forms.'

'But what if they do, and what if they come back and try to rob you?'

'Mum, I think you've been seeing too many gangster films.'

'Well I don't like it.'

'I shall only be on me own tomorrow morning. He might be back on Monday. Besides, he often leaves me on me own.'

'I still don't like it.'

'And remember, love,' said her father. 'Don't let anybody take a car for a test run; they might not bring it back.'

'Oh don't say things like that, Charlie. You're making me more nervous about it.'

'Honest, Mum. I'll be all right.' Sue grinned to herself. It was going to be rather nice to be in charge.

★   ★   ★

On Saturday morning Sue opened the show-room and settled herself down behind her typewriter. One or two men were wandering around the cars, but that wasn't anything new, Hunt's attracted a lot of people. After a while the

73

men came into the office.

'Fred Hunt around?' asked one, a tall, burly man with a tattoo on his hand.

'No, I'm sorry. Can I take a message?'

'Na. Tell him we'll catch up with him some other time.'

Sue picked up her writing pad. 'Who shall I say called?'

'Bert Rose and his son. Don't worry too much about it. I'll see him soon.'

Sue watched them from the window. She didn't like the look of them and was pleased that it was bitterly cold and they didn't hang around for long.

She looked up again surprised when the bell over the door rang once again.

'Ron. What are you doing here?'

'I've come to see if you're all right.'

'Yes I am, thank you.'

'Jane was telling Mum last night that you'd be all on your own, so I've come to look after you.'

'Thank you. That's very nice of you.'

He took off his coat.

'It's all right. You don't have to stay.'

'Yes I do. You see, Mr Hunt told me to look after you.'

Sue sent up a silent prayer. Ron had certainly flipped this time.

'Shall I make you a cup of tea, little Sue?'

'No thank you.' She was trying to think of something to get him out.

He sat at Mr Hunt's desk. 'This feels nice. I'd like to be the boss.'

Sue felt sick. 'Please, Ron. Go home.'

'I can't. I've got to look after you.'

Sue couldn't concentrate on what she was doing. She prayed desperately that someone would come in. She could have yelled with relief when she saw the parts van draw up outside. 'I'll just go and collect the parcels,' she said, walking to the door.

'No, I'll do that.'

'I've got to check it and sign for it.'

He was out of the door before she could stop him. She looked at the clock. Only another hour to go before she could close up.

Ron came back in with the parcel. 'I told him it'd better be all right or else I'll clock him one.'

'That's going to go down well. Put it down and I'll check it.' Sue took the invoice and saw that Ron had scribbled where she should have signed. After checking the contents she said, 'It all seems in order. I was wondering, could you take this round to Mr Field? You know, the workshop. You've taken stuff round there before.'

'I reckon I could do that for you.' He put on his coat and went out.

Sue was on the phone right away. It seemed to be ringing forever before Mr Field answered it.

'Yes, he's just walked in,' he replied when Sue asked him if Ron had arrived.

'Do you think you could keep him there for a while?'

'Course. What's the trouble?'

'Nothing. He just gives me the willies when I'm on my own.'

'Why? Has he upset you in some way?'

'No. It's just that I don't like it with only him around.'

'Don't worry, love. I'll see to it.'

'I'm going to lock up now and go home. I don't want him following me.'

'D'you think he might?'

'Don't know.'

'Well you are a very attractive young lady.'

'Just keep him there for a little while, please.'

'Course I will, love. Don't worry.'

Sue quickly put everything away and locked up, then she ran up the road as fast as she could.

* * *

'You're home early,' said her mother when she walked in.

'There wasn't a lot doing and Mr Field suggested I shut up.' Sue crossed her fingers behind her back. She didn't want her mum to know the real reason.

'Just as long as Mr Hunt don't think you're taking advantage of him not being there.'

'I wouldn't do that.'

'Not heard any more about how he is, then?'

Sue shook her head. She was dreading Ron coming home. She knew he would be angry.

'You all right, love? You look a bit peaky.'

'I'm fine.'

'It's this damp and cold weather. Enough to get anyone down,' said Granny Potts, who was huddled over the fire.

'I know. I worry about Charlie in this weather.'

Sue sat gazing into the fire. Should she tell

her parents about Ron? But what was there to tell? Everybody knew he was a bit weird. But lately he seemed to have got worse, and she was very frightened of him and what he might do to her.

9

Sue jumped up when she heard someone knocking at the front door. She guessed right away who it would be.

He looked angry when she opened the door. 'Little Sue. You didn't wait for me.'

'Who is it, Sue?' called her mother from the kitchen.

'It's Ron.'

There was no shouting for him to come in as there usually was when a neighbour called, and almost at once her mother was at her side. 'What is it, Ron? Is it your mum?'

'No, Mrs Reed. It's little Sue here. I was helping at the garage and she didn't wait for me to bring her home.'

'Sue didn't say you was back working at Hunt's.'

'I'm not. But I knew little Sue was on her own and so I decided to keep her company, but she come home without me.'

'Well not to worry, Ron. She's home now safe and sound. Goodbye.' Doris Reed began to close the door.

'But Mrs Reed,' Ron pushed the door open, 'I want to take little Sue out.'

'Not today, Ron. She's got some chores to do in here.' With that she closed the door, leaving him on the doorstep, and turned to Sue. 'If he puts his great big muddy footprints all over my nice white step, I'll clock him one.'

Sue grinned. 'Thanks, Mum. He's beginning to be a pain.'

'I'll have a word with Maud tomorrow. I don't like the idea of him hanging about the showroom while Mr Hunt's away.'

'Neither do I. Now come on, what're these chores you want me to do?'

'Sue, has he been threatening you?'

'No. Why?'

'You looked frightened.'

'I am a bit. But I expect he's harmless.'

'I hope so. You will tell us if he tries anything won't you?'

Sue turned and looked at her mother as she pushed open the kitchen door. 'Course.' Did her mother suspect that Ron had been acting funny?

★   ★   ★

It was later that evening when Jane came in to see Sue.

'Can we talk?' she asked when Sue opened the door.

'Course. Come upstairs. What's the trouble?'

'Did Ron come to see you at work this morning?'

'Yes. Why?'

'He's been telling Mum that he's gonner look after you. He's gonner take you to work on Monday and stay all day.'

'Oh no. I don't want him around. He gives me the willies.'

'I'm gonner tell Mum about how he threatened me. She'll have a word with him and I'll try and see if she can keep him at home.'

'How d'you reckon she'll be able to do that?'

Jane shrugged and grinned. 'She can always threaten him with the devil or the vicar; that usually does the trick.'

Sue smiled. 'You can be very wicked at times.'

'I know. Don't forget he had a go at me, and he's never done that before. I was very frightened but I never told her. I know he can be a pain, but he is still my big brother, and it's Mum I feel sorry for. Then again, I don't want him to do anything really wrong and they take him away.'

'D'you think he might?'

'I hope not.'

Sue felt full of guilt. 'I'll try and keep out of his way.'

'Thanks.'

Although they changed the subject to talk about the films they wanted to see, Sue was still concerned about Ron. Could he turn really violent? And what about poor Mrs Brent? She'd had more than enough to put up with since losing her husband. What would she do if Ron was taken away?

★ ★ ★

On Monday morning Sue was dreading going to work, and got ready as fast as she could in the hope that she would be out of the door before Ron realised it, but as soon as she opened her front door, there he was at the gate.

'Thought you might be early,' he said, his grin making his flabby face crinkle. 'I'm really looking forward to being with you all day. Just me and you. We can pretend that it all belongs to us. I'll be the boss and you can be me secretary. We're going to have a great day.'

Sue gave him a half-hearted smile. 'I just hope you don't get in me way, that's all.'

'I won't, I promise.' He loped along to fall into step beside her, and took her arm. She quickly brushed him away. 'Don't do that.' She didn't want him near her.

⋆　⋆　⋆

All through the morning, every time Sue looked up Ron was grinning at her. She wanted to scream at him but knew that wouldn't do any good. So much for Jane imagining that his mother would stop him coming here. Wait till she saw her friend tonight; she'd give her a piece of her mind.

'What's he doing here?' asked Mr Field when he came in with the work sheets and orders for spare parts.

'He came with me this morning.'

'Why's he sitting in the boss's chair?'

'Ain't got nowhere else to sit,' said Ron.

'Well I can tell yer, Mr H. ain't gonner like it if he walks in and catches yer.'

'I told you that, Ron. Now please, go home.'

'You heard what Sue said.'

'I ain't going.'

81

'You all right, love?' asked Mr Field.

Sue only nodded.

Mr Field came up close to her and whispered, 'D'you want me to chuck him out?'

Ron was at his side in a flash, and although Mr Field was a wiry man, he was no match for Ron, who towered above him. Ron grabbed his shoulder and swung him round, almost knocking the older man off balance.

'What you saying to my girl?'

'Take your hands off me.' Mr Field shook Ron off.

'You leave my little Sue alone.'

'Please, Mr Field. Please go.' Sue was fighting back tears.

'I don't want to leave you alone with this maniac,' Mr Field said, smoothing down his brown coat.

Once again Ron grabbed him. 'I ain't no maniac. And I'd never hurt my little Sue.'

'Let go of me.' Mr Field made his way to the door and, pointing his finger at Ron, said, 'Just you make sure you don't harm her, d'you hear? I'll pop round in a bit, Sue, just to make sure you're all right.'

'Thanks.'

Ron settled back in the chair. 'Never liked that bloke. He might be little but he always seems too big for his boots. If anybody else comes in to talk to yer, I'll clock 'em one.'

'You can't do that. This is a business. People come and go all the time. And Mr Hunt wouldn't be very pleased about that.'

'He'll be glad when he knows I'm here to

protect you, not like *him*.' He nodded towards the door.

Sue was grateful when Mr Field phoned to check on her. That made her feel a little safer.

*   *   *

It was dark when Sue began to put things away. All day she had been waiting for Mr Hunt to walk in. Why hadn't he phoned? Were his injuries worse than she had been told?

'You'll have to go outside while I lock up,' she said to Ron.

Reluctantly he went out.

The thought that was running through Sue's mind was that if only there was a back way out, she could run away from him, but it wasn't to be. Ron was standing grinning at her through the window, and she knew she had to go. She turned the key in the lock and began to make her way home with Ron close beside her.

'You gonner wait for Jane?'

'Yes I am. You can go on if you like.'

'I'll wait a little while, but I don't wonner walk along with her. She told me mum I was at Hunt's, and me mum told me off. She said I should keep away.'

Sue was surprised. So Jane had told her mum. This was the first time he'd talked about it. 'What did your mum say, then?'

'She was gonner send the vicar round to see me. But I said if she did I'd get very angry. I don't like that vicar.'

As soon as the bus came in sight, Ron walked

on. When Jane alighted, Sue tucked her arm through her friend's.

'How's your day been?' asked Jane.

'I've had him grinning at me all day.'

'I guessed he'd be with you.'

'So you told your mum.'

'Yes. But I didn't make that much of it, as yesterday was me dad's birthday and she was upset and spent most of the day in church praying.'

'That's all right,' said Sue.

'Your boss ain't back, then?'

'No, and I ain't heard from him. I was hoping he would phone, but I'm worried he might be worse than the hospital said.'

'What you gonner do if he is?'

'Dunno. I can manage for a little while, but I can't take anybody out on a test drive if they want to buy a car.'

'When he comes back you'll have to get him to teach you to drive.'

'I wouldn't mind. It would be nice if I could drive us about.'

They laughed together.

'We could go to the seaside, and just think, no more hanging about for buses from the pictures or dances,' said Jane.

'And we could go wherever Cy is singing.'

'Trust you to say that. You forget, you've got to learn to drive, then buy a car.'

'There's always something that gets in the way of our dreams.'

All thoughts of Ron had gone out of Sue's head, and all she could think about was that if she could get a car, she would be able to see more of Cy. She could even take him out. The thought of that really excited her, but first she had to persuade Mr Hunt to teach her to drive, then she had to save for the deposit on a car. That night she had a smile on her face as she dreamed of racing about in her own car with Cy Taylor at her side.

★   ★   ★

Today was New Year's Eve, and as they both had to be at work tomorrow, Sue and Jane had decided not to go out tonight. Besides, Cy wasn't going to be at the town hall. Sue sat at her desk, with Ron opposite her playing with a pencil, and wondered what the New Year would bring. She was worried about Mr Hunt. Why hadn't he got in touch? Harry Field had phoned and asked her the same question; he'd also asked if Ron was there, and when she'd told him he was, he'd wanted to know if she was all right. She'd reassured him that she was fine.

At twelve o'clock Sue looked up surprised and a little shocked when the door to Mr Hunt's flat opened and he came into the office.

'All right then, Susan?'

'Yes. Yes, I am.' She hurried round her desk and quickly pulled Ron out of the boss's chair. 'What about you?'

'Not too bad.'

'When did you get home?'

'Yesterday. I was at my mother's all weekend.'

'Why didn't you let me know you were out of

85

hospital? I've been worried sick about you.'

He smiled. 'Have you?'

Sue blushed and looked away. 'Yes, I have,' she said softly. 'Would you like a cup of tea?'

He sat down in his chair. 'Yes please. What are you doing here, Ron?'

'I've been looking after little Sue. I didn't like the idea of her being here on her own, in case anybody come in and tried to steal a car.'

'They can't do that without the keys, but it is very good of you to think of that. I'll have to pay you for looking after my business.'

Ron pulled himself up to his full six foot and grinned. 'Thanks, Mr Hunt.'

So much for Sue thinking the boss would be cross. 'You can go now, Ron,' she said.

'All right. But I'll meet you when you finish.' He put on his cap and left.

'You all right, Susan?'

'Yes. It's just that he gives me the willies.'

'Why? What's he said?'

How could she tell him? It sounded so trivial. After all Mr Hunt thought Ron had done him a favour by looking after her and his business.

'Nothing. What happened to you? Were you hurt very badly?'

'No, not really. Shook up more, but the car's a mess. I'll pop round and get Harry Field to bring it in. Now, what's been happening while I've been away?'

'Not a lot really. Mr Field has been busy, and I've just kept up with the paperwork. Not sold any cars.'

'Don't expect you to, not at this time of year.'

'Nobody even wanted a test drive.'

'Just as well, with me being away.'

'A Mr Rose and his son came in, but he didn't say what he wanted.'

'Thanks, I'll give him a bell later.'

Sue looked worried. 'They seemed a bit scary. Mr Rose had a big wolf tattoo on his hand.'

Fred Hunt laughed. 'I suppose they do look scary. Good job you couldn't see all his tattoos. But Bert Rose is all right. He's handy to have on your side and they do me favours sometimes. He's a bit older than me, but we was at school together. Anything else bothering you?'

'No.' Sue hesitated. 'Mr Hunt, I was wondering, while you were away, if you could teach me to drive?'

'What?' He laughed.

'Well if I could drive, perhaps I could go out with a customer if you couldn't.' Her voice was beginning to fade as she lost confidence.

He looked at her and steepled his fingers. 'I've never thought about that before. You know, that don't sound such a bad idea.'

Sue smiled. That was the first hurdle over. To get her own car would be a bigger challenge.

'We'll have to see about getting you a licence.'

'All I've got to do now is pass me test.'

'That'll take a little time.'

'I shall get there,' she said confidently.

10

'Harry and Bill've taken the breakdown and gone to collect my car,' said Mr Hunt, walking back into the showroom. 'It's a bit of a mess, and I'll be claiming off the other bloke's insurance, so can you get a letter off to my insurance company, Susan?'

'Yes, of course. Good job he stopped.'

'At least he had the decency to wait for the ambulance.'

'You didn't break any bones, then?'

'No. The bang on me head knocked me out cold, but d'you know, I didn't even break the windscreen. What worried the doctors and me was that I couldn't remember a thing for a day, not even me name. Believe me, that's very worrying.'

'That must have been awful. Thank goodness you're all right now and back here.'

'You going out tonight?' Mr Hunt asked out of the blue.

'No. Me and Jane have to work tomorrow, and besides, the band we like ain't gonner be at the town hall.'

'That's a shame. Where will you see the New Year in?'

'At home with me mum and dad.'

'That's a pity. Wouldn't you have liked to go out somewhere exciting?'

'I should say so. But wherever we go we have

to catch a bus, and that means we won't be home till about two, and me mum and dad ain't happy about that, especially as we all have to get up for work in the morning.'

'Sorry about that.' Mr Hunt smiled.

'I didn't mean . . . '

'No, I know.' So many thoughts were going through his mind. He looked at Sue, who was busy typing away. He would take her out soon, but New Year's Eve could be a bit intimate, what with all the kissing, and as much as he would have liked it, he mustn't rush things.

For the rest of the day Sue was happy. This was how she wanted it to be: Mr Hunt sitting at his desk, and her working away at hers.

★ ★ ★

The new year arrived, and on 20 January everyone was mourning the death of King George. Although Sue was upset, the biggest blow to her was that all the cinemas and dance halls were closed, and that would include the town hall, where Cy Taylor was due to be appearing.

'Don't know why everything has to close and we have to listen to that dreadful mournful music all the time.' Sue went and turned the wireless off.

'It's a mark of respect, young lady. Besides, it's only for one weekend, so you can do without till after the funeral,' said Granny Potts indignantly. 'If me legs didn't play me up so much, I would go and see him lying in state.'

'Mum, don't talk so daft. Have you seen the papers? The length of the queues would put me off,' said Doris. 'Anyway, you'd catch your death in this weather.'

'It must be nice to pay your respects, though.'

'You wouldn't catch me up there,' said Sue.

'No, well you youngsters are all the same. Mind you, I bet the new king will send a few hearts a-fluttering.'

Sue smiled. 'He is rather nice.' The papers had been talking about the new King Edward. He was young, and very handsome.

★　★　★

Every week Sue asked Jane if there was any news of when Jeff Owen's band would be at the town hall again, but so far there hadn't been any posters.

'I'll tell you as soon as I see 'em, won't I?' said Jane irritably as Sue asked the same question once again.

Sue's disappointment was eased a little when one morning a month later Fred Hunt said that if she wasn't busy on Sunday, he would take her out for her first driving lesson. She was over the moon.

'I can't believe he's letting you drive one of his cars,' said her father when she told him she was going out with her boss.

'He's coming round for me after dinner. When I pass me test I'm gonner get me own car.'

'And where do you think you're gonner get that kind of money from?' asked her father.

'I'll think of something.'

'Sounds like you're getting a bit above your station, young lady,' said Granny Potts. 'No one's got a car round these parts, especially a slip of a girl.'

Sue looked at her father and grinned. 'I'll be able to take you out, Gran, think about that.'

'Don't think I'd trust my life to you in a car, do you?'

★   ★   ★

All Sunday afternoon Sue was sitting at the wheel of a Ford on an old factory estate. Round and round they went, and again and again she crashed the gears.

'I'm sorry,' she said for the umpteenth time.

'Don't worry.' He held her hand gently over the gear stick. 'Double de-clutching is a bit difficult till you get used to it. Thank goodness you don't have to worry about that in the new cars.' He wanted to keep his hand on hers.

Sue crashed the gears again. 'Sorry.'

'As I said, don't worry. This car is in for repairs before we can sell it anyway.'

It took a while before she was changing the gears smoothly, and when they stopped he said, 'Once you've got the hang of handling the car, we can get your licence and get you out on the road. I know it's a bit humiliating having to have L plates — thank God they weren't used when I learnt to drive — but then you can start to think about taking your test.'

'Oh Mr Hunt. Do you really think so?'

'Don't see why not.'

As he drove her home, Sue was flushed with excitement. 'This is the best thing that has ever happened to me.'

When they turned into Lily Road, Fred looked at her. 'You know, you'll be such an asset to the firm.'

She was beaming as she got out of the car. 'Thank you so much. I'll see you in the morning.'

Fred Hunt gave her a wave as he drove off. To have her sitting next to him all afternoon had been such a pleasure. How could he tell her his feelings? Wouldn't it frighten her away?

★ ★ ★

Before Sue had time to get through the gate, Ron was at her side.

'What you doing going out with him on a Sunday?'

'I really don't think it's any of your business.'

'I don't want you going out with him, or anyone else for that matter.'

'Ron, what I do and who I go with is my business. Now get out me way before I call me dad.'

As she pulled the key through the letterbox she was seething. Ron was really beginning to get on her nerves. Everything she did, he seemed to be there watching her. She'd be glad when she could drive and had her own car; at least he wouldn't be able to follow her then. But was all that just a pipe dream?

'Well,' said her father when she walked in. 'How was it?'

'Good. I made a right mess of changing gear at first, but I got the hang of it in the end.'

'D'you know, you've got a boss in a million,' said her mother.

'I know. It's so funny driving, there's such a lot to think about.'

'You wasn't going round the roads, was you?' asked her gran.

'No. He took me round an old factory. When I've learnt how to drive the car, then he said he'll take me on the road.'

'I'll stay indoors that day,' said Gran.

'Gran, you don't go out much anyway. I'm just going in to Jane; be back later.'

'We've got crumpets for tea, so don't be too long.'

'No, Mum.' Sue picked up her coat and went out.

★　★　★

Jane was almost as thrilled as Sue and quickly ushered her upstairs to hear all about her afternoon.

'I can't wait till you've got a car,' she said.

'I've got to get the money first.'

'I bet he'll let you have one cheap.'

'I hope so.'

For what was left of the afternoon, they chatted about this and that. Eventually, Sue looked at her watch.

'I'd better go, me tea'll be ready.' She put on

her coat. 'Your mum at church?'

'Of course. It gets on my nerves being stuck here all day with Ron. Although he has been in his room all day. Mind you, I don't know what he's been up to, and I don't really want to know.'

Sue felt sorry for her friend. Jane didn't have a lot to look forward to. 'Look, next time I go out for a lesson, I'll ask Mr Hunt if you can come with me.'

Jane brightened up. 'D'you think I could?'

'Don't see why not. Anyway, I'll ask.' She opened the door, expecting to see Ron standing there.

'Little Sue, come and see what I've done.' He was calling from his bedroom.

Sue looked at Jane. 'What is it?' she whispered.

Jane shrugged. 'Dunno. He has been very quiet.'

'Little Sue, come on.'

'Jane, come with me.'

Together they made their way into Ron's room. It smelled musty, and there was an overpowering odour of paint. There was no light on, and the window was covered over with paper.

'Look. Look through this hole.'

Sue looked at Jane and stepped forward. The small hole cut in the paper looked down into her yard.

'I can sit here, and every time you go to the lav I can keep me eye on you.' He laughed. 'You see, this is a big eye.'

'You're sick,' said Sue, and rushed out of the room with Jane close behind.

'Sue! Sue, wait!' yelled Jane as she clattered down the linoed stairs after her friend. 'Let's go out and see what he's done.'

They went out into the yard and looked up. Covering his window was a huge painted eye. They couldn't see the peep-hole, which must have been in the iris.

'Your brother should be locked up.' Sue went back into the house and rushed down the passage.

'I'll tell Mum,' called Jane as Sue slammed the front door shut.

Ron sat on his bed with his head in his hands. He rocked back and forth. 'Go away. Leave me alone.' His head was pounding. 'I don't want to listen to you.'

★   ★   ★

'You'll never guess what that idiot Ron's done now.' said Sue as she barged into the kitchen.

'Calm down, love,' said her father. 'Then you can tell us.'

'He's not hurt you, has he?' asked her mother anxiously.

'No. Come outside.'

She led the way into the yard. 'See.' She pointed up at Ron's bedroom window, but the eye had been removed.

'What are we looking for?' asked her mother.

'He made a big eye that covered the window and he had a little hole in the iris that he looked out of. He said he would watch me every time I go to the lav.'

'How long has this been going on?' asked her father.

'This is something new, and I'm beginning to be frightened of him.'

'That boy's getting worse. Come on, let's go in,' said her mother. 'I'll have a word with Maud about this.'

Charlie put his arm round his daughter's shoulders. 'D'you want me to have a word with him? I could go in now if you like.'

'No, leave it to Maud,' said Doris.

'Mrs Brent's at church,' said Sue.

'Leave it to me, Charlie.'

'Well just you make sure she knows what's going on.'

When Jane came over later, she guessed that Sue had told her family about the incident. She let the Reeds know that she had told her mother what Ron had done, but that he had denied it, and although they'd searched his room, they couldn't find the eye anywhere.

That night Sue felt very troubled. How mad was Ron? What if he followed her one night and hurt her? She began to get cross with herself. She was starting to let her imagination get the better of her.

11

For weeks Ron had kept his distance and Sue hadn't seen him hanging around. One evening when she met Jane off the bus she commented on this.

'After that thing with the painted eye, Mum asked the vicar to come round and talk to him, so it might have done a bit of good.'

'Was he upset about it?'

'A bit, but don't you worry about it.'

Although Sue was pleased, she still wasn't sure he would leave her alone. Was he thinking up something else?

'By the way,' Jane tucked her arm through Sue's, 'you're never gonner believe it, but your fancy man and the Jeff Owen Band're coming to the town hall next Thursday night.'

Sue jumped in the air. 'Is he? Is he really? On a Thursday? That's unusual. They don't normally have good bands on a Thursday.'

'Could be because they didn't get here that time in the snow. Anyway, as that's my afternoon off, we can go together.'

'What can I wear?' asked Sue.

'You've got plenty of things.'

'I know, but I think he's seen all of 'em.'

'Do you honestly think he'll remember you, let alone what you was wearing?'

'No, I don't suppose so. I'm being a bit silly, ain't I?'

'Yes, you are.'

All day Thursday, Sue was getting more and more excited about meeting Cy again. When Mr Hunt asked her what she was singing when he walked into the office, she blushed and told him it was 'Sweet Sue'. 'Sorry about that, but I'm going dancing tonight and I do like the singer.'

'Sounds very interesting,' said Mr Hunt.

'He is so good looking. A bit like Tyrone Power. And you should hear him sing. He makes me go all funny.'

Mr Hunt laughed, but was concerned. He didn't like to think Susan could get hurt over this lad. But then again, she was young, and all young girls had crushes.

'He really is nice.'

'Well just make sure you don't make any mistakes while you're drooling over him.'

Sue blushed again and felt silly. Was she getting too familiar, and being told off in a polite way? 'I won't.'

★   ★   ★

That evening Sue hurried home and took extra care getting herself ready for her big night out, even though she didn't have a new dress and was again wearing the blue frock her mum had made her last Christmas.

As they stood shivering at the bus stop Jane said, 'I'll be glad when you've got that car. Just think, we'll be able to swan up to the dance in style. Mind you, the way you was making the car

98

jump forward on Sunday, it'll be a while before you'll be allowed on the road.'

'You enjoyed the ride out, now didn't you?'

'Course. Even though I bumped me head a few times.'

'Don't be so fussy, it was an afternoon out.'

'I know, and it was a bit of a laugh. Can I come out with you again?'

'If Mr Hunt says it's all right.'

'I like your boss, he's a really nice man.'

'I know. Right, here's our bus.'

'Thank goodness for that.'

The town hall wasn't as crowded as it usually was on a Saturday night, and when they walked into the dance hall Sue quickly made her way to the chairs near the bandstand.

When Cy stood up to sing, he gave her a wink, and she thought her heart would fly away.

'Did you see that,' she said in a loud whisper to Jane to make herself heard above the music. Her cheeks were bright pink and her eyes sparkling. 'He winked at me. He recognised me.'

'I bet he does that to all the girls.'

'I don't think so. Come on, let's dance.'

They always had to dance together till the boys got up courage to ask them. Then it was just a question of picking out the best dancers. Some of the blokes trod all over their feet, while others just wanted to hold them so tight they could hardly breathe.

All the time Sue was smiling at Cy Taylor.

When it was time for the interval, she said to Jane: 'Can you get me a glass of ginger beer? I'm going outside for some fresh air.'

'What? Are you mad? It's freezing out there.'

'I won't be long.'

She ran to the cloakroom and handed over her ticket. 'I'll be back in a minute,' she said to the cloakroom girl.

'You'll have to pay again,' said the girl.

'That's all right.'

Sue hurried outside and to her relief found Cy Taylor leaning against the wall having a cigarette.

'Hello,' she said casually, going up to him.

'Hello, babe.'

'You don't remember me, do you?'

He looked puzzled.

'Christmas Eve, when you were last here. You kissed me.' Sue was pleased the light over the back door was behind her, as she didn't want him to see how she was blushing and her knees were trembling.

'I've kissed a lot of girls, but I'm sure I would have remembered those luscious lips. Give us another taste to refresh my memory and then I'll let you know.'

Without hesitation Sue stepped forward and let him kiss her.

When they broke away he said, 'Not sure. I'll try again.'

As their lips met again, Sue was worried she would pass out with the sheer pleasure of his lips on hers. Then the door opened and a member of the band came out.

'Come on, mate. Jeff's yelling for you.'

'Bye for now, my pretty one. What's your name?'

100

'Sue.'

'Sweet Sue. I'll sing that just for you.'

Sue walked back inside in a daze, and after repairing her make-up in the cloakroom went across the dance floor to Jane.

'What you been up to? You look like the cat that's got the cream.'

'I've just been kissed by Cy.'

'What? Where?'

'Outside.'

'So that's where you've been while I've been sitting here like a long-lost soul and feeling like a wallflower. How did you know he would be outside?'

'On Christmas Eve I followed him, and it seems he always goes out for a smoke during the interval.'

'You crafty thing.'

'All's fair in love and war.'

'Sue, don't get too silly over this bloke. He's out of reach. They're not for the likes of us.'

'We shall see.'

For the rest of the evening Sue couldn't take her eyes off Cy Taylor, and when he sang 'Sweet Sue' she knew she was in love with him, truly in love, and nobody was going to get in her way and try to stop her.

★   ★   ★

That night in bed she went over and over the evening and how she was going to get Cy Taylor to take her out. The thought that was going through her mind was that if she had a car *she*

101

could invite *him* out; that way they would be on their own. She would make up a picnic and take him out into the country; no man would be able to resist that. She knew she was being silly but she didn't care, and went to sleep smiling, with the image of her and Cy driving along the open road and stopping in a field, where she knew she would let him make love to her.

★　★　★

'Did you enjoy yourself last night?' Fred Hunt asked.

'Yes, I did.'

'And did you see your hero?'

Sue grinned and nodded. She wanted to tell Mr Hunt that he'd kissed her, but she didn't think that would be right.

'Did you want to go out driving again on Sunday afternoon?'

'I wouldn't mind, that's if you've got nothing else to do. Could Jane come along?'

As much as he wanted Sue to himself, he said, 'Of course. I'll pick you up about two, will that be all right?'

'Thank you.'

'And Susan. I think you should get your driving licence, then we can go out on the road.'

She beamed. 'I've got it already. And thank you. You don't know how much this means to me.'

'That's good. Well in that case, I was wondering, are you doing anything the Sunday after next?'

'No.'

'How would you like to come out for a drive on the road?'

'I don't know. Do you think I'll be ready for that?'

'I would think so. I've got to see my mother and I was wondering if you would like to drive me down there. That way you can get some experience on the roads — they're not too bad on a Sunday — and I won't have to stay long at me ma's.' Also he wanted his mother to meet Susan.

Sue was taken aback and panic filled her. 'I won't have to drive your big car, will I?'

He laughed. 'No, not if you don't want to.'

'I shall be ever so worried.'

He smiled. 'You don't have to be. We can take one from the workshop, and besides, I'll be there looking after you.'

Sue smiled happily. Every day, it seemed, her dream was getting that little bit closer.

12

It was a warm spring afternoon in early April, and after what seemed to Sue a hair-raising journey, they arrived at their destination.

'It's a big house,' she said as she emerged from the car and stood looking up at the many chimneys.

'Yes, it is. Come on. Ma's waiting.'

With a great deal of apprehension Sue followed her boss inside, where two women hugged him; he introduced them as his mother and Aunt Rosa.

'Come into the front room,' said Rosa, taking Sue's coat. 'The fire's lovely in there.'

Mrs Hunt merely gave Sue a slight nod and said to her son, 'That's not your car. Where's yours? I thought you of all people would have had it repaired by now.'

'It's fine, but it's too big for Susan to handle, so we used this smaller one.'

'What d'you mean, too big for Susan?'

'She drove down here.'

'And who is Susan?' His mother fired the question at him in a way that made Sue feel very uncomfortable as she followed them into the well-furnished front room.

Mrs Hunt waved a hand at Sue to indicate that she should sit in a green velvet armchair that stood beside the wide French windows. Sue lowered herself down very nervously and perched on the edge.

'Susan works for me.'

'So what are you doing taking out someone who works for you, on a Sunday as well?'

'Susan is learning to drive, and I thought it would be good experience for her to drive down here. After all, the roads are very quiet on a Sunday.' He gave Sue a reassuring smile.

'What does a slip of a girl want to be able to drive for?'

'Ma, she will be a great asset to the business and to me.' He was beginning to get agitated with all these questions, and with the fact that his mother was talking as though Susan wasn't there. 'She can take punters out on test drives when I'm busy.'

'I think that's lovely,' said Rosa. 'I would have liked to have been able to drive during the war. It must have been wonderful to sit high up behind the wheel of an ambulance or a lorry.'

'Well you would. Anything to do with men.'

Ted came into the room. 'Wondered whose car that was outside. As it's a Ford, I thought it might be you, but the L plates threw me.' He shook Fred's hand. 'Anyway, how are you? How's the head?'

'Fine, thanks.'

'You gave us all a bit of a fright.'

'Not as much as I gave me.'

'So what's with the L plates?'

'Susan did the driving.'

'Clever girl.'

'I only crashed the gears a couple of times. But there's so much to think about.'

105

Fred smiled at her, and his mother took note of that.

For the rest of the afternoon the small talk continued, but as it was about family, most of it went over Sue's head. After the light tea, her boss said to Sue's relief that it was time to leave before it got dark.

When they went out to the car, Sue removed the L plates and then sat in the passenger seat. 'You'd better drive home.'

'Why's that?'

'I don't want to make a fool of myself.'

He laughed and gave his family a wave.

'Your mum doesn't like me.'

'Don't worry about her; she questions everybody's motive.'

★ ★ ★

They arrived home a lot quicker than it had taken them to get there.

'Thank you for this afternoon. It's been very interesting,' said Sue when they turned into Lily Road.

'You're going to be a good driver. We'll go out again next week, if that's all right with you.'

'I would love it. Thank you, Mr Hunt.'

As Sue pushed open her gate, she saw next door's frontroom curtains twitch. She knew Ron was watching her, but she would have been shocked and worried if she had seen the angry look on his face.

★ ★ ★

'How did you get on?' asked her father.

'Fine. It's a lot different driving on a road; you have to keep to your side and watch out for traffic.'

'Christ, I should hope you do,' said Granny Potts. 'What did he want to take you to see his mother for?'

'It was just somewhere to go, and he said he had to see his mum, so that killed two birds with one stone.'

'Seems funny to me, taking out someone who works for him.'

'Mum, it might be because he's lonely and wants a bit of company,' said Doris. 'So, where does his mum live?' she asked her daughter.

'It's a little village in Surrey.'

'What's the house like?'

'Doris, give the girl a chance.'

'It's all right, Dad. It's a big house and very grand. The rooms I went in had smashing furniture, and you should see the curtains, they went right down to the floor. And it's all on its own — not many people seem to live near them — and you should see the bathroom: it's enormous, with a lovely big bath and washbasin. I could have lived in there, and it was lovely having a wee indoors.'

'Is it hers?' asked her gran.

'No, I think it's his aunt and uncle's. His uncle's got a grocers shop and a couple of kids and some grandkids. I don't think his mum liked me.'

'What makes you say that?'

'Her attitude. But his Aunt Rosa's nice.'

'She's probably worried that our Sue's gonner make off with him; after all, he must be worth a bob or two.'

Sue laughed. 'Oh Gran, he's an old man.'

'There's many a young girl what marries an old man for his money.'

'Not me.' She wanted to tell them that her heart belonged to Cy Taylor.

★   ★   ★

At last the day came when Sue passed her driving test. When she was given that important piece of paper, she unconsciously threw her arms round Mr Hunt's neck.

'I'm sorry,' she said when she realised what she'd done.

Fred Hunt grinned. He hadn't been bothered by her reaction; in fact he'd enjoyed it. 'Not to worry. Now you'll be allowed to take a car out on your own.'

When they arrived back at the office he said, 'Before you take your hat and coat off, I want you to collect some spares that Harry's waiting for. Do you think you can manage that?'

Sue beamed. 'Course.'

'Well drive carefully. I don't want this car wrecked.'

As she drove, she felt very confident. When she arrived at the spares depot, there were a few men who were a bit surprised as they loaded her car.

'Fred Hunt let you drive one of his cars?' said one old man. 'Must have more money than sense.'

'He reckons I'm a good driver.'

'Well I wouldn't let a slip of a girl near my car if I had one.'

Sue only smiled as she got in the driver's seat and gave them a wave as she pulled away. She was singing as she drove back to the garage. The freedom that this was going to open up for her was beyond words. Now all she had to do was get together a deposit and then persuade Mr Hunt to let her buy a car of her own. That was a very tall order, but although she was under age to take out a hire purchase agreement, she was sure Mr Hunt or her dad would sign it for her.

⋆ ⋆ ⋆

It was well into the summer before Sue asked her boss about having a car of her own.

'You don't have to worry about buying one; all the time you work for me, you can borrow one from the forecourt.'

'Do you mean that?'

'Just for the weekend, mind.'

'Can I have one this weekend, then me and Jane could go out for the day?'

'I don't see why not.'

'Thank you so much.'

He would do anything to make her happy, but wished he could be with her.

The first time they went out, they giggled like a couple of schoolgirls.

'This is great,' said Jane. 'You are so clever learning to drive.'

'I know.'

'Will you be able to borrow it next weekend?'

'I don't know. Mustn't push me luck. Can't have one every weekend.' Sue wanted to wait till Cy Taylor was back at the town hall, then she would take him out on the Sunday. Slowly her dreams were coming true.

★   ★   ★

On Monday she felt happy and so grown up as she drove to work. It was lovely not to have to walk.

But her joy left her halfway through the morning when she looked out of the window and saw Ron in deep conversation with Mr Hunt.

Fear filled her. What did he want?

After a while Mr Hunt walked into the office, with Ron following on behind. 'Ron is coming back here to work.'

Ron was grinning. Sue felt as if her world was falling apart.

'I'm finding it difficult to keep the cars up to scratch, and he did make a good job of the cleaning.'

'Can't you get someone else?' she asked quietly.

Fred Hunt looked at her. What was worrying her? 'He's fine. And he's reliable. Does he bother you?'

'No.' She looked at Ron. How could she tell Mr Hunt about the eye and all the other things that made her flesh creep? It would make her sound silly. 'Does Mr Field know?'

'Who I hire has nothing to do with him.' There

was an edge to the boss's voice. 'Ron can start in the morning.'

That evening when she met Jane, Sue was full of it.

'You might not be very happy about it,' said Jane, 'but me mum will be more than pleased.'

'Just so long as he stops that silly nonsense about wanting to marry me.'

★   ★   ★

For a few weeks Ron did keep his thoughts and hands to himself and Sue began to relax in his presence. Every evening he insisted they walk as far as the bus stop together, but he still wouldn't wait for Jane and he did behave himself. Had the vicar's talk done the trick?

At the end of the month Sue asked Mr Hunt if she could borrow a car for the weekend.

'Got anything exciting planned?'

'Just going to the dance Sat'day night.' Sue wasn't going to tell him that she hoped to take Cy out on Sunday.

'That's nice,' was his answer. He knew she would be seeing that young man. Could he be a threat to his plans?

★   ★   ★

On Saturday morning the office door was thrust open and banged against the wall. Sue jumped and looked up.

'Where is he?' A man stood filling the doorway, his face contorted with anger.

111

'If you mean Mr Hunt, Mr Clarke, he's round the back.'

'I'm gonner bloody kill the conniving, cheating shyster.'

Sue didn't say a word. She had had dealings with Mr Clarke before. He was a big, muscular man who never wore a coat whatever the weather. He was tall and very frightening. Since buying his car, he had come in a few times and started shouting about the things that were wrong with it. Mr Hunt wasn't going to give in, though. He had told Sue that he had been at school with Mr Clarke, and that he was a bully. He had a few coal delivery lorries and was well known for cheating his customers and putting the fear of God into some of the old people.

Mr Clarke stormed out of the office, slamming the door behind him.

It was just a few minutes later that Sue heard the shouting. She looked out of the window and saw that Mr Clarke had Mr Hunt's head under his arm and was hitting him in the face. She ran out on to the forecourt.

'Stop it! Stop it!' she yelled, looking round frantically for help. 'I'll call the police.'

'You do that, love, and I'll tell them about how he cheats his customers,' snarled Mr Clarke between blows.

At that moment Ron came up behind the fighting men and hit Mr Clarke over the head with a large lump of wood. Mr Clarke fell back and Mr Hunt stood up, and after straightening his tie, smoothed his hair down.

'Bloody sod crept up behind me.' He looked at

the man lying on the floor. 'For two pins I'd smash his sodding head in. Thank you, Ron.'

Ron grinned. 'That's all right. Don't want anybody to hurt you or little Sue.'

Mr Clarke lay on the floor, moaning.

'D'you want me to give him a good kicking?'

'No. I'll sort this out.'

Sue could hear the phone ringing, so she went back into the office. She had seen her boss angry before, but not like this. She could see he was trying to keep his temper under control. She watched him pick Mr Clarke up, and could see that a lot of angry words were being exchanged. When Mr Hunt came into the office rubbing his fist, he smiled at her. 'Sorry about that.'

'Are you all right?'

'Yes. Just a couple of bruises and a scraped knuckle, but I'll live.'

'Will he be back again?'

'I would think so. Don't worry, Ron will look after you. That lad is such an asset.'

'What are you going to do about Mr Clarke?'

'Don't worry about him. I come from round this way, remember, and I know a few villains who'll dust him over for a couple of pounds.'

'I certainly wouldn't like to upset you,' said Sue cautiously.

'You have nothing to worry about.' He wanted to add, *and I'd kill anyone who upsets you.* Instead he smiled and made his way upstairs to his flat, thinking as he pushed open the door: *that includes that so-called singer if he breaks your heart.*

113

13

Sue was thoroughly excited as she drove to the dance. 'I still can't believe your boss would let you borrow one of his cars,' said Jane.

'He knows I'm a good driver,' said Sue confidently. 'Anyway, it ain't a new one.'

'Even so, it's ever so nice.' Jane ran her hand over the brown leather seat.

Sue felt very important as she parked the car, and when she got out she was aware that she was attracting some glances. Not many women of her age could drive, and certainly not many had a car. They must think she was well off.

Jane also took in the admiring glances, and she looked like the cat that had got the cream as she tucked her hand through Sue's arm and together they went inside.

As usual Cy Taylor took Sue's breath away when she walked in and saw him standing on the stage. He looked so handsome in his evening suit. She quickly made her way to the seat nearest the band.

'I suppose you'll be going outside in the interval?' said Jane, looking round.

'What do you think?' said Sue, gazing up at the band. She had already told Jane that if she couldn't take Cy out tomorrow, the two friends could go out together. Jane wasn't happy about being second best.

When Cy caught sight of her he gave her a

smile and a nod. Sue felt her knees buckle.

After the next few dances, when she was waltzed, foxtrotted and quickstepped round the floor, it was the interval.

Outside, Cy was leaning against the wall as usual, puffing thoughtfully on his cigarette. Full of confidence, Sue went straight up to him.

'Hello. Remember me?'

'How could I forget you?' He dropped his cigarette and ground it out with the toe of his shoe. 'I was hoping you'd be here tonight.'

'Were you?'

'Yer. It's nice to see a friendly face in the crowd.'

'Is that what I am, a friendly face?'

'And a very pretty one, I might add. In fact, I would say you are the prettiest one in this place.'

Sue knew she was blushing. She wasn't used to such compliments. 'Do you live near here?' she asked.

'Not really. I'm from up north, but I'm not home that much. Always on the road, you know.'

'That must be hard on your family.'

'Na. As long as I send the money home, me mum and dad are happy enough.'

'No wife, then?'

'Good God, no.'

Sue relaxed and moved closer, so that he could smell her Evening in Paris scent. She knew she didn't have much time for any preamble, so she just asked outright: 'Would you like to come out with me tomorrow?'

'Can't. Sorry, love.'

'Why?'

He laughed. 'Have to move on with the band tonight.'

'Where are you going?'

'Guildford.'

'Could I come and see you there?'

'Course. We're playing at the ballroom. Anyone can come if they buy a ticket.'

'I didn't mean to the dance.' Sue was almost quaking. She knew she was being very forward, but time was running out and he would be called in very shortly. 'No, I meant could I see you tomorrow afternoon? Take you out for a drive?'

'What?'

She crossed her fingers behind her back. 'I've got a car.'

'You have?'

'Yes.'

'And you can drive?'

She nodded. 'What do you think?'

'I think that sounds a very interesting idea. Ain't used to having a chauffeur, especially a lady one.'

The door opened and the drummer called out: 'Come on, Casanova. Jeff's waiting.'

'Where and what time tomorrow?' asked Sue urgently.

'Pick me up at Guildford station about three. By the way, what's your name again?'

★   ★   ★

'I can't believe you've asked him out,' said Jane as they were driving home. 'What you gonner tell your mum and dad?'

116

'Dunno. I'll think of something. I can always say I'm going out with Mr Hunt.'

Jane sat back. 'What if he don't turn up?'

'He will. I just know he will.'

'Well let's hope Mr Hunt don't come and ask your mum and dad for the car back tomorrow.'

'He won't do that.' Sue was beside herself. Tomorrow she was going to be alone with her heartthrob.

★ ★ ★

A couple of times throughout the morning Doris asked her daughter if she felt all right.

'I'm fine,' came the reply. 'Why?'

'You look a bit flushed, that's all. Are you worried about taking Mr Hunt out again?'

'No.' Sue hated lying to her mum, but she knew her mother would never let her go if she thought she was going to meet a singer she knew nothing about.

'Is Jane going with you?'

'No. It's business. I'll just pop next door.' Sue left the house in a hurry. She didn't want to tell any more lies and she was afraid she was getting herself in too deep.

'Little Sue, this is a nice surprise. See you've got the car outside. We going for a ride then?' asked Ron, who was waiting for her in the passage.

'No. I've got to go out.' She was worried that Jane might say something to Mrs Brent and Ron might overhear it, and that it would get back to Mr Hunt and possibly her mother.

117

'I like working for Mr Hunt. He's ever so nice to me, and after I hit that bloke he said he reckons I could be very useful if anyone comes round wanting a fight.'

'We don't get too many coming round wanting a fight, thank goodness,' said Sue, following Ron into the kitchen.

'Hello, Sue,' said Jane as her friend walked in. 'Didn't hear you knock.'

'Didn't have to. Mr Nosy here was looking out of the window.'

Jane tutted and turned back to the sink to continue peeling potatoes. 'D'you know, Ron, I bet you know the business of everybody who lives in this road.'

He grinned and touched his nose. 'I sure do.'

'Well scram now. Sue and me want to talk.'

With a downcast look on his face he reluctantly walked out of the room.

'Right. That's got rid of him. Was there anything special you wanted?'

'No, not really. It's just that . . . ' Sue looked at the closed door and hesitated. 'You won't say anything to your mum, will you, you know, about me meeting Cy?'

'No. Course not.'

'That's good. Only I've told my mum I'm meeting Mr Hunt, and if Ron hears different, well, anything could happen.'

'Are you getting cold feet?'

'No. Just as long as he turns up.'

'You worried he might not?'

Sue shrugged. 'I shall know in,' she looked at her watch, 'three hours' time.'

*   ★ ★

Sue parked the car outside the station and waited. An hour later she was still sitting waiting and was feeling cross and stupid. How could she have been so silly as to believe he would turn up? She was about to drive away when she caught sight of him jumping off a bus. She hurriedly scrambled out of the car. 'Cy!' she called.

When he caught sight of her he gave her a wave.

Sue ran up to him. 'You came?'

He kissed her cheek. 'Sorry I'm late. Jeff wanted to have a rehearsal.'

Sue didn't care. He was here with her now. 'Shall we go for a drive?'

'Why not? I could do with some relaxing. It's been a bit tense back there.'

As they drove along Sue wanted to sing. She hadn't known she could be so happy.

'I've got to be back at six,' he said, breaking into her thoughts.

'That's all right.' Soon they were in the country. 'Shall we stop near here?'

'If you want. I love the look of concentration you have. It makes your lovely eyes sparkle. How long have you been driving?'

'Not that long.'

'This certainly is a novelty,' he said, grinning. 'I've never known a girl who could drive, and who has her own car.'

'This ain't mine. It belongs to my boss. I work for a garage that sells cars.'

119

'And here was me thinking I'd found a rich heiress.'

Sue panicked. 'Is that why you came out with me?'

'Na. It's because you're pretty and I like you.' Sue relaxed. He liked her.

'He must be a good boss if he trusts you with one of his cars.'

'He is.' Sue pulled the car over on to a grassy spot. 'D'you fancy a walk over towards those trees?'

'That sounds like a very good idea.'

As they walked across the grass, Cy held her hand. It was a warm afternoon and Sue was wearing a cotton summer dress; Cy was dressed in a white shirt and flannels. She knew they made a handsome couple.

After a short while he stopped and, turning her to him, kissed her lips. It was a long, hard kiss and Sue felt her senses reeling.

Cy looked around. 'Let's sit down,' he said, holding on to her.

In a daze she sat beside him as he continued to kiss her.

'I think you're great,' he said when they broke apart.

'And I think you're wonderful,' she said breathlessly.

He began to undo the top button of her dress. 'Do you mind?'

Sue shook her head. She wanted to tell him that he could do what he liked.

He kissed her neck as his hand went inside her dress. 'You have such pert tits. How many blokes have been round these?'

'No one.' She closed her eyes.

'You mean you ain't ever done it?'

'No,' she gasped as his hand went down to her thighs. Slowly it travelled up past her stocking tops and suspenders, and as she was wearing camiknickers his fingers quickly found her very private parts. She was both excited and frightened, and as she tensed he looked at her and smiled.

'Just relax.'

'But suppose someone can see us.'

'They can't see where me hand is. Don't you like it?'

'Yes,' she whispered as she lay back and once again let him smother her face with kisses. She knew she was besotted with him and all her common sense left her.

'God, you're wonderful.' He kissed her lips with such passion.

Sue couldn't believe this was happening to her. She had feelings she had never experienced before. She wanted him to make love to her. She wanted him to be the first. She could feel his fingers pressing into her and knew that, as he was so close to her, he also had feelings for her.

'If it was dark, I'd have you.'

Sue couldn't believe that he wanted her as much as she wanted him. She found herself saying: 'Can I meet you somewhere?'

He sat up. 'You mean that? You want me to be the first?'

She nodded. This was what she wanted more than anything else in the world. Was she being a bit forward? Would he think she was easy? But then he knew he was the first, and why should she go along with convention? This was the man she loved and one day would marry.

She could hear children yelling, and suddenly she felt guilty and sat up.

'What's wrong?'

'Nothing.'

'Don't worry about them.' He went to pull her down again.

'What if they recognise you?'

He grinned. 'D'you think they might?'

'I don't know. Their mum might.'

'In that case we'd better be off. Can't let the image suffer.'

Sue brushed herself down as they walked back to the car. When they were settled inside, Cy looked at his watch.

'If there was more time I'd get you to park in some secluded spot and have you now.'

'I can't do that. Not in the boss's car.'

'Why not? He's not to know.'

'I would rather it be in a bed.'

'That's OK. It was just a thought.' He kissed her cheek. 'Better get going. Jeff starts going on if any of us are late.'

14

Sue took Cy to the ballroom where he would be performing that evening. How she wished she could have stayed with him. She smiled, contenting herself with the thought that next month she was going to be alone with him in a hotel he knew in Euston. As she drove home singing, her head was in the clouds and her thoughts were on his kisses, which were still lingering on her lips. She knew she was a romantic, but she didn't care. He had wanted her and had made a date, giving her the address of the hotel. He had said he would phone her at work if something else came up and he couldn't make it.

She didn't mind that she might not be able to get a car. That didn't matter; she would be more than happy to fly to him on wings if need be, to give herself to the man she loved.

'Did you have a nice afternoon?' asked her mother as she walked in.

'Yes thanks.'

'Go anywhere nice?' asked Granny Potts.

'No, not really.' Sue crossed her fingers behind her back. 'Mr Hunt wanted to show me the new model that a friend of his is selling; he's got a showroom over Euston way.' She looked away as she felt herself blushing. Although telling lies was beginning to come easy, it still bothered her.

After tea, Jane came in. In the privacy of Sue's

bedroom she wanted to know where they'd been. 'And did anything happen?' she asked as she plonked herself on the bed.

'No, course not.' Sue nervously patted the back of her hair. 'We went for a ride in the country, that's all.'

'And he didn't try anything on?'

'No, course not,' said Sue again, trying to make it sound convincing. She moved over to the window and looked out on to the roof of the lav in the yard below. She wasn't going to tell even her best friend what had happened.

'Did he kiss you?'

'Yes.'

'What's he like? Is he a good kisser?'

'He's all right.' How could Sue tell her friend that his kisses were wonderful and full of the promise of what was going to happen in two weeks' time?

'When you seeing him again?'

'I don't know. He's got the office phone number.'

'D'you think he'll ring you?'

Sue only shrugged. She couldn't tell Jane that she was going to a hotel and letting him make love to her. But what if he changed his mind?

'You sound as if you've lost interest.'

'No, I haven't.'

'I know: he was a bit of a letdown, not as good as when he's standing there all dressed up and singing.'

Sue smiled. She would let Jane go along with that idea.

The following morning Sue felt obliged to drive Ron to work.

'This is smashing,' he said as he sat next to her. 'I ain't ever been in a car before; well, not with you driving. You're a clever girl, my little Sue. Jane was a bit fed up yesterday.'

'Why?'

'She was annoyed with you 'cos you didn't take her out.'

'She knows I was with a mate.' Sue was getting worried. She had told her mother one thing; now she was telling Ron another. 'I said I'd take her out some other time.'

He shuffled in his seat. 'Good. Can I come with you?'

'I don't know. I'll have to ask Jane if she wants you to.'

'That means no.' He looked this way and that as they drove along. 'I'll have to give this car a good clean; look at all those dog ends.' He wound down the window. 'And it stinks of smoke. Didn't know you smoked.'

Sue felt her stomach lurch as she glanced down at the small ashtray. She had forgotten that Cy smoked all the time. She smiled at Ron and said sweetly, 'Don't tell your mum, 'cos she'll tell mine or Mr Hunt, but my friend smokes.' That wasn't a lie, as Cy *was* her friend, soon to be her lover. 'Ron, let it be our little secret.'

He grinned. 'I like that. Me and you having a secret.'

125

Despite her fears, in many ways Sue felt sorry for him. At times he could be so childlike.

★   ★   ★

'Did you and your friend have a good day out yesterday?' asked Fred Hunt, who was sitting at his desk when Sue walked in.

'Yes thanks.'

'Go anywhere interesting?'

'Only for a ride out into the country.'

'It's nice this time of year.'

'Yes, it is.'

'Did you go to the dance on Saturday?'

'Yes.' Sue was getting worried. Why was he asking all these questions? Had he seen her?

'Was your singer there?'

'Yes, he was.' Sue smiled.

'That's good. So you weren't disappointed?'

'No.'

Sue was pleased when the phone rang, as she had to get down to work and it took her mind off worrying what his next question would be.

Fred looked across at Susan. She was blossoming into a lovely young lady.

★   ★   ★

It was the middle of July, and the weather was hot and sultry. All morning Sue sat with the door wide open as she typed away. Every time the phone rang, her heart jumped into her mouth. She was terrified it would be Cy telling her that he couldn't make it this afternoon.

At long last it was one o'clock and time for her to leave. She stood up as Mr Hunt walked into the office.

'You've been in a bit of a dream today, Susan. Are you feeling all right?'

'Yes thank you. It must be this weather.'

'It is a bit warm. I'm surprised you didn't want to borrow a car for a trip to the seaside tomorrow.'

'Didn't really give that a thought.'

'It might be worth doing next weekend; that's if you want to.'

'I think that would be lovely. I'll tell Jane. Is it all right if I go now.'

'Course. Sorry. I didn't mean to keep you. Have a nice weekend.'

'I'm sure I will.'

Although Ron was outside waiting for her, Sue still had a spring in her step. She had already told her parents that she would be going out for the afternoon and evening. When they asked who with and where to, she'd told them she was seeing an old school friend who had come into the showroom with her father, who was buying a new car. She had told Jane the same thing, but she wasn't sure Jane believed her, especially when she asked her friend's name. Sue had had to remember who had been at college with her. So that was another lie.

She knew Cy could only stay for a few hours, as he would be singing in the evening. It was a private do, so she couldn't even go with him. He did suggest they meet up after and spend the night together, but Sue knew she couldn't do that, not stay out all right.

As she sat on the underground, her thoughts were racing and her palms sweating. When other people did this sort of thing how did they feel? Did she look guilty? Had Cy done this before? How did he know about this hotel? She quickly dismissed all these negative thoughts. He had told her the band often stayed there.

For two weeks the one question that had continually invaded her thoughts was, could she become pregnant? The idea that she could have a baby horrified her, even if it was Cy's. Would he marry her? What would her parents say? She would lose her job. Fear began to grip her, even though she remembered the girls at college saying you couldn't fall for a baby the first time you did it.

When she got out at Euston station, she felt a little calmer as she walked along the road to meet her lover.

* * *

The hotel wasn't what she was expecting; it was just a large, dingy-looking four-storey house. It didn't look over-clean. Her mother would kill her if she took fleas back home with her.

She looked all around her, almost expecting someone to walk past and recognise her, then she walked slowly up the stone steps, which didn't look as if they'd been swept for weeks. She pushed open the door and stepped into a dingy hall that smelled of cabbage cooking. In front of her was a tiny desk with a row of keys on hooks

128

on the wall behind. A tall, stern-faced woman who was sitting behind the desk stood up. Her piercing eyes and hair pulled back into a severe bun were very intimidating.

She addressed Sue. 'Yes. Can I help you?'

Sue wanted to turn and run away. This wasn't what she was expecting. She looked round, bewildered. Had she got the right address?

'I'm meeting a Mr Cy Taylor here,' she said, her voice hardly above a whisper.

'Oh yes. Room four. Up the stairs and first door on the left.' It was so matter-of-fact. The woman didn't want to know anything about her. Did people come here all the time just for . . . ? Sue didn't dare ask if he was up there already and waiting for her. Without looking back, she made her way slowly up the stairs and knocked nervously on the door of Room 4.

The door was suddenly jerked open and Cy was standing there. Pulling her into the room, he took her in his arms and kissed her long and hard.

'I was worried in case you'd changed your mind.'

All Sue's fears disappeared. He was here and she was in his arms. And he'd been was worried she wouldn't turn up. His kisses were hard and demanding. Hardly stopping for breath, he moved her round the room towards the bed and began pushing her skirt up.

15

Sue lay next to Cy, under the scratchy sheet. After the fury of removing their clothes, they had done it. Now he lay on his back with his eyes closed and she looked at him in wonder. He was so good looking, and they had made love! His kisses had thrilled her beyond words and when his hands explored her body she wanted to cry out in ecstasy. He appeared to know what he was doing, so Sue just lay there and let him take her. It wasn't as magical as she'd thought it would be, but she didn't care. She was a woman now, and she was next to the man she loved so very much.

He opened his eyes and smiled at her. 'That was great. You are very special and I love every inch of your body.'

He put his arm round her and Sue felt a thrill as he caressed her again. He levered himself up on his elbow and she could feel herself blushing as he looked into her face. She had been both surprised and shocked at seeing him naked, and the sight of his manhood had frightened her. This was something she had never seen before, and although she had insisted that they draw the curtains, they were very thin and didn't keep much light out. She wished it had been dark, then she wouldn't have felt so embarrassed. But when he kissed her, she'd felt all her inhibitions leave.

He sat up and lit a cigarette and puffed the smoke into the air. 'Right, how about something to eat? Making love always makes me hungry.'

Sue was taken back at the remark and looked at him, surprised.

He swung his legs over the side of bed. 'What's wrong?'

'Nothing.'

She watched as he stood dressing himself. After he put on his shirt he bent down and looked in the speckled mirror, then with both hands slicked down his straight dark hair. 'Come on, get dressed,' he said. 'I'm starving.'

Sue felt tears sting her eyes. She knew that it probably hadn't been his first time — after all, women must throw themselves at him — but hearing him talk to her like that made her feel as if she had been used.

He turned and looked at her, then came round to her side of the bed. 'When you look at me like that, I want to do it again. You are so lovely, even with your hair all tousled. Come here.'

As he took her in his arms, her tears began to fall.

'What is it? What's wrong?' He gently pushed her away from him and looked into her face. 'I know I was the first, but I thought you wanted it?'

'I did,' she sobbed.

'I didn't mean to hurt you, but I got a bit carried away.'

Sue pulled the sheet up to her face and buried her head. He tugged the sheet away and kissed her wet cheeks. 'Now come on, get dressed and no more tears. Let's go and get something to eat.'

As she sat on the side of the bed and discreetly got dressed, her thoughts were in turmoil. Half of her had regrets and she suddenly felt guilty. What would her mum and dad say if they knew what she'd done? And what about Gran?

She hung back as they went down the stairs. What would that woman behind the desk say? Much to Sue's surprise, however, she was smiling at Cy.

'Will you be back for a meal before you go to work?' she asked.

'I would think so. The others should be here this afternoon.'

'The rooms are all ready for them.'

Cy put his arm round Sue's waist and gently ushered her through the front door.

'She's a bit frightening,' said Sue when they were outside.

'She can be a nosy cow. She'll be telling all the band that I had a girl here this afternoon.'

'She wouldn't, would she?'

'She's done it before.'

Sue had to ask. 'So you've brought other girls here?'

'Only a couple of times. It gets very lonely on the road with just a bunch of blokes to keep you company. That's why the band call me Casanova.'

'Has there ever been anyone special?' asked Sue quietly.

'No, not till now that is. I could get very fond of you, Sue.'

132

Sue felt happy. Even though he'd had other girls, he was telling her that he was fond of her.

They sat in a café and Cy ordered egg and chips. Sue didn't feel hungry and settled for a cup of tea and a cake.

As she watched him eat, she asked, 'When will you be coming back to the town hall?'

'Dunno. Never sure of the dates till Jeff tells us.'

'Hope it's not too long.'

He reached across the table and took hold of her hand. 'I'll let you know as soon as I can. Perhaps we can have another afternoon together?'

'I'd like that.'

★   ★   ★

As Sue sat on the train taking her back home, it was Jane who filled her thoughts. What would she say if she knew what Sue had done that afternoon? Would she be able to tell? Somehow Sue felt different. She smiled to herself. She was now a woman in every sense of the word, and it made her glow inwardly knowing she had a secret.

★   ★   ★

Gran was sitting in the yard. 'Hello, love. Did you have a nice time?' she asked as Sue came out.

'Yes thanks. Where's Mum?'

'Just popped over the road. Said we needed

133

some more milk. I think she thought you might be bringing your mate back.'

'No. She had to get home.'

'Grab a chair and come and sit in the sun for a little while. It'll do you good. You look a bit pasty-faced. 'Sides, it'll soon disappear behind the houses.'

Sue brought out a chair. She sat down, leaned back and closed her eyes, letting the sun warm her face, then gave her gran a quick sideways glance. She couldn't believe that at some time in her life Gran must have done it, and what about her mum and dad? She couldn't imagine them entwined like she had been with Cy. It didn't seem right somehow.

'Did you have a nice time, Sue?' asked her mother, coming into the yard.

'Yes thanks.'

'You didn't bring you friend back, then?'

'No. She had to get home.'

'Mum, you'll never guess,' said Doris. 'You know that Maisie Webb who lives in the next street?'

'Can't say I do.'

'Course you do. You're always going on about how she flaunts herself. Wears all those slinky frocks, always done up to the nines. Fur coat and no knickers, they reckon. Well. They was saying over in the grocer's that she's gone away, and guess what? They reckon she's having a baby. Can you imagine the family's shame? They reckon her father's going mad and has threatened to kill the bloke. But she won't say who it is.'

Sue froze. What if her parents found out what she had done?

'You're quiet, Sue,' said her mother. 'You all right?'

'Yes. I was just thinking about that poor woman.'

'You look a bit flushed.'

'Must be the sun,' said Granny Potts. 'She was looking very pasty when she came home.'

'Yes. It could be the weather. As I was saying, that Maisie brought it on herself, if you ask me. She should be ashamed, bringing that kind of disgrace on her family.'

'That's the trouble with today's youngsters, think only of themselves.' Gran pulled her shawl round her shoulders. 'It's started to get a bit nippy. I'll think I'll go in.'

Sue stayed out in the yard for a while. The thought that was filling her mind was, thank goodness you can't get pregnant when you do it the first time. But what if Cy wanted to do it again? Was she prepared to take the risk?

She glanced up at Ron's window. He was looking down at her. How long had he been up there, staring at her? That made her feel even more uncomfortable. He gave her a wave and blew a kiss. She got up and went inside.

★　★　★

That evening when Jane came in, she wanted to know if Sue had had a good day with her mate. 'Where did you go?'

'Only round the West End shops.'

135

'Did you buy anything?'

'No. Just looked and had a cup of tea and a cake, that's all.'

'Are you seeing her again?'

Sue shrugged.

'Doesn't sound as if you had a good time, then. I expect she's changed since your college days.'

'Yes. We both have.' Sue hated to keep up this pretence. 'I'm gonner ask Mr Hunt if I can have a car for next weekend, then perhaps on Sunday we could go to the seaside for the day.'

Jane's face lit up. 'Could we? That would be smashing. If the weather stays this warm, perhaps we could have a paddle.'

'Why not.' Sue was pleased she was able to make her friend happy.

16

Saturday was very warm, and Sue asked Mr
Hunt if she could have a car for the weekend and
told him why. Ron, who was standing close by,
grinned at her.

'Can I come with you and Jane to the seaside?'
he asked.

'No, you can't.'

'They won't want you to tag along,' said Mr
Hunt, laughing.

'Just as long as they don't try and get off with
any blokes,' Ron said very seriously.

'What they do won't be any of our business.
Just as long as the car comes back in one
piece, that's all I'm worried about.' Deep
down that wasn't what Fred was concerned
about at all. He knew he had to declare his
love for Susan before she was whisked away
by someone else. But what if she rejected
him? And why was Ron so concerned? Did
he have a soft spot for her? Then again,
anybody would; she was a lovely and very
likeable girl.

Sue noted that her boss wore a worried frown.
'You all right, Mr Hunt?'

'Yes, I'm fine.'

'I promise I'll look after the car.'

'I know you will. Just you go and have a nice
time.'

When she finished work at midday, she

137

reluctantly asked Ron if he wanted a lift home. As he sat next to her in the car, she could feel his eyes on her.

'Ron, stop staring at me.'

'I can't help it. You are so very beautiful, and I want you to be my girl.'

'Don't start all that nonsense again. I thought I'd made it very clear. I don't want to be your girl.'

When she stopped the car outside their houses, Ron took hold of her hand. Sue quickly pulled it away.

'Stop it. What are you doing?'

'I just want to hold you. You know I would do anything for you.'

'Just leave me be.' She opened the door. 'Come on, get out.'

Ron stood and watched her go through her gate. 'If anyone ever hurts you, my little Sue, I'd kill 'em.'

'Thank you, Ron, but I can't ever see that happening. I'm a big girl and I can look after meself.'

'I'll always be here for you.'

'Thank you, Ron. Goodbye.' She pulled the key through the letterbox and went inside.

★ ★ ★

On Sunday morning, Sue and Jane were laughing as they made their way to Brighton.

'I love this,' said Jane, waving to a group of cyclists as they passed them. 'You are so

138

lucky being able to drive and your boss letting you have a car.'

'I know. Mind you, I do have to put me own petrol in it.'

'Oh, what a shame.' Jane threw her head back and laughed.

For the rest of the day the sun shone and they lay back on the stony beach soaking up the sun. They had brought a picnic lunch, and for both of them it was a perfect day out.

'I wish we could do this every weekend,' said Jane after a painful trip over the stones to get into the sea. They stood holding their frocks up as they paddled.

'I can't take advantage of Mr Hunt.'

'He must like you to let you have a car.'

'He does, and he knows I'll be careful.'

'If we do this again, I reckon we ought to get one of those.' Jane pointed to a young woman in a swimsuit. 'She's wearing a nice one; mind you, I don't like her hat.'

Sue laughed. 'What does she want a swimming hat on for if she's only going to go in up to her knees?'

'Dunno, p'raps she reckons it looks good.'

'Those blokes seem to think so as well. Look, they're splashing her.'

'And she ain't running away, just standing there all coylooking and giggling.'

'Can't say I fancy showing meself off like that,' said Sue.

'I would, and I've made up me mind. I'm getting one of those.'

'Do you mean one of those blokes?'

139

'Hopefully,' said Jane.

Sue hadn't seen her friend so happy for a very long time.

As the afternoon wore on, Sue reluctantly decided it was time to go home. She had been pleased her friend hadn't enquired any more as to what she'd done last Saturday afternoon. To Sue, learning to drive was proving to be the best thing she had done in her life.

★　★　★

Two weeks later, Sue was drooling over Cy again. As soon as she walked into the dance hall, he winked at her and her knees turned to jelly.

'S'pose you're going outside again in the interval?' said Jane. She was definitely a bit narked.

'What do you think.' Sue wanted to find out when they were going to meet up again.

As soon as she was outside, she ran up to Cy and put her arms round his neck. He kissed her.

'Guessed you'd be here. I've got to tell you, we're doing the rest of the summer season in Blackpool.'

Sue stepped back, shocked. 'Blackpool? That's miles away.'

'I know. Can you get up there?'

'No.'

'What about for a holiday? We could spend all day on the beach and the nights in bed making love. Sounds great to me.'

Sue was both upset and thrilled. He wanted

140

her to spend time with him, but she knew she wouldn't be able to. 'Would you really want me to come up to see you?'

'Course I would.'

'I'll try. I can take a holiday. I'll see what my boss says.'

'Good.' He kissed her with all the passion she had come to expect.

When she walked back to Jane, she knew she was looking down.

'What's wrong with you? He's dumped you?'

'No. They're doing a summer season at Blackpool.' What would Jane say if she told her that Cy wanted her to go with him?

'So what you gonner do, go after him?'

'I wouldn't mind.'

'I can just see your mum and dad giving you their blessing as you go off into the sunset to meet lover boy.'

'I know it will be a bit awkward, but I'm gonner try to go up there.'

'Well I reckon you're raving mad.'

'I've got a week's holiday; why don't we both go?'

'I can't afford a holiday. What about that mate of yours from college?'

'That's a good idea. I'll phone her.'

She wanted to throw her arms round her friend; she had just given her an excuse to go to Blackpool. But what would Jane say if she knew that Sue had already been with him?

★   ★   ★

141

Sue was thrilled. Cy had written to her twice in the first week he was away, asking her how soon it would be before she could get up to see him. When she told him she had managed to get a week off at the end of August and couldn't wait to be with him again, he replied that he was counting the days. Sue had been making plans, and told her parents that she was going with her friend from college.

'Can't say I like the idea of you going all that way on your own,' said her mother when Sue told her about the holiday.

'But I won't be on my own.'

'Why don't you bring her home one Sunday? We'd like to meet her.'

'Your mother only wants to see if she's a nice girl and not one who flaunts herself,' said Granny Potts.

'I'll see if she can come one Sunday.'

'That'll be nice.'

★ ★ ★

At the beginning of the week Sue asked if she could have a car over the August Bank Holiday weekend. She needed cheering up, as it had been two weeks since she'd seen Cy. Although he had written to her and told her how much he missed her and how he was really looking forward to their week together, it wasn't the same as being with him.

'Are you sure you'll be all right?' asked Fred Hunt. 'The roads will be very crowded.'

Sue smiled. 'I promise I'll be careful.'

'I know you will. Going anywhere nice?'

'I thought Jane and I could go to Brighton again. She's bought herself one of the new swimsuits.'

'Can she swim?'

'Don't think so.'

'And what about you?'

Sue blushed and looked down. 'I've got one as well, though I can't swim either. But we want to look the part on the beach.'

Fred didn't say what was on his mind. The thought of her in a swimsuit was enough. 'Well, have a good time.'

'We will. And thank you, Mr Hunt, very much.'

The way she looked at him, for a moment he thought she was going to kiss him, but that was only wishful thinking. Why was he so stupid over her? No girl had ever affected him like this before. Besides, what would such a young, lovely-looking girl want with a man years older than her?

* * *

Jane and Sue had a wonderful weekend. On Sunday they went to Brighton, and on Monday to Greenwich. On Tuesday, when she got back to work, Sue was thrilled to see another letter from Cy waiting for her. She had told him to send her letters to Hunt's; that way her mother wouldn't query them.

Dear Sue,
  I thought I'd let you know not to bother

143

*to come up as me and my wife have made it
up and she's here with me and I don't want
any trouble. She don't know about you.*

*Sorry to let you down. I was really
looking forward to spending a week with
you.*

See you at the dance next month.
Love and kisses,
Cy xxxxxx

Sue sat and stared at the letter. Was it true?
Had he got a wife, or was he just fobbing her off
because he had found someone else? She was so
unhappy, she wanted to cry. How could he do
this to her?

'Did you have a nice weekend?' asked Fred,
coming into the office.

'Yes thank you.'

'Everything all right? You look a bit down.'

'I'm fine. And so is the car.'

He smiled. 'That's good. Now can you go and
collect some spares for Harry Field? I've got the
order form here. I'd go meself but I'm expecting
an important client and I don't wonner miss
him.'

'No, that's fine.' Sue collected the order form
and her handbag and was off. She was glad to
get out of the office. She knew that once she was
alone in the car, she would park somewhere and
cry. How could Cy do this to her? Why had she
been so stupid? But whatever she thought, it all
came back to the fact that she loved him.

★ ★ ★

For the rest of the day Sue felt she was in a dream and couldn't really concentrate. As usual, Ron walked with her after work as far as the bus stop. She was aware he'd been talking, but wasn't listening to what he was saying.

'Are you going to wait for Jane?' she asked.

'Course not. Little Sue, you look ever so down in the dumps. Is everything OK?'

'Yes thank you, Ron. You go on, I'll wait for Jane.'

She knew that as soon as Jane stepped off the bus she would tell her everything. She had to confide in someone; she couldn't keep this bottled up any longer.

'My dopey brother gone on?' asked Jane, pulling Sue's arm through hers. 'That was a smashing weekend. I've been telling 'em at work all about it. They reckon you must be the luckiest girl round here. To be able to drive and borrow your boss's car.' She stopped suddenly and looked at Sue, who had tears running down her face. 'What is it? What's wrong?'

'Jane, I've been such a fool.'

'Why? What you done?'

Sue wiped her eyes and blew her nose. 'Can we go somewhere? I've got something to tell you.'

'Course. We can go and sit in the park. Is that all right?'

Sue nodded.

As soon as they sat down Jane asked, 'Well, what is it?'

'I should be going up to Blackpool at the end of the month.'

'I know that, don't I? So what's upset you? Can't your mate go?'

Sue shook her head.

'Well that ain't the be all and end all. It's a shame but it ain't worth getting yourself all upset over.'

'I wasn't going to be with me mate. I made all that up.'

Jane sat upright. 'So who was you going with?'

'I was gonner spend a week with Cy.'

'How? When did you make the arrangements?'

'At the dance.'

'And your mum's found out?'

'No.'

'I know, he can't make it.'

'Read this.' Sue handed Jane her letter, and Jane quickly read it.

'The cheeky sod. He's been leading you on all this time. If you ask me, it's a good job you found out before it was too late. The bloody liar.'

Sue began crying again and Jane put her arm round her friend's shoulders. 'Don't cry. He ain't worth it. Good job you found out before you and him . . . you know.'

'We already have.'

'What? When?'

'A couple of weeks ago, when I said I was going out with that girl, well I met him at Euston and we went to a hotel and we . . . '

Jane pulled her arm away and sat back. 'No. You never did.'

Sue couldn't answer.

'I always thought you was a silly cow, now I know. And him a married man. The slimy sod.

I bet he thought it was a right laugh, him being the first.'

'Don't, Jane. I didn't know he was married. He might just be saying that 'cos he's got another girl.'

'Well he ain't gonner tell you that, not all the while it suits him. You are so stupid.'

'Don't you think I know that?'

'You all right? You know, have you had the curse since you . . . you know?'

'I'm due this week, but you know me, I'm always all over the place. Besides, you can't fall the first time you do it.'

'Who told you that load of codswallop?'

'The girls at college.'

'And you believed them? There's a few of 'em at work that thought that and finished up in the family way.'

'P'raps they only said that and it wasn't their first time.'

'I dunno. But I thought you'd have more sense than to believe everything that toad told you.'

'Don't go on at me. Don't you think I feel bad enough as it is?' Sue gave a loud sob. 'Who'll want me now I'm damaged goods?'

'Stop being so dramatic.'

'I can't help it.' She began crying again.

'Right. Now come on, dry your eyes and let's make our way home. Otherwise you'll have your mum sending out the police and fire brigade for you.'

'I know. That can be a bit of a pain.'

'You're lucky to have a family that really cares for you.' Jane stood up quickly. 'Come on.'

147

Sue felt guilty. She had everything. 'I'm sorry to burden you with my troubles,' she whispered.

'Don't worry. That's what friends are for.' Jane linked her arm through Sue's, and Sue knew she was lucky to have such a good a friend.

Before they left the park, Sue went to the water fountain and bathed her eyes. 'Do I look all right?'

'They're still a bit puffy. Put a bit of powder under 'em.'

Sue got out her little pot of Phul Nana powder and dabbed at her face, hoping it would hide her red and blotchy eyes.

'Come on, you'll do,' said Jane, trying to be light-hearted. How she hated Cy Taylor. She knew her friend was suffering, but what bloke was worth all this?

17

'Hello, love,' said Granny Potts as Sue walked into the kitchen. 'It's been a bit warm today.'

Sue kept her head down; she didn't want her gran to see her blotchy face. She couldn't answer right away as she was frightened she would burst into tears again.

'Your mother's bringing in the washing; she looks fair done in. They've been scrubbing all those wooden floors in the school hall today. I ask you. In this weather as well.'

Sue knew that when the children were on school holidays, her mother had to go in and do extra work.

'Just going to the lav,' she croaked.

Outside, she hurried past her mother and locked herself in the lav. When she felt a little calmer, she came out.

'You was in a bit of a hurry there.'

'Yes. Jane and me went round the park and so I was bursting. Don't like using the lavs in the park.'

'Thought you was a bit late. Take this lot for me, love. I'm feeling a bit tired.'

'Gran said you've been scrubbing floors.'

'It's hard work trying to get 'em clean.'

'I wish you didn't have to do that, Mum.'

'I like to earn me bit. Don't want your father thinking he has to keep me and me mum.'

'He don't think that.'

'No, I know. But I like to pay me way.'

Sue didn't argue. They had been over this conversation before. She picked up the basket of clean, dry washing that her mother had folded neatly. 'I love the smell of clean washing when it comes off the line.'

Her mother smiled. 'It's much better than having to drape it round everywhere in the winter trying to get it dry. You all right, love? You look a bit down.'

'I am,' said Sue, following her mother into the scullery. 'Mum I won't be going to Blackpool after all.'

Her mother stopped in the doorway. 'Oh Sue. Why ever not?'

'That so-called friend has let me down. She said she can't afford it.' Sue could feel the tears welling up again; she was telling more lies.

'I am so sorry. I know how much you was looking forward to it.'

'Yes, I was.'

'Not to worry. Cheer up. It ain't the end of the world. There'll be other times.'

But to Sue it *was* the end of the world.

★ ★ ★

That evening when Jane came in, the two girls sat in Sue's bedroom.

'So what did you tell your mum?'

'I said me so-called friend had let me down.'

'Well in a way that's true. What you gonner do now you've got that week off?'

Sue shrugged. 'Dunno. Not much to do. I wish

150

you were off too and then we could go out together.'

'So I'm second best again, am I?'

'You know you're not. At least I can rely on you. You don't let me down.'

'You wonner remember that when the next bloke comes along.'

'There won't be a next one.'

Jane laughed. 'Why's that? You gonner be a nun?'

Sue smiled. 'That might not be a bad idea.'

For the rest of the evening they sat and talked. Sue was grateful she had a true friend like Jane, who was always there for her.

★　★　★

On Sunday morning as Sue sat at the table she wasn't feeling so good.

'This not going on holiday has certainly got you down,' said her mother, pouring her a cup of tea.

'Don't get upset about it, love,' said her father. 'You're young and there'll be other times you can go away.'

'Do you want a bit of toast?' asked Gran.

'No thanks.'

'You look like you're coming down with something. Why don't you go back to bed?'

'I think I will, Mum. I'll take a bucket up with me as I feel a bit sick.'

In her bedroom Sue was afraid. She had an inkling of what might be wrong with her. She hadn't seen a period since she went with Cy. Was

151

she having a baby? She threw herself on the bed and cried. So much for everybody telling her it wouldn't happen the first time. What would Cy say when she told him? He couldn't marry her, as he already had a wife. What a mess she'd made of her life. Why had she been so stupid and naive? What would her mum and dad say? Such a disgrace to bring on them.

The knock on the door made her sit up.

'It's only me, love,' said her mother. 'Can I come in?'

'Course you can.'

'Sue, you been crying?'

Sue nodded. There wasn't any point in denying it.

Her mother sat on the bed. 'You don't want not going on this holiday to get you down. Your dad and me have just been talking about it. What if during that week you're off we all go to Clacton for a few days. As it's the school holidays I'll be off and Dad reckons he could get a couple of days holiday as well. Gran reckons it'll do us all good.'

Sue threw her arms round her mother and cried, 'I don't deserve you.'

Her mother held her tight and gently patted her back. 'There, there. Now come on. You're gonner make yourself ill behaving like this.'

'I'm sorry.'

'Well stay up here for a bit. You might feel a bit better later on. Is there anything you want?'

Sue shook her head.

When her mother had closed the door, Sue

burst into tears again. What would they say if they knew the truth?

★　★　★

On Monday, as Ron and Sue went to work, she was still feeling a bit sick but had so far managed to control it.

'Little Sue, are you all right? You don't look very well.'

'I'm fine, thank you, Ron.'

As soon as she walked into the office, Mr Hunt said the same thing.

'I must look really pasty. You're the second person who's asked me that.' She gave him a wan smile. 'I'd better put a bit more rouge on.'

★　★　★

The few days' holiday they had at Clacton, Sue tried hard to enjoy herself. The weather was fine and just sitting on the front was relaxing. She could see it was good for her mother to be waited on for a change. The boarding house was clean and the landlady pleasant, and Sue was reluctant to go home at the end of the week, as all the stark realities would have to be faced again.

★　★　★

In the middle of September, Jane told Sue that the band would be coming to the town hall the following week.

153

'Shouldn't think you'll wonner go and see that scumbag.'

But Sue knew she had to see him. She had to tell him. So far she had managed to keep her morning sickness under control and nobody suspected. Her mother knew that her periods had always been erratic and so didn't question her.

'What about you, Jane? Do you fancy going?'

'Wouldn't mind. Then I can give you-know-who a piece of me mind.'

'No, you can't do that. I don't want him to know that he's upset me that much. I'll have a quiet word with him and find out if he really is married or whether he just said that to put me off.'

'Please yourself. But if it was me, I'd wonner tear him apart.'

Sue smiled grimly. She knew she had to see Cy to tell him about the baby. But what would his reaction be?

★   ★   ★

Sue was very nervous when she walked into the dance hall. Cy was on the stage singing, and despite everything, he still made her heart flutter. Letting her imagination run riot, she hoped he would tell her he wasn't really married and that he would marry her. In a dream, she waited for the interval.

Jane plonked herself down next to Sue when she'd finished being whirled round the floor in a quickstep. 'I wish you'd cheer up. You

154

look a right misery.'

'Sorry, Jane.' All the while she was looking at Cy, who had hardly acknowledged her.

'I hope you ain't thinking of going out to talk to him in the interval.' Jane nodded towards the bandstand.

'I've got to. I've got to find out the truth.'

'Do you honestly think he's capable of telling the truth? He's a bit like you, living in a fantasy world.'

The band began to leave the stage, and Sue got up.

'Won't be long.'

Outside, Cy was leaning against the wall, smoking. When he saw her, he straightened up and took her in his arms. She pulled away.

'What is it? What's wrong?'

She felt like slapping his face. How could he be so insensitive? 'Why did you say you were married and that your wife was in Blackpool?'

He grinned. 'Don't take it to heart. I should have known better. The tart I picked up wasn't half as good as you, or as good looking.' He tried to kiss her, but she moved her head away.

'I'd arranged my holiday and everything.'

'Yer, I'm sorry about that, but when I wrote that letter I was a bit drunk. I was desperate for some female company, and this girl just happened to be around.'

'So it wasn't your wife?'

He laughed and looked over at the other members of the band, who were huddled together, laughing and smoking. 'No, it wasn't. Come on, Sue, give us a kiss. I quite fancy

155

another afternoon together.' He started to nuzzle her neck.

She pushed him away. 'I've got something to tell you.'

'I hope it's good.' He went to put his arm round her.

'There's no easy way to say this. I'm having your baby.'

For a moment or two he looked stunned and was speechless. 'What?'

Sue suddenly had courage she hadn't known she possessed. 'I think you heard.'

'You can't be.'

'I am.'

'Is it mine?'

'I can't believe you've just asked me that.'

'Well, is it?'

'Of course it is. What are you going to do about it?'

'Nothing.' He ground his cigarette out with his shoe. 'You ain't the first to try and pull this stunt.'

Sue felt herself crumple. 'I thought we could get married.'

'Sorry, darling. But what I told you in the letter was true; you see, I am already married.' He went to move away, and Sue grabbed his arm.

'But Cy, wait. What am I gonner do?'

'Dunno. Get rid of it. That's your problem.'

'What?' she almost screamed.

He pushed her aside and looked over at his mates again. 'Shh. Keep your voice down. But I'll tell you something. It was nice while it lasted.' With that he turned and went inside.

Sue stood and stared after him. Her world was falling apart. What was she going to do now?

★   ★   ★

The band was just returning to the stage when Sue went over to Jane, who was sitting laughing with a young man. She didn't look at Cy. 'Come on, Jane, we're going.'

'What? I ain't finished me drink.'

'Leave it.'

'Hang on a minute, darling,' said the young man, standing up. 'I just bought this lady a drink and she's gonner sit here with me and finish it.'

'Please yourself.' Sue gathered her handbag and left.

She hung around the cloakroom for a while, and when Jane didn't appear, she decided to leave.

She was standing at the bus stop crying when Jane came up to her. 'Thought you might have waited.'

'I had to get out. I couldn't face him again.'

'So he is married?'

Sue could only nod.

'What can I say? At least you'll get over him. Now come on, dry those eyes and let's get home. After all, it ain't the end of the world.'

But Sue knew that for her it was.

18

On Monday morning as Sue made her way to work, she wasn't listening to Ron as he lumbered along beside her. Her thoughts were on Cy and most of all on what had happened to her. All Sunday he had dominated her thoughts. He was married. Why had she been so besotted and let him make love to her, with the result that now she was going to have his baby? How could she have been such a stupid idiot to think that he had loved her? She was so ashamed, and all she could think about was what she should do. Her overriding thought was she had to get rid of the baby. She knew that was so very wrong, but what else could she do? Where could she start looking? If only she worked with other women, in a factory or a shop, someone would be able to help her. She was tempted to ask Jane, but didn't feel she should burden her with her troubles. After all, Jane still didn't know.

'You look a bit down, young lady,' said Fred.

'I'm sorry.'

'Is something bothering you?'

'No,' she said quickly, and smiled, hoping that would stop him from asking any more questions.

'Look, why don't you take a car this weekend, then you and your mate could go and have a day out.'

'Thank you. That would be nice.'

Fred looked at her. He knew something was

upsetting her. He should be the one taking her out, trying to bring the happy smile back. Perhaps he could suggest it nearer the end of the week. He could always say there wasn't a car available. He gave her a slight nod as he left the office. Yes, that was it. He would take her out on Sunday to a nice tea room somewhere in the country.

On Saturday when Sue asked which car she should take, Fred said he was sorry, but the one she could have had hadn't been repaired. Sue looked at him suspiciously. As far as she knew, all those on the forecourt were roadworthy.

'That's all right, we'll go out some other time.'

'Susan, I know you're disappointed, so why don't I take you and your friend out in mine? How about if we go out into the country and perhaps go to a tea room or something?'

'Oh no. Thank you all the same, but we couldn't put you to any trouble. We can wait.'

'Please, Susan, I would like that. I don't get out a lot, only to the pub or to me ma's, so this will be a nice change, taking two young ladies out for the afternoon.' He would have preferred to take her alone but he knew that would be pushing his luck. This wouldn't be like the Masons' do, when he'd had an excuse to invite her; this was just a ride in the country.

'Well only if you're sure and not doing anything.'

'I'm sure.'

★　★　★

159

That evening Jane knocked on the door. 'Where's the car? I thought we were going out tomorrow?'

'Come in. We are. We're going out in Mr Hunt's car.'

'What, that big posh thing?'

'Yes.'

'He's letting you borrow that?'

'No. He's taking me and you out tomorrow afternoon. He wants to take us to the country and have something to eat.'

'Why's he doing that?'

'He reckons I need cheering up.'

'Well he's not wrong about that. You ain't been the same since you saw you-know-who. I tell you something Sue, you've got a boss in a million.'

'I know.'

★　★　★

On Sunday afternoon, Fred drove up to the Reeds' house. He had never been inside before, as Susan was always waiting for him when he took her out for her driving lessons. Today he had taken extra care with his appearance, as he wanted to make a good impression on her parents. He walked up to the front door and knocked. Ron was standing at his gate.

'Good afternoon, Ron.'

'You taking my girl out?'

'I am taking Susan and her friend out, but I didn't know she was your girl.'

'Well she is.'

Fred smiled when Sue opened the door.

'Come in, Mr Hunt. Jane's here and we're both ready.'

He was ushered into the kitchen and introduced to Sue's parents and grandmother.

Doris Reed didn't want to show that she was very impressed with this well-dressed man who was taking her daughter out. 'I thought you would have better things to do than to take a couple of girls out for a ride,' she said.

Charlie glared at his wife and, shaking Fred's hand warmly, said, 'This is very kind of you.'

'It's my pleasure. To take out two lovely young ladies is an old man's dream.'

'You're not an old man,' said Doris quickly.

'These two young things think I am.'

'We're ready, Mr Hunt,' repeated Sue. She couldn't believe how her mother was behaving, almost as if she disapproved. Sue wanted to get out as soon as possible.

As soon as they left, Granny Potts said, 'What was wrong with you, Doris? You was acting as if you didn't like him.'

'No I wasn't, but I hope he doesn't think we approve of him taking our daughter out.'

'It's Sue's decision, though, and we did let him take her to the Masons' do and teach her to drive.'

'I know that, Charlie. But our Sue's a very lovely innocent young girl and she could have the pick of the bunch.'

'Well they've got Jane with them, so that should put any ideas about hanky-panky right out of his head,' said Gran.

'I hope so.'

'What's brought this on? You've not worried about it before,' said Charlie.

'I dunno. She looks sort of troubled just lately. I'm worried that he might have some hold over her.'

Gran laughed out loud. 'You don't half come out with some crackpot ideas at times.'

'I'll have a word with her when she gets home. If she ain't happy in that job, she could always leave,' said Charlie.

'I think you're seeing things that ain't there,' said Gran. 'She's old enough to make up her own mind about whether she wants to leave. Besides, look how good he's been to her. Teaching her to drive, letting her borrow a car whenever she wants. No, I just reckon he's a sad lonely bloke.'

'That's what worries me, Mum. That's just what worries me.'

★   ★   ★

Sue and Jane sat in the country tea room.

'This is lovely,' said Sue, looking round at the old-fashioned decor.

'Look at those old pictures behind you,' said Jane, trying hard not to point.

Sue turned her head. 'They are nice. Thank you so much, Mr Hunt, for bringing us here. We ain't used to being in such a posh place.'

'I told you, it's my pleasure. And, I might add, I'm getting a few envious glances from some of the men. I reckon they think I'm your uncle.'

Jane laughed. 'I wish you *was* my uncle.'

162

'Ah, here's the tea,' said Fred, sitting back.

They watched as the young waitress in a black frock and frilly white pinny put the silver tea pot, sugar bowl and milk jug on the table, which was covered with a spotless white tablecloth. A plate of small sandwiches and a two-tiered stand of fancy cakes followed.

When the waitress walked away, Fred said, 'Now come on, girls. Enjoy.'

Sue was pleased that her morning sickness had died down. 'This is really nice.'

'You wait till I tell me mum,' said Jane, taking another sandwich.

When it was time to leave, Sue and Jane went to the Ladies.

'D'you know, I reckon if you played your cards right, he'd take you out.'

'I went out with him once, remember.'

'That was only because he didn't have anybody else to take.' Jane looked in the ornate mirror. 'No, I reckon he's a bit sweet on you.'

'Don't talk daft. He's me boss.'

'I know. But he does look at you in a special way.'

'No thank you. Oh, don't get me wrong, he's nice enough, but I want a young man. I don't want to be an old man's darling.'

'Yer. And look where that got you.'

Sue quickly turned on Jane. Did she suspect? 'What d'you mean?'

'All right. Keep yer hair on. What I meant was all that mooning over you-know-who, only to find out he's married.'

'Well, yes, I was a bit of a fool. Come on, Mr

163

Hunt will think we've fallen down the hole.'

All the way home, Sue thought about what Jane had said. Did Mr Hunt think of her as more than his secretary?

★ ★ ★

As the month wore on, Sue was beginning to worry that her mother might suspect something was wrong. She did ask her when she was due again, and Sue somehow managed to fob her off, but for how long? She also felt that some of her skirts were getting a little tight. Soon Jane would notice something was wrong. She had to do something quick, but what?

She stood at the window of the office and looked out at the rain falling like stair rods. When the phone rang, it made her jump.

'Yes, Mr Field. I'll tell him as soon as he gets back. Do you want me to order the spares? I'll do that right away.'

Later that morning Mr Hunt hurried into the office. He took off his trilby and banged the water off it. 'It's chucking it down out there. There's water everywhere. I'm going up to change me clothes. Everything all right here?'

'Mr Field phoned. That car that Mr Mitchell's in a hurry for needs a new exhaust. He wanted to know if I could order one, so I have. Is that all right?'

'That's fine. When can they deliver?'

'They're not sure. Might be this afternoon.'

'That's good.' Mr Hunt left the office and went upstairs to his flat.

During the afternoon the clouds cleared. When the phone rang, Sue put her hand over the mouthpiece and said to her boss, 'It's the spares place. They can't deliver today. What shall I tell them?'

'I'll be over later.'

'Mr Hunt will come over and collect the exhaust.' She put the phone back on its cradle.

'That's a damn nuisance. I didn't want to go out again today. I think I've got a cold coming on. I wish some of these places would get their business in order.' He stood up. 'I won't be long.'

Sue watched him walk across the forecourt. As he was about to get into his car, a man came up and banged on his windscreen. Mr Hunt was out of the car like a shot. He grabbed the bloke by his coat and pushed him back out of sight. She couldn't see what was happening. Where was Ron? He was always around when there was trouble, and it wouldn't be the first time he had sorted somebody out for Mr Hunt. Was this someone coming back for revenge? She knew he had made a few enemies over the years; he had told her that went with the job, as some people resented his wealth. Sometimes she had seen some shady-looking men talking to her boss, and sometimes a wad of money would be handed over and the invoice wasn't filed. But that was nothing to do with her.

Sue went outside. Should she call the police? Where was Ron?

Fred was punching the bloke in the face. Both of them had bloody noses.

'Stop it!' she yelled. 'Stop it or I'll call the police.'

The man broke away and started to run off.

'Come into the office,' said Sue taking Fred's arm.

'I'm all right.'

'Who was that?'

Fred wiped his bloody nose. 'He said I owed him money as the car he bought broke down and it cost him to get it repaired.'

'Where is Ron?'

'I sent him round to the workshop. I'll just get cleaned up, then I'll go and get those spares.'

'No, I'll go.'

'Are you sure?'

'Of course. It ain't the first time, is it?'

'No. But drive carefully, the roads are still very wet.'

'I'll be all right. At least it's stopped raining.'

As Sue was driving along, her thoughts were all over the place. Was that man really a customer? Sue hadn't recognised him. What was Mr Hunt involved in? Was he telling her the truth? Anyway, why was she worried? She had enough on her plate. Her thoughts were on this baby again. What could she do about it?

'Hello, Sue,' said Mr Bennett, who was in charge of the garage where they got their spares. 'How are you today?'

'I'm fine, thank you.'

'Thought his nibs was coming to collect this.'

'He got held up.'

'Right, let's put it in your car. Bugger, it's started to rain again.'

Sue quickly got in the car as the heavens opened up once again. 'Bye,' she called out, but her voice was lost in the sound of the rain drumming on the roof.

She drove back slowly. Thank goodness the traffic wasn't very heavy. The windscreen was misting up, and the wiper was having a job to clear the water. After a while it packed up altogether.

'Damn. That's all I need.' She began to cry. 'Don't you think I've got enough problems without you sending all this against me?' she shouted to the sky. Leaning forward, she peered through the windscreen, trying to see. She wound her window down and tried to wipe the outside of the screen with her hand. As she did so, she accidentally pulled on the wheel with her left hand. Quickly she tried to straighten up, but it was too late, as a lamppost suddenly appeared out of the gloom in front of her.

19

'Get those wet things off. There's a cuppa all ready for you,' said Granny Potts to her daughter as she walked into the kitchen.

'Thank Gawd that rain's stopped for the time being,' said Doris, taking off her black felt hat. 'I thought Charlie might be home be now; they can't work in this weather. The decks get too slippery.'

'You look fair done in.'

'I swear those kids take a great delight in chucking paper all over the floor. And when they put the chairs up on the desks, they leave 'em at such an angle that they fall down at the slightest touch.'

'Little sods. Never mind. Sit down and rest your feet for a while. Dinner's all ready.'

'I don't know what I'd do without you, Mum.'

'Well I hope I can look after you for a while yet.'

They drank their tea and settled down in a comfortable silence. The only sound was the rain beating on the window and the ticking of the clock.

At six o'clock, Charlie walked into the kitchen.

'Don't often see you home first,' said Granny Potts, going to the table and lifting the tea pot. 'Cuppa?'

'Not half. Bloody awful day. It's running like a river down the high street.'

'That Sue's only got silly shoes on. Her feet'll be soaking wet when she gets in.'

'She's not in yet?' asked Charlie. 'She's a bit late.'

'He might have wanted her to stay on a bit longer,' said Doris.

The knock on the front door made them look at one another.

'Who's that?' asked Charlie.

'I dunno. Can't be Sue,' said Doris. 'I'll go and see. 'Oh, hello, Ron. What you doing here? Is it your mum?'

'No. Is little Sue home?'

'No. Ain't she with you?'

He shook his head. 'She ain't been in all afternoon.'

'What, she's not been to work?'

'Yes, but she went out for some spares and she ain't back yet.'

Doris's hand flew to her mouth. 'Was she in a car?'

Ron nodded. 'Mr Hunt phoned the spares place and they said she'd been and gone.'

'You'd better come in.'

Ron snatched his cloth cap from his head and followed Sue's mum down the passage.

'Charlie, Charlie! Sue ain't been at work this afternoon. She had to pick up some spares and Ron said she ain't come back. What d'you think could have happened?'

'Mr Hunt says she's a very good driver, so there's nothing to worry about,' said Ron quickly as he shifted from one foot to the other.

'Oh my Gawd,' said Granny Potts. 'You don't

think anything's happened to her?'

'No,' said Charlie. 'We would have heard be now. She's probably had a breakdown and couldn't get to a phone.'

'That's just what Mr Hunt said. I'd better be going. Jane will be in in a minute and she'll be ever so mad that little Sue didn't wait for her. Bye.'

As Ron left the room, Doris slumped in her chair. 'D'you think something might have happened?'

'No, course not. As I said, she's probably had a breakdown. All I hope is that he lets her have a car to come home in. She don't need to be traipsing about in this weather.'

To ease the atmosphere, Granny Potts said, 'I'll see to the dinner and put Sue's in the oven.'

The food was dished up but everybody just picked at it, and when the clock struck seven Charlie stood up.

'I can't sit here waiting, I'll have to go and try to find out something.'

'Where?' asked Doris.

'Perhaps I should go along to the phone box and phone Fred Hunt; he might know something be now. Or I could try the police station.'

'Oh Charlie, don't say things like that. I'm worried enough.'

'So am I, love. So am I.'

It was then that they heard a rat-tat-tat at the front door. Everybody just stared at each other.

'I'll go,' said Charlie.

Somehow neither Doris nor her mother was surprised when Charlie came back into the

170

kitchen accompanied by a policeman and Mr Hunt.

'Oh my Gawd, what's happened?' asked Granny Potts.

Her daughter's face was ashen. 'What's happened to my Sue?' she asked softly, dreading the answer.

'I'm afraid she's been in an accident,' said the policeman.

'Is she . . . is she . . . ' repeated Doris, unable to say the words that were spinning around in her brain.

'She's been injured and she's in the hospital. We went to see Mr Hunt here, as it was one of his cars and had the firm's name in it, and he told us who was driving and where Miss Reed lived.'

'Can we go and see her?' asked Charlie.

'Yes, of course. Mr Hunt has said he will take you.'

Charlie glared at Fred. 'Was there something wrong with the car?'

'No. It was perfectly sound. I am so sorry about this. Susan's a good driver, but the weather was bad.' Fred looked down at the floor. The thought that was running through his mind was, had the car been at fault?

'I'll get me coat and hat,' said Doris. 'Mum, if Jane comes in, tell her what's happened.'

'Course I will. Give Sue my love.' Granny Potts was trying hard not to cry. Her precious granddaughter injured. What a blow for them all. She silently prayed that Sue would be all right. 'Is she badly hurt?' she asked the policeman.

171

'I'm afraid I don't know. All I was told was that I had to go to the garage and find out who the driver was.'

Fred Hunt stood nervously turning his grey felt trilby over and over. 'If you're ready, we can be off. It won't take too long to get there.'

Doris got into the car feeling as if she was in a dream, and with Charlie sitting next to her, holding her hand, she prayed.

*   *   *

Jane wasn't very happy when she turned the corner of Lily Road. She was wet through and the first bus hadn't even bothered to stop as it was full up. After waiting what seemed to be for ever for the next one, she found it crammed with wet smelly people, and to make matters worse she had to go upstairs with the smokers. She was very fed up and glad to get out in the fresh air again. When a car passed her, she looked up and was very surprised to see Mr Hunt driving and Mr and Mrs Reed sitting in the back. Where were they going? Jane hastened her step and decided to drop in on Granny Potts first before going home. She hadn't been surprised that Sue wasn't waiting for her at the bus stop, not in this weather.

'Jane, I thought it would be you. Come in, love. You're wet through. Have you been home yet?'

'No. I saw Sue's mum and dad in Mr Hunt's car. What's happened?'

'Sue's had an accident. She's in hospital.'

172

Jane sat down hard and the colour drained from her face. 'How bad is she?'

'We don't know. The police went to the garage 'cos that's where the car come from, and Sue's boss came with the copper and now he's taken 'em to the hospital.'

'Was there something wrong with the car?'

'We don't know. But Gawd help the bloke if there was. Charlie will kill him.'

'Sue's a very good driver.'

'So everyone keeps saying. D'you want a cuppa?'

'No thanks. I'll go on home. Ron will go mad when he hears. He's got a very soft spot for Sue.' She gathered up her handbag and went to the kitchen door. 'I'll see meself out.'

Granny Potts settled down again. Somehow she knew she was in for a long wait.

★   ★   ★

'Jane, you're home at last. I'll get you a towel to dry yourself. You all right? You look like you've seen a ghost.' Maud Brent didn't normally fuss round her daughter like this.

'You know?'

'Know what?'

'About Sue.'

'Only that Ron's upset that she isn't home. I do worry about him and his feelings for her.'

'She's had an accident and she's in hospital.'

'No, I didn't know.'

'So why all the fussing?'

173

'I'm not fussing. Just thought you looked a bit wet, that's all.'

Jane snatched the towel from her mother. 'You don't usually bother to worry about me.'

Her mother tutted and sat down. 'Now what's this about Sue?'

'She's had a car accident and is in hospital, that's all I know. Granny Potts told me, but they don't know anything else.'

'I'll go and pray for her.' Maud Brent went into the front room to her shrine.

Ron hadn't said a word all the time Jane was talking. Now he spoke. 'You said my little Sue's had an accident?'

'Yes, Ron.' Jane shut the kitchen door to block out the sound of her mother's mournful chanting from the front room.

'Which hospital is she in?'

'I don't know.'

'I'll have to go and see her.'

'I don't think they'll let you in. You ain't family.'

'Not yet I ain't, but I will be when she marries me.'

'Stop talking a load of crap.' Jane wasn't worried about the consequences if Ron attacked her; her thoughts were on Sue. She rubbed her hair with the towel.

Ron began putting his coat on.

'And where are you going?'

'To the hospital.'

'You don't know which one she's in.'

'I'll go to every one in London. I'll find her.'

'Please yourself.' Jane was too tired and

worried to argue with her brother; she was more concerned about her friend. She could hear her mother chanting loudly in the front room. My God, it's like living in a madhouse, she thought. All I want is for my friend to be home safe and well.

20

When the Reeds arrived at the hospital, they were ushered into a small room. Fred Hunt told them he'd wait outside in case they needed a lift home. He had his own reasons for hanging around too: he wanted to know how badly Susan had been injured, but he couldn't let her family know his feelings for her.

Charlie paced the floor. 'Why won't someone come and talk to us, tell us what's happening?'

'Sit down, Charlie, for Gawd's sake. You're making me head spin. They'll come and tell us in their own good time.'

'How can you sit there all calm?'

'I ain't calm. Me heart's beating like a hammer. Oh Charlie, I couldn't bear it if anything happened to her.' She buried her head in her hands and began to cry.

Charlie sat next to his wife and put his arm round her heaving shoulders. 'I'm sorry, love. I know how you feel. I'm sure they're doing all they can for her. Now come on, wipe your eyes. You don't want our Sue to see you like this; it'll only upset her.'

Doris blew her nose and wiped her eyes, then gave her husband a weak smile. 'You're right. I don't want to upset her.'

A few minutes later the door opened and a young man wearing a white coat with a stethoscope hanging round his neck walked in.

He held out his hand. 'I'm Dr Banks. I'm looking after Susan.'

Both Charlie and Doris stood up and shook his hand.

'Please, sit down.'

They did as they were told, and he sat in another vacant chair.

'I don't know how much you know about the accident.'

'Nothing. Nothing at all,' said Charlie, sitting on the edge of his seat.

'Well I'm afraid Susan will have some scarring to her face.'

Doris gasped and quickly put her hand to her mouth.

The young man went on. 'Her head hit the windscreen and she was cut by the glass, but hopefully the scars will fade in time. She also has a broken leg and a badly twisted foot, though we hope that will straighten in time. She is young and should heal quickly.' He looked at them intently. 'I'm afraid we couldn't save the baby.'

'Baby? What baby?' asked Charlie.

'Oh dear. Didn't you know your daughter was pregnant?'

Charlie shook his head and looked at his wife. 'Did you know?'

Doris's mouth had dropped open. 'No, I didn't. Sue was having a baby? How could that happen?' She turned to the doctor. 'Have you got the right Susan Reed?'

'I'm very sorry. This must be a shock.'

'You can say that again,' said Charlie with a look of disbelief on his face.

'How far gone was she?' asked Doris.

'Almost three months.'

'Three months, and you didn't know about it?' said Charlie to his wife. He was beginning to get angry. 'What sort of mother are you not to know?'

Doris began to cry.

'Mr Reed, this isn't something you should be worrying about just now. Please don't show Susan how this has upset you. Don't talk about it.'

'Can we see her?' he asked.

'Yes, but just for a short while. Remember, she has been in an accident and she's still a bit woozy and drifting in and out of consciousness. She needs her rest.'

With a great deal of apprehension, they followed the young man. He held open the door to a small room.

Doris tried hard to stifle a gasp as she looked at her daughter. Sue's head and part of her face were bandaged and her hair was matted with dried blood. Doris heard her husband choke back a sob.

The doctor whispered, 'That's a cage to keep the bedclothes off her foot, and her leg's in plaster. It looks worse than it is. Susan, your mum and dad are here.'

Sue opened the eye that wasn't covered with a bandage. A tear ran slowly down her cheek. 'I'm so sorry.'

'Remember, not too long,' said the doctor as he left the room.

Doris sat beside her daughter and clutched her

hand. Sue winced. 'I'm sorry, love. I don't want to hurt you.'

Charlie, who had been trying to compose himself, came round to the other side of the bed and sat on a chair. 'Hello, love.' His voice was thick with emotion.

'Dad,' whispered Sue. 'I'm so sorry.'

He gave her a smile. 'You ain't got nothing to be sorry for. You're alive and in one piece, that's all we're worried about.'

'Where do you hurt?' asked her mother.

'All over. Me back, me leg, and me stomach. All over.'

'Don't worry about it now. They'll soon have you up and about,' said her father.

'I hope so.' Sue closed her eye.

After a short while a nurse came into the room. 'I think you'd better go now. Sister will give you Susan's clothes and tell you the visiting hours.'

'Thank you,' said Charlie. 'Come on, love, let Sue get some rest. We'll be back tomorrow.' He kissed his daughter's cheek.

'Bye, love.' Her mother did the same, but just as she stood up, Sue put out her hand.

'Mum.'

Doris froze. What was she going to tell her?

'Mum. Tell Mr Hunt I'm sorry about the car.'

'Don't worry about that,' said Charlie. 'Just you get yourself better.'

Sue lay back and closed her eye again.

Outside in the corridor, Doris began to weep. 'Oh, Charlie.'

179

Charlie gently knocked on the sister's office door.

'Come in.' The woman behind the desk rose as soon as she saw them and put out her hand. 'Good evening. I'm Sister Lee. Please take a seat.'

Charlie and Doris shook her hand and sat down opposite her.

'Your daughter looks bad at the moment, but I can assure you that when the bandage is removed and she has been cleaned up, she will look a little better.'

'But the doctor said she will be scarred.'

'Well yes, but we won't know how badly just yet.' She went on to explain the hospital's procedure then, after a moment of laboured silence, she stood up, which was a signal for them to go. 'Here are your daughter's clothes.'

'Thank you,' said Charlie as he took the paper bag she was holding out to him.

They left the sister's office and walked along in the corridor. Charlie put his arm round his wife's shoulders. 'Come on, love, let's get home. Your mum will be all anxious to know how she is. We can come back tomorrow.'

'What about this baby?'

'What about it? It don't exist any more.'

'I know. Should we tell Mum?'

'Dunno. Is there any point?'

'I dunno. The shock . . . And who was the father?'

'Well whoever it was, I'll give him more than a piece of me mind if I ever catch up with him.'

'Why didn't Sue tell me?'

180

'Don't ask me. I tell you, Doris, this has really upset me. I didn't think our Sue was like that.'

'She's young and pretty and . . . ' She stopped. 'Oh Charlie. What if her face is a mess? She'll never . . . '

He patted her hand. 'Remember, looks ain't everything.'

'I know, but when you're only eighteen . . . '

'Come on, let's get on home.'

When they stepped outside, Fred Hunt hurried towards them.

'How is she?'

'You still here, Mr Hunt?'

'Please, call me Fred.'

As they approached his car, Charlie could see from the dog ends on the ground that he had been smoking rather a lot. 'Not too good, I'm afraid. She's got a broken leg and the doctor said her foot's a bit twisted.'

'Will she be all right?'

'We hope so. But she could be scarred from the glass in the windscreen.'

'Oh no. That's awful. Susan's such a pretty young lady.'

As they drove home, Doris was crying softly. After a while Charlie broke the silence.

'Fred, do you want to came in for a cup of tea?'

'That's very kind of you, but I don't want to intrude. You'll want to talk amongst yourselves. If you like, I can run you to the hospital tomorrow. I'm not doing anything.'

'That would be very nice,' sobbed Doris.

'Visiting is for half an hour at three.'

'I'll be round at two thirty, so you can be the first in.'

'Thank you.' Doris wiped her eyes and sat back. She now had to face her mother. Should she tell her about the baby? And who *was* the father?

★　★　★

Sue lay back. Her thoughts were in turmoil. She had been told that she had lost the baby, but had her parents been told? What a mess she'd made of her life. She gently touched the bandage on her face. What if she'd lost the sight in her eye? She knew she could be scarred. Who would want her now? She felt so miserable. Her leg and foot hurt, and her stomach and back. She was feeling very sorry for herself and began to cry. She drifted off into a troubled sleep, but suddenly she could see the lamppost coming towards her and there was nothing she could do. She screamed out.

A nurse came running into the room. 'It's all right, Susan.' She patted her hand. 'You're having a bad dream.'

Sue cried and held on to the nurse. 'I want me mum.'

'Of course you do. Now try to get some rest. I'll give you something to help you sleep.'

Sue wanted her mum, but she also wanted Cy. She wanted him to hold her and tell her he still loved her, even if she was ugly with red scars all over her face, and that he wanted to marry her and they could have other babies, but she knew that would never be. So what did the future hold for her? Would anybody want her? She closed her eye as she drifted off again.

21

As soon as the Reeds arrived home, Jane was knocking on their front door.

'I've been looking out of the window waiting for you and saw Mr Hunt's car drive up.'

'Jane, come in. Yes, he kindly took us to the hospital,' said Mrs Reed.

'I know, Granny Potts told me.' Although Jane was dreading the answer, she had to ask. 'How is me old mate?'

Doris Reed waited till they were in the kitchen before she spoke. 'Not so good, I'm afraid.'

Tears filled Jane's eyes. 'Was she conscious? Could she speak to you?'

Doris nodded. 'We did speak to her for a little while, although she wasn't really doing much talking.'

Granny Potts hadn't spoken; she just sat in the chair looking bewildered.

'We saw her doctor.' Doris had to stop as she wiped away a tear.

'Sit down, love,' said Charlie.

Jane did as she was told.

'D'you want me to make a cuppa?' asked Granny Potts softly.

'No, Mum, you must listen to what the doctor told us first.'

Charlie quickly raised his eyebrows at his wife.

'He said that her head hit the windscreen and

some of the glass went in her face. She could be scarred.'

'Poor little cow.'

'He also told us that she's broken her leg and twisted her foot.'

A sob came from Jane. 'To think we was all so proud of her being able to drive.'

'I know.' Doris fiddled with her hands.

'Was the car to blame?' asked Granny Potts softly.

'No,' said Charlie. 'They reckon it was the weather.'

Granny Potts sat and looked at her daughter's worried face. 'That it?' she asked.

Doris looked at Charlie, then said angrily to her mother, 'Ain't that enough for you then?'

'Course it is, but I'm worried you might be keeping something back.'

'Why should I do that?' Did her mother know about Sue's condition? Had Sue confided in her? After all, they had always been very close.

'Don't know, to spare me feelings, I suppose.'

'No, Mum, that's it.'

'All right, keep yer hair on. I'll go and make us all that tea now.'

'Sorry, Mum, but I'm a bit wound up.'

'I can understand that. You gonner stay for a cuppa, Jane?'

'No, I'll go on home.' She didn't want them to see the tears that were ready to fall. 'Will you be going to the hospital tomorrow?'

Doris nodded. 'I'm afraid it's only relations that can visit.'

'I know that. But give her my love.'

185

'Course.'

'I can see meself out.' With that Jane left.

Doris picked up the paper bag. 'I'd better sort Sue's things out.' She began pulling out the clothes. 'Oh my God.'

'What is it?' asked Charlie.

She held up her daughter's coat. The front was stiff with a deep stain that had turned from red to a rust colour. 'We can't keep this.'

'No, course we can't. Give it here. I'll take it out and burn it.' Charlie quickly took the coat from his wife. 'We'll get her a new one when she comes home.'

Outside, he leant against the wall, buried his head in the coat and cried. He didn't want his wife to see him. Men weren't supposed to cry.

⋆ ⋆ ⋆

Ron threw open the door as soon as Jane walked through the gate. He had been very angry when Jane had told him to stay at home, telling him, 'they don't want everybody in there,' so he had stayed at the window, waiting for her. 'How is she?'

'Let me get in.'

Maud Brent came out of the front room and followed her son and daughter into the kitchen. 'Well, how is she?'

'She's not good. She went through the windscreen and she's been cut by the glass. And she's got a broken leg. The doctor said she could be badly scarred.'

Ron sat in a chair and hugged himself. 'My

beautiful little Sue.' Huge tears ran down his podgy face as he rocked back and forth. 'I went to lots of hospitals, but I couldn't find her. My beautiful little Sue. I'll always love you.'

'Ron, stop that,' said his mother. 'You wailing won't help Sue. I'll go and pray.'

'That won't help her either,' said Jane angrily. 'Only the doctors can do that.'

'Prayers do help.'

Jane looked at her brother and her mother. She had to get away from them. 'I'm going up to my room to write her a letter.'

★　★　★

After Granny Potts had gone to bed, Doris sat back exhausted, nursing the cup of cocoa Charlie had made her. He sat in the chair opposite her.

'You didn't tell your ma about the baby.'

'No. I didn't see the point. I was even wondering if she knew.'

'How could she?'

'Her and Sue have always been very close.'

'I know, but . . . '

'What if Sue don't know that we know?'

'That's a point. What about Jane?'

Doris finished her cocoa. 'She didn't seem as if she knew. I think we'd better wait till Sue tells us about it herself.'

'But what if she don't?'

'Then we'll just have to keep her secret.'

'I'd like to know who it was.' Charlie looked angry.

'She may tell us one day.'

'Have you finished your cocoa, love?'

She nodded.

'Come on then, let's be off.'

Doris stood up. 'I don't think I'll be able to sleep, I'm too worried.'

'I know, but come on, give it a try. Remember, we've got to put on a brave face for Sue tomorrow.'

Doris gave her husband a wan smile. It was comforting to have a strong man at her side. As she followed him up the stairs she felt very sorry for Maud next door. She had no one to lean on and her son didn't help. Still, at least he was working now, thanks to Sue.

★ ★ ★

Dead on two thirty, Fred Hunt knocked on the door. Charlie opened it.

'We're all ready,' he said.

Doris looked at the huge bunch of flowers on the seat next to her. 'Mr Hunt, are these for Sue?'

'Yes. I hope you don't mind, but I was over at the market this morning and I thought they might help to cheer her up.'

'That's very kind of you. They are really lovely, must have cost a few bob.'

'She deserves them. She's a good girl.'

Charlie looked at Fred Hunt. Was this conscience money? Was the car faulty? How would he find out?

Doris also looked at Fred and thought to

herself that Sue wasn't such a good girl after all. In her eyes, good girls didn't have babies.

★   ★   ★

'Susan. Susan.' Someone was gently shaking her. 'Susan, wake up. The doctor's here.'

Sue opened her eye. Why was it that every time she went to sleep, someone woke her up? 'Hello,' she said wearily.

'Hello, Susan. How do you feel today?'

'Rotten.'

'Do you have any questions to ask me?'

'Have I lost the sight in me eye?' she whispered, dreading the answer.

'We don't think so. The glass seems to have missed the eye itself.'

'Will I be badly scarred?'

'I'm afraid I can't answer that really truthfully. We will have to wait and see when all the stitches come out.'

Sue turned her head away from him and began to cry.

'Come on now. Try to be a brave girl. Your family will be here this afternoon.'

'I don't want to be brave.' She wanted to talk about the baby, to ask if she could have children in the future. She wanted to know if her parents knew. But she put those thoughts to the back of her mind. She couldn't face the subject yet. The doctor was talking.

'We are taking you to the big ward and I'll be around later on to see how you are. Try to rest.' He patted her hand.

Fat chance of that, she thought, as a nurse came up with her dinner.

★   ★   ★

At three o'clock the ward door was opened and everybody rushed to make the most of the half an hour with their loved ones. The Reeds had been told that Sue had been moved, and they stood for a moment or two trying to find her. When they saw she was at the very end of the ward, they hurried towards her.

'Sue love, it's me and your dad.' Doris laid the flowers on the bed and gently touched her daughter's hand, making her jump.

'Mum. Dad.' Sue opened her eye. 'What time is it?'

Charlie gave her a weak smile. 'Why, love, you going somewhere, you got a date or something?'

'No. It's just that I don't know if it's morning, noon or night in here. Mum, I want to come home.'

Doris wanted to sweep her daughter into her arms and run off with her; she looked so young, small and vulnerable. 'And I want you home, love. We all do.'

'Everybody sends their love. And Mr Hunt's sent you these flowers.'

'They are really lovely, look.' Doris held them up.

Sue gave them only a cursory glance. 'Tell him thanks.' She closed her eye again.

For the full half-hour hardly any words were exchanged. And all too soon the bell went for

190

the visitors to leave.

Doris kissed Sue. 'We'll be in tomorrow.'

Charlie was finding it difficult to hold back the tears, but it would never do for his daughter to see him so upset. 'Bye, love,' was all he could manage as he bent over and kissed her cheek.

Outside, Fred was waiting. 'How was she?'

'Not so good,' said Charlie, blowing his nose loudly.

'She liked the flowers,' said Doris.

'That's good. I'll get some fruit for her tomorrow. That's if you'll let me bring you.'

'You don't have to,' said Charlie. 'It's very nice of you, but we can get the bus.'

'It's no bother. Besides, it's the least I can do. I'm very fond of Susan.'

Doris looked up quickly. Why was he so worried? Did he know about the baby? Had he been the father? No, that was impossible. She tried to sort out in her mind who it could have been. Sue was always out with Jane; did Jane know? Did Sue have a boyfriend? She did spend a lot of time with Fred Hunt, and she was young and very pretty.

All through the journey home Doris looked at the back of Fred Hunt's neck. Why was he so concerned about her daughter? She knew she was letting her imagination run away with her, but if the baby had been his, he had a lot to answer for.

Charlie was also giving Fred Hunt a sly look. Why was this man so worried about his daughter? After all, she was just an employee.

191

Was the car to blame and he was worried about it? He could finish up in court. Charlie knew he had to go to the police to try and get to the bottom of this.

22

After her parents left, Sue let her muddled thoughts take over. When she closed her eye, the crash suddenly loomed up in front of her, and she winced as she felt pain in every bone in her body. She tried to remember the police trying to get her out of the car, but at the time she had been drifting in and out of consciousness. She had never known pain like it and had cried out with every movement. The blood that had filled her eyes and mouth had been warm and sticky. Her stomach had been racked with searing pain as she had been crushed against the steering wheel. Cy Taylor and the baby filled her mind. Well, that problem had gone for ever now; but what about her future? She knew she was going to be horribly disfigured and could even be blind in one eye. She began to cry silently. Who would want her now? Would Mr Hunt still employ her? She should have been killed, then all these worries wouldn't have mattered. The pain in her ankle was almost unbearable and her head throbbed.

'All right, love?'

Sue opened her eye to see an old lady standing beside her bed.

'I'm Florrie. I'm in the bed over there.'

'That's nice,' said Sue and closed her eye again. She wished she could turn over; she didn't want to talk to anyone.

'Nice flowers. From the boyfriend?'

'No. Me boss.'

'That's nice of him.'

Sue wanted to scream at her to go away, but the old lady sat down on the chair beside her bed.

'You look like you could do with a bit of cheering up.'

'I'm all right.'

'Your mum and dad are very worried about you. Looked fair worn out, they did.'

Sue opened her eye. In all of this she hadn't really given a lot of thought to her parents or Granny Potts. 'I expect they are,' she said softly, feeling full of guilt.

Florrie patted her hand. 'Keep yer pecker up, love. Tea's just coming round so I'd better hop back into bed.'

Sue returned her thoughts to her lost baby. Was it a boy or a girl? Could they tell at this stage? Did her parents know about it? Had the doctor told them? If so, what did they think of her? All these questions were buzzing round in her head. She remembered how her mother had gone on about that girl Maisie. At least she was going to have her baby, despite what everybody thought of her.

'Susan, your tea's here.' A young nurse rearranged her pillows. 'Try and eat something.'

Sue looked at the food. How could she eat? She just wanted to be left alone to die.

'When will the doctor be round?'

'Not till tomorrow now. Why? Are you in pain?'

Sue nodded.

'I'll give you something to help with that.'

A few moments later the nurse returned and Sue quickly swallowed the pills she gave her. She just wanted to sleep. With a bit of luck, when she woke up again she would find that all this had been a bad dream.

★ ★ ★

Ron was pacing the floor. 'When they gonner let her come home?'

'I don't know, when she's better.' Jane was getting fed up with her brother, who hadn't stopped talking about his 'little Sue'. She was worried enough about her friend without him keeping on.

'Why won't they let me go and see her?'

'I've told you a hundred and one times. They only let family visit.'

'Well I'm very nearly family. When she comes out we can be married.'

Jane was exasperated. 'Look, why don't you go next door and talk to her mum and dad. They'll put you in the picture and they'll tell you if you can marry her. Remember, she is still under age and you'll need their consent.'

He sat down hard in the armchair with a bewildered look on his face. 'What if they say I can't?'

'Well in that case, you'd better look for someone else. I'm going up to bed.'

★ ★ ★

Fred Hunt was also pacing the floor. If only he could get in to see Susan. Why did the hospital have to have such strict rules? He had been racking his brains to find some way of seeing her. There must be someone who was willing to accept a few quid and let him sneak in. Tomorrow he'd ask around and see if one of his mates knew someone who could help him.

The phone rang and he wasn't surprised to hear his mother on the other end of the line.

'So, how is the young lady?' she asked. Fred had told them about the accident.

'Her parents said she's in a bit of a state.'

'I expect she is if she went through the windscreen. Frederick, I'm very worried.'

'We all are, Ma.'

'Now listen. Are you sure it was nothing to do with the car?'

'I'm pretty sure the car was sound. Why?'

'I don't want you to finish up in prison.'

He laughed. 'I'm not going to finish up in prison.'

'Well just you be careful. Make sure that car was all right.'

'I will, Ma. Good night.'

'Good night, son.'

Fred put the receiver back on its cradle and stood looking at it for a while. What if the car's brakes were faulty? He would never forgive himself if they were. First thing Monday he'd go and see Harry and get him to write out a report about the car's state of repair, just in case the police wanted to know.

★ ★ ★

On Sunday Fred took the Reeds to the hospital again, but they told him there wasn't anything new to report and they returned home in silence.

Very early on Monday morning, he was woken by the bell on his front door being rung loudly and constantly. He looked at the clock. 'Christ. It's only six o'clock.' He dragged himself out of bed. 'Who the bloody hell's calling at this time in the morning?' he mumbled to himself as put on his dressing gown and made his way down the stairs. He wrenched open the door. 'What d'you think you're doing . . . ?' He stopped when he saw a policeman standing on his doorstep.

'Mr Fred Hunt?'

'You know that.' This was one of the bobbies who often had a wander round the showroom. Fear gripped him. Had Susan died? Had they found a fault with the car? Trying to remain calm and detached, he asked, 'Who wants to know?'

'Can I come in?'

'If you want.' Fred stepped to one side and the policeman entered. 'What's this all about, officer?' He knew he had to be careful and mind his Ps and Qs.

In the small living room, Fred beckoned to the officer to sit down.

'I'll stand if you don't mind, sir.'

'Please yourself.'

The policeman undid the button on his top pocket and took out a notebook. Reading from it he asked, 'Do you know a Mr Rose?'

Fred grinned. 'Sure. What's old Bert been up to?'

'It seems he and his son have been involved in a robbery, but he said he was with you that night.'

'He would say that.'

'Do they come here for a game of cards?'

'Sometimes.'

'Mr Rose said that on Sunday the sixth of September the three of you were here and had a few drinks and played cards.'

'Could have.'

'Can you prove it?'

'How can I?'

'In that case, sir, you'll have to come with me to the station to sign a statement.'

Fred was at his wits' end. How could those two stitch him up like this? They'd had disagreements in the past but they had always stuck by each other and often helped each other out of trouble. He had to find out what this was all about.

'I think there might have been some mistake.'

'Well in that case you've got nothing to worry about, sir.'

'Can I get dressed first?'

'Course.'

Fred was racking his brains trying to think why Bert Rose would say this. He hadn't seen the man for months. Then he suddenly remembered Susan saying something about a Mr Rose coming to the showroom when he was out; she had mentioned his tattoo. When was that?

He never had bothered to find out what they had wanted; was it an alibi?

★ ★ ★

Later that morning Ron wandered round to the workshop. He didn't like Harry Field but he didn't know who else to ask. 'Mr Field,' he called out. 'Mr Field, are you there?'

Harry Field scrambled out from under the car he was repairing. 'Oh, it's you. What do you want?'

'It's Mr Hunt. He ain't opened up yet.'

'What d'you mean?'

'I went to go in and it's all locked up.'

'He's probably out.'

'But who's gonner answer the phone? It was ringing when I got there.'

'Don't worry about it.' Harry went back to what he was doing.

'But Mr Field . . . ' Ron was getting angry. He didn't like being ignored, especially when he was trying to be polite to someone like Harry Field.

'Look, lad, sling your hook. I'm too busy to worry about you or Fred Hunt.'

Ron dragged him out from under the car by his feet.

'Leave me alone, you silly sod. I don't know where he is and I've got a job to do, so get out of here or I'll tell the boss you're a menace and you'll get the sack.'

Reluctantly Ron walked away. He didn't want the sack. He was so happy working for Mr Hunt. He grinned to himself. Everything was good;

199

even his demons had stopped talking to him, and he was saving all the money his mother allowed him to keep so that he could marry his little Sue. He didn't care if she only had one eye and scars all over her face. He would kiss her and make her better. He settled himself down on the doorstep and waited for Mr Hunt.

★　★　★

By the time they arrived at the police station, Fred knew he had to be as vague as he could when answering the copper's questions.

'You say you don't remember the night of Sunday the sixth of September?'

'No. Christ, I can't even remember what I had for dinner last week, let alone what I was doing weeks ago.'

'But you know Albert Rose and his son?'

'Yes, I told you. We went to school together, and sometimes they came round for a game of cards.'

'I see. Wouldn't have thought he was in your league moneywise.'

'Just 'cos I got a few bob don't mean to say I turn me back on mates.'

'Couldn't be that they do a few favours for you now and again?'

'What d'you mean?' Fred had to be on his guard. He could say that Bert and his son had been with him; you never know, it might be useful.

'Come off it, Fred. We all know that you sometimes do dodgy deals.'

'Can you prove that?'

'You know we can't; you're a bit too clever.'

'Thanks. Can I go now?'

'We might call on you again. Unless you come across a diary that tells you where you were on that night. Then you call us.'

'I'll do that.' Fred picked up his trilby and stood up.

Outside, he lit a cigarette and drew long and hard on it. It tasted good. He was glad to get away from the police station. He had to think. He didn't want to upset Bert and his son, but what had he been doing that night?

★ ★ ★

'Ron, sorry you had to wait. I had something important to do.'

Ron stood up quickly when he saw his boss arrive and snatched off his cap. 'That's all right, Mr Hunt. Your phone's been ringing and I couldn't get in to tell the person you wasn't here.'

'That's all right. If it was that important, they'll ring back. I'd like a cuppa.'

'I can do that for you.' Ron bustled away to the tiny room where the gas ring for the kettle was. 'Thought you might have gone to see my little Sue.'

Fred looked at him. '*Your* little Sue?'

'Yer.' Ron grinned. 'I'm gonner marry her. I don't care if she's got scars and only one eye. I'm still gonner marry her.'

'What does Susan say about this?'

He looked down. 'She says no. But she will if no one else wants her.' The whistle from the kettle sent him scurrying back to the kitchenette.

Fred sat and stared at the desk Susan would normally be sitting at. He felt sorry for Ron with his wild dreams. His thoughts went back to Susan. If only he could get to see her. He couldn't bear the thought of having to spend the rest of his life without her. He knew he was acting like a lovesick youth, but he didn't care.

'Here's your tea.'

'Thanks, Ron.'

'What d'you want me to do?'

'You could clean up that car that Harry brought from the garage on Saturday. Might be able to sell it this week.'

Ron smiled. He knew in his mind that Mr Hunt wouldn't sack him. He was too useful.

Later that morning Harry Field came into the office. He had been shocked when Fred told him on Saturday what had happened. 'How's Sue?'

'I've not been in to see her — as you know, it's family only — but I don't think she's that good from what her folks say.'

'I'm really sorry to hear that. She's a lovely girl.'

'She could be badly scarred.'

'Poor kid.'

'I've been taking 'em to the hospital.'

'Tell 'em to give her my regards.'

'I will.'

'You was a bit late this morning. I had his nibs worrying the life out of me wondering where you was.'

'Sorry about that. But I had to go out.' Fred wasn't going to say he was at the police station; Harry might read more into that than there was.

'Do you think you'll be able to manage without Sue?'

'Dunno.' Fred looked at the papers on his desk. 'I was going to come and see you when I got a chance. That car Sue was driving. Was the brakes sound?'

'Course they was. Why? The police say different?'

'No. Do you think you could give me a written report?'

'Course. You don't doubt me, do you?'

'No. But it's best to be prepared, just in case.'

'I'll do that, Fred. Look, if things get a bit, you know, on top of you here . . . well, I was talking to Jen about all this and she said she wouldn't mind coming in for a few days to help out, just till Sue gets back.'

'Thanks. I could kiss you.'

'No. Don't do that. At least she knows the business.'

For the first time in days Fred smiled. Jen did know the business; before she married Harry, she had worked for Fred.

'I'll get her to come in tomorrow and you can sort out what days you want her in.'

'Thanks, Harry. That's one load off me mind.'

When Harry had left, Fred looked out at Ron. When he'd finished that car, he could sweep the site. That should keep him busy for a while.

Fred went to Sue's drawer. He had to check his diary and see if anything would jog his memory about where he'd been on the Sunday that Bert and his son said they were here.

He pulled out a load of books and papers.

'Mr Hunt.'

Fred jumped and the things he was holding slid to the floor. 'Ron. You frightened the bloody life out of me.'

'Sorry. What you doing in little Sue's desk?'

Fred was scrabbling on the floor picking up papers. 'If you must know, I've got someone coming to work here for a little while and I want to make sure there's nothing outstanding.' He wanted to tell Ron that it was none of his business, but he knew he had to be polite to him, as he was never quite sure how he would react.

'I'll help.'

'No, that's all right. I can manage.' Why was he feeling so guilty? This was his office. He could do what he liked. 'You can go and sweep the forecourt if you've finished that car.'

Ron grinned. 'All right.' With that he scurried out.

Fred picked up his diary. Then he bent down to retrieve a small black book. It fell open, and some words scrawled in large capitals caught his eye: HE'S BLOODY WELL MARRIED AND TOLD ME TO GET RID OF IT.

He looked at the date. September the twelfth. This was Susan's personal diary. Why had she left it in her drawer? And who was she writing about? He quickly put the book in his pocket. He would give it to her parents when he saw them tonight, but right now he had to tell the police that Bert and his son had indeed been here that night. Who knows when he might need a favour in return.

23

It didn't matter how hard he tried not to think about it, for the rest of the day Fred Hunt was aware of Susan's diary in his pocket, and every few minutes his fingers found their way to it. He thought about the words written in large black capitals and wondered what they meant. Was she seeing someone who was married? Halfway through the morning, as he was sitting at his desk, a terrible thought struck him and he put his head in his hands. What was it she was trying to get rid of? Was she talking about a baby? Was she expecting? If that was the case, who was this bloke? Did her parents know? He realised he had to try and get into the hospital and pass the diary over to Susan herself, rather than her parents. He had to find out if what he suspected was true. If there was a baby, was she still carrying it? But how could he ask such a thing? She would quite rightly accuse him of reading her very personal diary.

★   ★   ★

At six thirty Fred was sitting outside the Reed's house. Visiting time during the week was from seven to seven thirty. All day he had pondered over the diary, and he could still feel it almost burning a hole in his pocket. Should he give it to her parents? Did they know she might have been

206

expecting? He was in such a dilemma.

'Thanks, mate,' said Charlie as he held open the car door for his wife. 'You all right? You look a bit worried.'

Fred smiled. 'Everything's fine, thanks, and you?'

'As well as can be,' said Charlie, settling himself beside Fred.

When they were comfortable Fred said, 'Let's hope you see some improvement.'

'I hope so. I'll be glad when they take those horrible bandages off her face and head, then we'll know if she's still got the sight in that eye.' Doris wasn't talking to anyone in particular as she stared out of the window.

'Have they given you any idea when they'll let her home?'

'Not yet. We might hear more this week,' said Charlie.

★ ★ ★

As Sue lay in bed with nothing to occupy her mind, her thoughts went to her lost baby. Nobody had mentioned it. She didn't know if it had been a boy or a girl. Would it have looked like Cy? For a brief moment she began to fantasise about life with Cy and a baby, then reality came back. Had the doctor told her parents? If so, why hadn't her mother said something? Were they waiting till she was home? What a mess her life was in.

At visiting time Sue knew she had to try and cheer up for her parents' sake. 'Hello, Mum,

207

Dad,' she said as they came up to her bed and sat either side of her.

'You sound a bit better.'

'I do feel a bit better, but I'm a bit worried as tomorrow they're gonner take this off.' She touched her bandage, then fingered her hair, which was still matted with dried blood. 'Then I'll know if I can see out of this eye. Mum, I'm so scared.' She brushed away the tear that was rolling down her cheek.

Doris held her daughter as best as she could. 'Of course you are, love. We're scared an' all.'

Charlie took hold of his daughter's hand and gently patted it. He swallowed hard. 'Do they say when you might be allowed out of bed?' He looked at the cage that was still under the bedclothes.

'Might be this week, then at least I'll be able to move about. Then if I get on all right with crutches they'll let me home.'

'That will be wonderful. Your gran can't wait to spoil you.' Doris tried not to sound worried.

'It must be better in this ward with other people,' said her father, looking around.

'Dunno. They seem like a lot of old women, and they wander over for a chat when all I want to do is sleep.'

'They're only trying to be friendly.' Charlie gave a nod to Florrie, who was without visitors.

All too soon the sister was ringing the bell for them to leave. Doris stood up.

'That boss of yours is very good. He insists on bringing us here.'

'Sue,' said her father as he stood up too, 'were the car's brakes all right?'

'Yes, Dad,' she said softly. 'Please don't blame Mr Hunt for what happened. It was the weather, and probably I'm not experienced enough. So tell him not to worry.'

The bell went again, and this time it was being rung with exasperation.

★ ★ ★

As soon as he saw them, Fred put out his cigarette and hurried round to open the car door. 'How is she?'

'They're gonner take the bandages off tomorrow.' Doris had tears rolling down her face. She dabbed at them with her handkerchief. 'Sorry.'

'You don't have to be.'

'Mr Hunt, what if she can't see out of that eye?'

'I can't answer that, but I can tell you that her job will always be there for her.'

'Thank you.'

'She also said they might let her get out of bed this week.' Charlie settled himself in the car. 'Then when she learns to use her crutches she's talking about coming home.'

Fred turned round to look at Doris. 'That's got to be good news.'

'Yes.' But so many practical things were racing round Doris's head. They would have to bring her bed downstairs, though thank God the lav was outside. She was also worried that the baby

209

still hadn't been mentioned. Would Sue ever tell them?

★ ★ ★

When Fred arrived home, he made himself a cup of tea and, taking Sue's diary from his pocket, went to sit in his armchair. He was just about to settle down when the doorbell went. 'Who the bloody hell's this?' he said out loud as he went down the stairs.

''Allo, mate,' said Bert Rose.

'What d'you want?' Fred looked up and down the road. 'I thought you was in clink.'

'I was, but thanks to you we're out. And I've just come round to say thanks. Fancy sharing this?' He held up a bottle of whisky.

Fred stood to one side to let him in.

'Thought me and the boy was in trouble this time,' Bert said over his shoulder as they went up the stairs.

In the small sitting room Fred went to the sideboard and got out two glasses. 'So, why did you pick on me for your alibi?'

Bert poured a generous amount into each glass. 'To us.' He sat in the armchair.

Fred sat at the table. 'Well?'

'We've looked after each other in the past, and I thought . . . Well, you never know if you might want a favour done at some time. After all's said and done, I have been of use to you in the past.'

'That's true. So was it a good job?'

'Na. Not worth all the hassle. Didn't get much at all.'

210

'That's not what the police said.'

'Well they would say that, wouldn't they?'

Fred looked into his glass. His thoughts were drifting off. 'Look, why don't you and the boy come round for a game of cards on Sunday?'

'Yer, we'd like that, taking a few bob off you. What time?'

'Any time in the evening. I might have to go to the hospital in the afternoon, but that's no trouble.'

'Not anyone we know?'

'The girl who works for me, Susan, she's had a car accident. If the family want me to bring her home, then that's where I'll be, but I don't think it'll be Sunday night.'

'Poor little cow. Is she badly hurt?'

'I don't know. I'd like to see her, but only family can visit.'

'Why's that? Here, you ain't sweet on her, are you?'

Fred picked up his glass. 'Don't be daft. She's just a kid. No, it's just that I'd like to tell her her job's still here. She's got enough to worry about without the thought of losing her job; besides, she's good worker.'

'You could always drop her a line.'

'Suppose so.' Fred swirled the amber liquid round in his glass.

'D'you know, I reckon I could get you in.'

Fred sat up. 'Do you think you could?'

'Leave it to me. Here, she wasn't in one of your dodgy cars, was she?'

'No. The car was fine.'

'See what I can do, mate. Sounds as if you've

211

got a soft spot for her.'

'She's a nice girl.'

'Yer, she seemed like that. She was very polite, and good looking as well.'

'She might not be now; she went through the windscreen.'

'Bloody hell. No wonder you're worried about her. Leave it to me, Fred, I'll see what I can do.' Bert stood up. 'Better be going.'

'Thanks, Bert. See you next Sunday.'

Bert gave him a playful punch on the arm. 'Well I owe you one, remember.'

When Fred had closed the front door he thought about Bert and his son. If Bert could get him in to see Susan without her parents being there, that would be one favour repaid.

Susan's diary was still filling his thoughts, and he was in two minds about whether to give it to her parents. Why had she left it in the office? Was it because she didn't want them to find it? He decided that for the time being he would put it in his safe. Out of sight, it was out of mind.

★ ★ ★

The following day Fred was on the lookout for Bert, hoping he would come up with some way of getting him into the hospital. That evening he took the Reeds to see their daughter.

Mrs Reed came out in floods of tears. Fred put out his cigarette and hurried over to them.

'What's wrong?' he asked an anxious-looking Charlie, who was holding his wife's arm.

'She's had the bandages off, and, Fred, she

looks bloody awful.'

Doris let out a mournful sob.

'Has she lost the sight in her eye?'

'No. But she's got this ugly red scar right across her eye, cheek and forehead. It looks worse at the moment as the big black stitches are still in.'

Fred gave Charlie a cigarette.

'Thanks, mate. The doctor said it would look better when they come out, but the scar will take a long while to heal.'

Doris broke down in tears.

'Come on, love. Get in the car.'

Fred felt so helpless. 'Has she seen herself?'

Charlie nodded. 'She wouldn't talk to us; she just lay there and cried.'

'She's only eighteen and her whole life's before her, but who will want her now?' Doris buried her face in her handkerchief.

'Poor Susan. It must have been a shock for her.' Fred knew then that he had to see her and tell her that he would look after her whatever she looked like.

24

Sue was frightened when the sister came to her bedside after swiftly and efficiently drawing the curtains round her bed. She helped her to sit up. What was going to happen to her now? 'When can I go home?' she asked the doctor who had been following Sister and was holding her file.

The doctor gave her a dazzling smile; even in this situation Sue could see he was good looking. 'You must be patient. We have to take these out first.' He gently touched her cheek.

'I just wonner go home.'

'Of course you do. We'll be getting you out of bed sometime this week and then we'll see how you manage.'

Sue touched her cheek too. The skin felt rough and wrinkled. She could feel the stitches. 'Will I look any better when these come out?'

'Yes. And in time the scar will start to fade.' He sat next to her and looked serious. 'But I'm not going to build up your hopes of it going away altogether. I'm afraid it will always be there.'

Tears ran slowly down Sue's face.

The sister looked at her and gently tapped the back of her hand. 'A bit of make-up will help to disguise it.'

'I'm more than pleased that you can see out of this eye,' said the doctor as he peered into her eye with his torch. 'You were very lucky.'

Sue didn't feel lucky.

'Let's take one step at a time,' said the doctor. The curtains were pulled back and they left her bedside to go on to the next patient. Sue turned over and looked at the window. Outside, everybody was going about their everyday lives, but hers had been shattered. She felt so miserable. How could she get in touch with Cy? Would he come to her bedside? She didn't think so, even if he was allowed. She would write him a letter and give it to her mum to give to Jane; she would pass it on. With that thought, she settled down.

★ ★ ★

For the rest of the week Fred was hoping Bert would turn up, but by Friday there hadn't been any sign of him. Perhaps he would have some news for Fred on Sunday when he came for the game of cards.

When Sue's parents saw their daughter on Friday she had had her stitches out and was sitting in a wheelchair. The ugly scar stood out bright red against her pale skin. Doris held her daughter in her arms, and it took her all her self-control not to weep.

Her father hugged her. 'It's great to see you out of bed.' Unable to look her in the eye, he glanced at her plaster and asked, 'How long before that comes off?'

'The doctor said it would be weeks, but at least now I can get around and sit on the commode. Those bedpans are awful.' Sue was trying so hard to sound positive. 'Mum, could you ask Jane to get me some Pond's cold cream? The doctor said that would help to soften my skin.'

'I can get that for you,' said her mother, only too pleased to be able to do something.

'Is Mr Hunt still bringing you every night?'

'Yes. He's very concerned about you. He told us that Harry Field's wife is helping out while you're in here.'

'She used to work for him before she got married. Mum, I don't think I'll be able to go back there to work.'

'Why not?' asked her father.

'Well look at me. I'll put all the customers off with my ugly face.'

'Don't talk daft. Mr Hunt said your job will always be there for you. As your mum said, he thinks a lot of you.'

Doris looked at her daughter. She was right; the scar was ugly. 'You look a lot better now those dreadful stitches are out.'

'But I'm going to be left with this.' Sue touched her scar and shuddered. Who would want to look at a face like this, she thought, let alone kiss her?

Fred was waiting outside as usual and could see that Sue's parents were upset. 'Is everything all right?'

'She's had the stitches out and it doesn't look very nice,' said Charlie.

'It'll be all right in time,' said Fred, trying to ease the situation.

'I don't think so,' said Doris.

216

They drove home in silence, each one with their own thoughts.

* * *

On Sunday evening when Bert and his son arrived, Fred's first words were, 'So much for getting me into the hospital.'

'Hold on, hold on,' said Bert. 'Bloody hell, let me get me money and cards out before you start carrying on like some old woman.'

'We're not using your cards for a start. I've lost money to you before with your cards,' said Fred, putting his own pack on the table.

'All right then, we'll play with yours. But I think we'd better have a drink first.'

Fred poured out three glasses of whisky.

'Cheers,' said Bert.

'Cheers,' said Fred and Bert's son together.

Bert began to shuffle the cards. 'Now before we start, I've spoken to someone at the hospital, and they said that if you go round the back any afternoon and ask for Jimmy Cole and drop him a drink, he reckons he'll be able to get you in. D'you know what ward she's in?'

'No.' Fred could hardly contain his elation. 'But I'll find out tomorrow night.'

'Right, that's the business over. Now let's see about taking some of that money off you.'

Fred smiled. He didn't care about the money. Whatever he lost would be worth it; he could be seeing Susan next week.

* * *

On Monday evening, as soon as he'd dropped Sue's parents off, Fred made his way round to the back of the hospital. He wanted to find out the lie of the place.

'What you doing round here?' asked a porter who was outside emptying a large bin.

'I'm looking for Jimmy, Jimmy Cole.' Fred tried to make it sound casual and as if he knew him.

'Gone home. Goes home about four this week. He's on earlies.'

'Thanks, I'll catch him there.' Fred sauntered away. Now he knew he had to get here before four.

When the Reeds came out, Fred, after enquiring about their daughter's progress, asked, 'By the way, what ward is Susan in? I think Harry's wife would like to drop her a line to let her know that she's only temporary, just till Susan comes back.'

Charlie looked at Fred. 'She don't have to write; Sue understands.'

'Oh.' Fred was disappointed with the answer.

'I don't want to offend you, mate, but Sue don't want to work for you.'

Fred was taken aback. 'Why? Why ever not?'

'It's not that she didn't like the job,' said Doris. 'But she says she can't face people again.'

'That's silly. We all love her and she's very efficient.' Fred was devastated. 'What's she going to do, then?'

'She don't know. Let's get her home first, then we'll worry about that.'

'Yes, of course.' Fred knew now that he had to

218

see her. 'But Jen would still like to write to her.'

'I think she'd like that,' said Doris. 'She enjoys getting letters, it makes her feel she's not forgotten. She's in Ward D2.'

'Thanks. And you can tell her she'll never be forgotten.'

★　★　★

Jane was surprised to see Mrs Reed standing on her doorstep when she opened the front door. She gasped. 'Is Sue all right?'

Doris smiled weakly. 'The doctor told us she's progressing as well as can be expected. But she is very down.'

'Come in. I'm sorry I've not been in for a day or two.' Jane was feeling guilty at not calling in every night. On Friday they had told her that Sue had had her stitches out, and that she didn't look that good and was very down. Poor Sue. She must feel that her life was finished. All weekend her friend filled her thoughts, until she felt she just had to take herself off to the pictures, not that she could concentrate on the film. She missed her friend so much; she had no one to talk and laugh with.

Doris put up her hand. 'We only saw you Friday, so please don't worry about it. We can't expect you to hang around all the time waiting for us to come home. Anyway, Sue gave me a letter for you.'

'Thanks. I'll answer it right away. I wish I could get to see her.'

'If only you could. It would help to cheer her

219

up. But she does look forward to your letters.'

Jane was fingering the envelope. 'This feels like a thick one. I wonder what's she got to say?'

'I'll leave you to read it in private. I know what you girls are like.'

As Doris left, she too wondered what was in that letter. Had Jane known about the baby? Had Sue told her she'd lost it? If only she could ask someone. If she could talk to her daughter about it, would that help to lift Sue's depression?

★   ★   ★

Jane hurried to her bedroom to read Sue's letter: When she opened the envelope, another one fell out. She picked it up. It was addressed to Cy Taylor.

Jane sat on the bed and looked at the sealed envelope she was holding. 'Oh no, Sue,' she groaned. 'Give him up. Remember he's married.'

She began reading her own letter.

Dear Jane,

As you can see, I've enclosed a letter for Cy. Do you think you could go along when the band are around and give it to him?

I expect Mum's told you I've had the stitches out and that I look really awful. I shall never ever go dancing again and I won't even want to go to the pictures, only when it's dark and no one can see me.

If you can find a new friend I really won't mind. And tell Ron that no one will want to marry me now, not even him, as I look hideous.

From your ugly friend,
Sue

Jane could feel the tears trickling down her cheeks and began crying uncontrollably. Sue hadn't put the usual kisses at the bottom of her letter. Jane wanted to go to the hospital and hold her friend and tell her that she would be there for her for ever. That she'd always love her whatever she looked like and if anybody took the mickey out of her she'd thump 'em.

'Jane. Are you all right?' Her mother was tapping gently on her door.

Jane went and opened it. Ron was also standing in the doorway and their mother pushed him to one side. Since Sue's accident, her mother had been supportive and understanding. Jane threw her arms round her and cried bitterly on her shoulder.

★ ★ ★

On Tuesday afternoon Ron looked up from the car he was cleaning and saw Mr Hunt. He was looking very smart and was carrying a large bunch of flowers.

'Going anywhere nice, boss?' Ron asked. He wanted to know if Mr Hunt had a girlfriend, and if he did, what about little Sue? After all, he did take her out sometimes.

Ron was confused and concerned about his little Sue. Jane had been very upset when she'd

221

had a letter from her friend. He had stood and watched his mother comfort her, and then, when they'd gone downstairs, he'd picked up the letters Jane had dropped. He'd read the one to his sister, then looked at the other one and could feel anger raging inside him. His little Sue had written to Cy Taylor, but not to him. He knew he was the singer with the band that played at the Town Hall. Why was Sue writing to him? Was she in love with him? He would find out when this singer was around and go and give him a piece of his mind. He would tell him that little Sue had had an accident and that he wouldn't want her any more. Ron smiled to himself. Now that Mr Hunt had a girlfriend and little Sue was ugly, that would leave the way clear for him.

25

Fred Hunt was annoyed with himself. It was unusual for him to feel so nervous; he was acting like a silly lovesick schoolboy on his first date. His hands were sweating as he gripped the steering wheel. Was there also some guilt mixed in with his feelings? After all, Susan had been driving one of his cars, and had it really been up to scratch? Harry said it was roadworthy, but sometimes they did cut corners. He looked at the flowers on the seat next to him. Were they too much? He would have to leave them at reception; he didn't want to make it too obvious that he was visiting.

He parked the car and made his way to the back of the hospital. There appeared to be a lot of people bustling about. He couldn't believe he was doing this; it was so out of character and absolute madness. God only knows what his mother would make of it. He looked about him. How would he know where to find Jimmy Cole? What did he look like?

An attractive young woman glanced over at him. She was carrying a bundle of washing. She smiled as she came up to him. 'You look lost. Can I help you at all?'

'I dunno. D'you know Jimmy Cole?'

'Everybody knows Jimmy. He's a porter but sometimes he can be found in the laundry room. I'm just going there, so if you'd like to come with me I'd be more than pleased to show you where he hides out. If he's not there, then someone will know where he is. I'm Nurse Stannard, by the way.'

'Thanks.' Fred fell into step beside her.

'A friend of yours, is he?'

'In a way.' Fred had to choose his words carefully. 'What ward are you on?'

'Mostly I'm in emergency, but I go on the wards sometimes. I'm still training and hope to be a sister one day.'

'I'm sure you'll go a long way.' As they moved into the bowels of the hospital, Fred could see that this might be very sad for any boyfriends she might have, as nurses weren't allowed to work after they were married.

'Here we are.' She pushed open a door and the heat and noise hit them. 'Jimmy, Jimmy!' she called out. 'Are you hiding in here? Here's a friend of yours who's come looking for you.'

A short, balding, rotund man came up to her. He wiped his wet forehead with a piece of dirty cloth. 'Who is it, Mary?'

'It's me, Jimmy.' Fred quickly stepped forward and shook his hand. 'How are you, me old mate?'

For a moment or two Jimmy looked bewildered, then the penny dropped. 'Hello, Fred.'

Nurse Stannard smiled. 'I'll just take this lot over to Sally.'

Jimmy took hold of Fred's arm and gently moved him away from the noise.

'That's better, we can hear ourselves talk now.'

'Thanks for seeing me. Bert said all I've got to do to is stand you a drink and you'll get me into Ward D2.'

Jimmy looked anxiously up and down the corridor. 'Yer, that's about the score.'

'Will a pound be OK?'

'Yer, that'll do.' He quickly put the note that Fred was holding out into his pocket. 'She must be very special.'

'Yes, she is.'

'I'll get you a brown coat and show you how to get to the ward. You'll have to push a wheel chair about, and if anybody asks, you're fetching a patient to take to X-ray. We do that all the time so nobody takes a lot of notice. Wait here and I'll get you a coat.'

Fred was exhilarated; he couldn't believe it was going to be this easy. Then fear gripped him. What if she didn't want to see him? The last thing he wanted was to upset her.

When Jimmy returned he was holding a brown coat. 'This should fit.'

Fred put it on quickly.

'Right, follow me,' said Jimmy.

To Fred it seemed they were going round in circles, but at last Jimmy grabbed a wheelchair from a corridor and they made their way to Ward D2.

'This is it. I'll ask the sister where Miss . . . What's her name?'

'Reed. Susan Reed.'

'Hello, Sister,' said Jimmy breezily as they walked up to the doors. 'Got to take a Miss Reed down to X-ray.'

'Have you? Are you sure? I've not been told about this. I'll just check my notes.' She went into her office.

Fred stood trying to look through the small round window in the door of the ward.

'I think there's been some mistake,' said Sister. 'I'll phone down to X-ray and find out.'

When she went back into her office Jimmy said to Fred, 'Right. In you go.'

'What?'

'In you go, go on, don't hang about.'

'But when she comes out, she'll see I've gone.'

'Don't worry. I'll sort that out. And if anybody asks, you're just picking up a patient's notes. We do that all the time too. Go on, get a move on before she comes back out.'

Fred pushed open the door and walked in. As he made his way down the ward he glanced at the bedridden women. Some of them smiled at him. He began to panic. He couldn't see Susan. Had she been moved? Would he recognise her?

He was almost at the end of the ward when he spotted her. She was sitting in a wheelchair with her plastered leg stuck out in front of her, and she was staring out of the window. 'Susan,' he said softly.

She turned her head quickly and it was all he could do to stop himself from gasping. The scar was indeed very ugly.

'Mr Hunt.' She put her hand up to cover her face. 'What are you doing here?'

'I've come to see you.'

'Well you've seen me, so now you can go.' She turned away from him.

226

'Susan, listen to me. I've not risked life and limb to get in here just to walk away the minute I see you.' He looked towards the door. 'I can only stay a little while, but I had to come to tell you that whatever's happened, your job's still there.'

She laughed. 'You've done all this just to tell me my job's safe?'

'Well, not just that. As you know, I'm very fond of you.'

She looked at him, bewildered.

He stumbled over his words. He knew he was rushing things, but he didn't have time for all the preliminaries. 'I'm sorry. I don't mean in that way.'

'I'm sorry as well, Mr Hunt. I'm sorry you've gone to all this trouble, but as you can see, I won't be going out much in the future, not looking like this.'

He wanted to pick her up and run away with her. He loved her and it hurt him to see her looking so down. 'Susan, there's something else.'

'What?'

'When I was going through your desk looking for any outstanding bills, I found your diary.'

She blanched. 'Did you read it?'

'Good heavens, no. I was going to give it to your mother, but it fell open at the last entry, and I'm afraid that as I picked it up I did read that page. Susan, are you in any trouble?'

She looked up at him. 'Not now. And thank you for not giving it to my mum. I'm sure she would have read it.'

The door was pushed open and Jimmy stood there beckoning to Fred to come out.

'Looks like I've got to go.'

'Thanks. Where is my diary?'

'In my safe. If you want, I can give it to your mother.'

'No. Keep it till I come out.'

Jimmy had started to walk towards him. 'Come on. Quick.'

'I must go.'

'Bye.'

Sue watched Fred hurry down the ward. At the door he turned and waved. He had come here to see her, but why? Surely not just to tell her her job was safe and that he had her diary. Thank God he hadn't given it to her mother. But how much had Mr Hunt seen? Did he know about Cy and the baby? She sat back bewildered. Whatever his motives, he was a nice man, and he obviously must think a lot of her, but as he said, not in a romantic way.

★   ★   ★

Grabbing Fred's arm, Jimmy hurried him past the sister's office without a word. It wasn't till they were safely in the corridor that he spoke.

'Blimey, nearly got caught that time. She was giving me a right ticking-off.'

When they got outside, Fred took off his brown coat and handed it back to Jimmy. 'Thanks, mate, and here's another pound for your trouble.'

'Thanks, Fred,' said Jimmy, pocketing the note. 'Nearly a week's wages in half an hour, now that's not bad going. Bert said you was a good 'un.'

'That's comforting to hear.'

Jimmy laughed. 'Yer, it's always best to keep on the right side of him. And if you wonner come back, just call fer me.'

'Thanks, mate.' Fred touched Jimmy's shoulder as a sign of appreciation as he walked away.

When he got in his car he looked at the flowers. He'd better not take them in now. He didn't want to have questions asked in case he got Jimmy into trouble. He'd give them to Mrs Reed tonight.

As he drove home, Susan's sad face filled his thoughts. He knew now that he had to ask her to marry him. He wanted to try and make her life as good as he could. But could she ever learn to love him?

★ ★ ★

Later that evening, as he was taking Susan's parents back home, Fred felt relieved when he realised that Susan hadn't told them of his visit to the hospital this morning. All day he had been mulling over what to say if they asked him why he'd been there. He'd decided on telling them that he'd had to pick up one of the doctor's cars, and on the spur of the moment had asked if it was possible to see her. But as nothing was said, he relaxed.

'She loved the flowers,' said Doris. 'Though

229

you shouldn't keep wasting your money on flowers; they don't last long.'

'I don't mind. I don't want her to feel we've forgotten her.'

26

It wasn't till the end of October that the doctor came to Sue's bedside and told her that she could go home at the end of the week. She accepted the news with very mixed feelings.

'Doctor?'

He looked up from the notes he was studying. 'Yes.'

Sue looked around and gave a nervous little cough. There was a question she had to ask but had been avoiding. 'Do my mum and dad know I was going to have a baby?' she said softly.

He sat on the chair beside her bed. 'Yes, they do.'

Sue swallowed. 'Were they very angry?'

'At the time they were in shock and more concerned with your injuries. Do you intend to talk to your mother about it?'

'I don't know.'

'I think you should.'

'If . . . and that's a big if, 'cos I don't think anybody will want me now.' She touched her cheek. 'But if I ever got married, perhaps to a blind man, would I be able to have children?'

The doctor took hold of her hand. 'Susan. At first you're going to feel very self-conscious about your scar, but in time it will fade, though it will never go away completely. But people will see you for what you are, a very nice young lady. And in answer to your question, I can't see any

231

reason why you shouldn't be able to have children.'

A tear ran slowly down her cheek.

'Come on now. You should be happy to be going home.'

'I don't think I am.' How would she feel when she was home? In here she felt safe, away from people staring and whispering.

*   *   *

That evening Mr and Mrs Reed came out of the hospital with smiles on their faces.

'She's coming home,' said Charlie to Fred.

'That's great news, when?'

'Could be Friday. I can't get time off; we've got a few ships in and Gawd help anyone who's not there.'

'Don't worry. I'll collect her. What time?'

Doris looked at her husband, waiting for him to speak.

'I'm sorry, mate, but she don't want you to bring her home.'

Fred tried to hide his disappointment. 'But how's she gonner get home?'

'I'll have to get a taxi,' said Doris.

'But that's daft when I've got a car and the time.'

'That's what we told her, but she was adamant.' Agitated, Doris opened and closed the clasp on her handbag. 'I don't know what to do.'

Fred looked at her. He could see she was near to tears. 'Look, don't get upset about it. I'll bring her home.'

'But she don't want anyone to see her.' Doris took a handkerchief from her handbag.

'Just tell her you couldn't get a cab.' He wanted to tell them that he had seen her and he wasn't shocked.

'Thanks, mate. We've got a couple of days to try and make her see sense,' said Charlie.

'I'll have to get her a new coat. We had to burn her other one.'

'I could send Jen out for one if you haven't got time,' said Fred. He was determined to make himself useful.

'That's very kind of you, but I can ask Jane, her mate. She works at the Co-op and she knows what Sue will like, and she'll get staff discount.' Doris shuddered.

'Come on, love, let's get you home, you're shivering.'

She smiled at her husband. 'It's this wind, and I am a bit cold.' But the main reason she was shivering was because she was seeing all the problems in front of them.

★   ★   ★

On Friday afternoon the sun was weak and it wasn't very warm, but Fred was happy because Susan was coming out of hospital. He was about to go over to Mrs Reed and the nurse who was pushing Susan in a wheelchair when he noticed there was some sort of dispute going on.

'It's that car,' said Doris pointing to where Fred had parked.

'Mum, I told you I didn't want Mr Hunt to take me home.'

'But, Sue, he offered, and I can't afford a taxi and I certainly can't see you getting on a bus.'

'It seems a very nice car to me,' said the nurse.

'It is. Sue's just being silly. He won't mind what you look like.'

The nurse stopped and looked at Sue. 'I know it's going to be hard for you. But people will accept you.'

'That's easy for you to say.'

'Yes it is. But these are people who love you and are concerned about you. You mustn't let them down. Now come on. Let's put you in that posh car.'

Sue kept her head down when they got alongside the car.

'Hello, Susan. Will you be better in the front?' Fred had opened the door and was waiting to help lift her in.

'No thanks.'

'It's good to see you.'

'Is it?' She was struggling to stand up, and with the help of the nurse managed to get on to the back seat.

Her mother sat next to her, and the nurse stood beside the door and looked in. 'Bye, Susan. I'll see you when you come back to have your plaster off.' She closed the car door.

They drove home in silence. Every now and again Fred looked in the rear-view mirror, hoping to give Susan a reassuring smile, but all the while she kept her head down.

* ★ ★

Granny Potts was at the front-room window waiting for them. As soon as she saw the car pull up she hurried to open the front door as fast as her feet could take her.

'Oh lovey. It's so good to see you again. We was all so worried.'

'Hello, Gran.' Sue managed to get through the gate just as Gran flung her arms round her and kissed her.

'Let's get inside, Mum,' said Doris. She turned to Fred. 'Would you like to come in for a cup of tea?'

Fred noted that Sue looked at her mother and shook her head.

'Thanks all the same, Mrs Reed, but I'd better get back.'

'Yes. Of course. Thank you so much for all you've done for us. When Sue feels like visitors you'll have to come to tea.'

'Thanks. I'd like that.' He watched them disappear into the house and the front door close. How long would it be before he saw her again?

★ ★ ★

That evening when someone knocked on the door, Doris looked at the clock and said, 'That'll be Jane.'

'Tell her I don't want to see her.'

Doris was getting angry with her daughter. All afternoon she had sat with her hand over her face. 'Sue, you have to see her sometime.'

'Why?'

'She's your friend and you can't shut yourself away for ever.'

'Why not?'

'Susan, stop being silly. Besides, you should thank her for getting you that nice coat.'

'She got paid for it, didn't she?'

'Doris, leave the girl alone,' said Granny Potts. 'She'll see her all in good time.'

Gran had been shocked at the scar on her beautiful granddaughter's face. It was red and angry-looking; no wonder the poor child was upset and didn't want to see anyone. It would take a long while for her confidence to come back, if ever. Gran only hoped that she had managed to conceal her own reaction when she first saw her.

Doris went and answered the door. 'Jane, I'm sorry, but she's being very silly. She don't want to see you.'

'But why?'

'She's very self-conscious about that scar.'

'So? She's me mate. I don't care what she looks like.'

'I'm sorry, Jane.'

Jane turned and began to walk away. 'She can't hide away for ever.'

'I know, that's what I told her.'

Jane was upset when she returned to her own house.

Ron flung open the door and said, 'Well? How is she? Can I go in and see her?'

'No you can't.'

'Why not?'

'She ain't seeing anyone.'

'But she saw you.'

'No she didn't. Come on, let me get in.'

Ron stood to one side and let her pass.

'How was Sue?' asked her mother.

'I don't know. She don't want to see me.' Jane was trying hard not to cry.

'The poor girl. I'll go and pray for her.'

Ron stood grinning to himself. He would wait in the yard for his little Sue to go to the lav. She'd have to come out sometime, then he'd tell her that he loved her and wanted to marry her.

27

On Saturday evening Sue sat looking out of the front-room window. Her bed had been brought down from her bedroom so that she didn't have the bother of trying to get up the stairs every night. Even though her mum and dad and gran were trying to do everything to make her life more comfortable, she still felt very sad and guilty. Her mother still hadn't said anything about the baby. Sue wanted to tell her all about it, but didn't know how to.

She watched the drizzling rain; it looked cold and miserable outside, just like her mood. She was fed up with reading. She missed going to work. Would she ever pluck up enough courage to face people again? Mr Hunt had said her job would always be there. Mr Hunt . . . Sue thought about her diary. Had he read it? Would he do such a thing? Should she ask him to bring it to her here? If he sent it, her mother would want to know what it was. Her mind was flitting from one thing to another. Did he know about the baby? What did her mother think? Should she talk to her gran about all this?

She saw Jane coming down the road with her head bent against the weather, and watched as Jane opened the gate. She was going to come in here. Sue cringed into the background. She didn't want Jane to see her, but if she knocked, her mother would invite her in. But Jane didn't knock; she just pushed something through the letterbox. Sue clomped her way up the passage, but she couldn't bend down to pick up the note that was lying on the mat.

'Was that the letterbox I heard?' asked her mother as she came out of the kitchen.

'Yes, it's from Jane. I can't pick it up.'

Doris bent down and, picking up the piece of paper, handed it to Sue. 'You know, you can't keep hiding away.'

'Why not?'

'You've got to face the world one day, so why not start with Jane?'

'It's the expression on people's faces that I can't stand.'

'I know, love, but once they get over the first shock, they'll come round and then they'll not even notice it. Mr Hunt didn't say anything when he brought you home.'

Sue ignored that remark. 'I'll just go and read me note,' she said as she hobbled along to the front room.

'Please yourself.' Her mother walked away. She was beginning to lose her patience with her daughter, but she couldn't be angry with her for long as the sound of her crutches thumping on the floor upset her.

Sue closed the door behind her. She knew it bothered her mother when she shut herself away, but at the moment she wanted to be alone. She didn't even want to talk to her gran. She sat on the bed and opened the note.

Dear Sue,

I know you don't want to see me, but just to let you know that I did give Cy Taylor your letter. You never said if he answered it.

Remember I'm only next door and when you feel like talking to me I shall be there.

Your best mate,

Jane xxx

Sue guessed her friend had been to the dance with someone from work. She couldn't expect Jane to lock herself away as well. She folded the piece of paper and let her tears fall. Her life had been ruined. Everybody thought she was very clever at being able to drive, but now here she was sitting all alone and feeling very sorry for herself.

Perhaps her mother was right: she should see Jane. After all, they had been friends all their lives. She would love to talk to her. Sue was remembering when Mr Hunt had first seen her in the hospital. He hadn't looked too shocked. And he'd never told her parents that he'd been to visit her. Her thoughts returned to Jane. As her mother had said, once her friend got over the first shock it wouldn't be so bad. Perhaps they could sit in here without the light on. That was it, she'd go and tell her mother that. She clomped her way into the kitchen.

'Hello, love, you feeling better?' asked her gran.

'No, not really.'

'You'll feel better when you've got that lot off.' Granny Potts nodded to her plaster leg.

240

Sue gave her beloved gran a weak smile. 'Mum, could you ask Jane to come in a bit later on?'

'Course.'

'We can sit in the dark so she don't have to look at me.'

'Well if that's what you want, but I still reckon you're being silly.' Doris didn't show too much enthusiasm, but she was very pleased that her daughter was making the first move.

★ ★ ★

Doris waited till she knew that Jane would have finished her meal before she went next door.

'Hello, Mrs Reed,' said Ron, who opened the door almost as soon as she knocked.

'My, but you're quick off the mark. Is Jane about?'

'Yes, she's upstairs. How's my little Sue? Does she want to see me soon?'

'I don't think so, Ron. But give her time.'

'Mrs Reed. I thought I heard voices,' said Jane as she came down the stairs. 'Is everything all right?'

'As well as it can be. Jane, if you're not going out tonight, Sue said would you like to come in for a bit of a chat?'

'I'd love to. I'll just get me coat.'

'Can I come?' asked Ron.

'I don't think so,' said Doris. 'It'll be all girl talk.'

He grinned. 'I know. Give her my love and tell her I want to see her and talk to her about

241

something very important.'

'I will, Ron. I will.'

★ ★ ★

'Are you there, Sue? Can we have the light on? I can't see a thing,' said Jane as she bumped her shin against Sue's bed.

'No, I don't want you to see me.'

'If you ask me, I think you're being a bit dramatic. Still, that's your way, always was the drama queen.'

'Is that what you think?'

'Yes.'

'But you haven't seen how ugly I look.'

'No, and the way you're behaving I don't suppose I ever will. Are you going to stay locked away for ever?'

'I thought you were my friend and wanted to be with me?'

'I was . . . am,' Jane hurriedly corrected herself.

'I didn't ask you to come in here to nag me.'

'Somebody's got to, and if I've got to sit here in the dark all evening then I'm going home.' Jane knew she was being horrible, but she didn't care. All she wanted was to make her friend realise that everybody loved her for herself. She brushed her tears away.

'Why are you crying?'

'It's you. Oh Sue, you're making me sound so mean and horrid.'

'I'm sorry. Come and give me a cuddle.'

Jane fell into her friend's arms and they cried

together. When at long last they broke apart, Sue, who was sitting near the light, switched it on.

'See, I am pretty ugly.'

Jane looked at her friend's face. 'What can I say?'

'Now you can understand why I don't want anyone to see me.'

'But we don't care what you look like. I see lots of people who have scars and they live normal lives.'

'How can I live a normal life. I can't go out to work.'

'Why not? Has Mr Hunt given you the sack?'

'No, but I can't sit in the office and talk to customers looking like this.'

'If you ask me, you're making a big thing about this. Now come on, let's change the subject. How long before you have that plaster off?'

'A couple more weeks, I think.'

'That'll be better, at least you'll be able to get around then.'

'Not got anywhere to go, though, have I?'

Jane ignored that and asked, 'Did Cy Taylor write to you?'

'No. Not that I thought he would. Not after what happened.'

'Well, he was married after all.'

'Yes, I know. Who did you go to the dance with?'

'A girl called Pat, she works in the office.'

'Was it good?'

'All right. But I missed you and I kept looking

243

at Mr Smarmy and thinking how much I wanted to punch him on the nose then tell everyone what a rotter he was.'

'Did you? Did you really?'

'Yes, I did, I really did, after the way he treated you,' said Jane softly.

Sue knew then that she had to tell someone about what had happened, and after all Jane was her best friend. 'Jane, I'm going to tell you something but you mustn't breathe a word of it to anyone.'

Jane giggled. 'Course I won't, But you're making it sound ever so interesting. Is it about Mr Hunt?'

Sue shook her head. Suddenly she had doubts. Should she tell Jane about the baby? But she needed to tell someone, and so far her mum hadn't mentioned it.

'One of the reasons I had the accident, apart from the weather, was because I had something on me mind.'

'But you're a good driver. Was there something wrong with the car? Your dad did think that, you know.'

'No, it wasn't the car.'

Jane sat forward; she could see her friend was nervous. 'What is it, Sue?' she asked quietly.

'It was the rain but also I wasn't really concentrating because I was thinking about the baby.'

'What baby?' asked Jane softly. She thought she knew what her friend was going to say.

'Cy Taylor's.'

'You're going to have his baby?'

'Was. I lost it when I had the accident.'

'Oh Sue. Do your mum and dad know?'

Sue nodded. 'They do now. The doctor told them.'

'And?'

'They haven't said a word.'

'Did he know?'

'Yes.'

'And?'

'He told me to get rid of it.'

'What? The wicked bugger.'

'He didn't want to know and I think he was worried his wife might find out.'

'Sue. Did you have the accident on purpose?'

'No. As I said, it was the bad weather and I wasn't concentrating.'

'How far gone were you?'

'A couple of months.'

'And you kept this to yourself all that time?'

Again Sue nodded.

'You've been carrying this secret all by yourself?'

'I wanted to tell you, but I thought you'd say 'I told you so'.' Tears were streaming down Sue's face.

Jane put her arms round her friend and hugged her.

They jumped apart when Sue's mother opened the door.

'Thought you might like a cuppa.'

'Thanks, Mum.'

She looked at their tear-stained faces. 'Don't go upsetting yourselves too much.'

'We're all right,' said Sue as she wiped her

eyes. 'Just getting a bit silly about old times, that's all.'

Doris closed the door. What had they been talking about? Had Sue told Jane about the baby?

Sue waited till her mother had gone, then said, 'I want you to do me a favour.'

'Anything, you know that.'

'Would you go and see Mr Hunt for me?'

'Course. Why, you want to make sure your job's all right?'

Sue shook her head. 'No. You see, he came to visit me in hospital.'

'He did? How did he manage that?'

'I don't know. It seems he knew someone.'

'What did your mum and dad say about that?'

'I never told them. He wanted to tell me that he's got my diary.'

'Seems a bit of a lame excuse if you ask me. I always said that he fancied you.'

'Don't talk daft.'

'Anyway, how did he get hold of it?'

'I left it in me drawer. I told him not to send it, 'cos me mum would want to know what it is. And I don't want him coming here.'

'But he's already seen you,' Jane said very softly.

'Yes.'

'And?'

'A bit like you, after the first shock he didn't seem to notice.'

'See. What did I tell you?'

'Anyway, if you could get my diary I would be a lot happier.'

'Do you think he read it?'

'Dunno. I did have an elastic band round the page and he said it fell open. And he asked me if everything was all right.'

'Did you write about the baby in it?'

Sue nodded. 'And all about Cy.'

'Bloody hell. Don't worry, I'll go in the morning. Is he likely to be home on a Sunday?'

'I would think so, unless he goes to his mum's. Thanks, Jane. I knew I could rely on you.'

'Just as well. See, I knew you would need me sometimes.'

'Come here. I'll always need you.'

Jane went to her friend and they hugged each other.

Sue was feeling happier than she had done for a long while.

28

On Sunday morning Jane was very anxious as she made her way to Hunt's Motors. Was she too early? Would he be up?

All night her thoughts had been about Sue. She had been going to have a baby. Cy Taylor's baby. Now that was all over and she had to try and start living again. But how could she, with that scar? A lump came into Jane's throat. Poor Sue. How could she help her?

Jane looked at the cars in the front of Hunt's garage, and the price cards on the windscreens told her some of them were pretty expensive. Whenever she'd seen Mr Hunt he always appeared very well dressed; he must be quite rich. She went over to the door that led to his flat, and rang the bell. She could hear him running down the stairs. What if he had a woman in there? Mind you, that would give Sue a laugh.

'Yes,' he said on opening the door. At least he was dressed.

'Mr Hunt, remember me? I'm Jane, Sue's friend. I came out with you a couple of times when Sue was learning to drive, and you took us both to a tea room once, remember?'

He was still a bit bleary-eyed and stood for a moment looking at her. 'Yes, of course. I'm sorry, come on in.' He stood to one side and she passed him. 'It's up the stairs and the door on the right.' He followed her up.

'This is a nice room,' she commented for something to say.

'It's only an old bachelor's flat. At least I can keep an eye on the stock down there.' He laughed. 'And I don't have too far to go to work.' He walked over to the window, clearing the newspapers, the few crocks and a full ashtray off the armchair and table as he moved round the room. 'Sorry about the mess. I don't normally have visitors on a Sunday. Please, sit down.'

'That's all right.' Jane perched on the edge of the armchair.

He pulled out a dining-room chair and sat down. 'Would you like a cup of tea?'

'No thank you. I've just come here for Sue's diary.'

'I thought you had. I'll go and get it, it's in me safe.'

He left her alone and went down the stairs to the door Jane had noticed when she came in. She guessed it led to the office. She went over to the window and looked out at the houses opposite. Smoke was drifting from the chimneys, adding to the gloom. She jumped when he returned, and sat back down.

He handed her a small black book and with a smile said, 'Tell her I didn't look in it.'

'Thank you.' Jane turned the diary over in her hands and said nervously, 'Mr Hunt, you've seen Sue. Do you think she'll ever get over this?'

He sat down. 'I honestly don't know what to say. You're her best friend. And I've seen you two together; you're more like sisters. I expect she can talk to you.'

Jane quickly put the diary in her handbag. 'I am very worried about her.' She could feel the tears welling up.

'There will always be a job here for her, you know.'

'Thank you. But at the moment she don't even want to go out.'

'I can understand that. She must try to see that looks ain't everything.' He could have kicked himself as soon as the words came out of his mouth.

Jane dabbed at her eyes. 'Sorry.'

'No, it's me that should be sorry.' He had to ask the question that was at the back of his mind. 'Was Susan in any sort of trouble?'

Jane looked up quickly. 'What d'you mean?'

'I suppose I shouldn't be asking these sorts of questions, but you see, I'm very fond of her.'

Jane looked taken aback.

Fred noted her expression and knew he had to laugh it off.

'Not in that way. She's a good worker and, well, she was nice to have around. She brought a bit of sunshine into an old man's life.'

Jane smiled at him.

'That boy she was very fond of, the singer, has he dumped her?'

'You know about him?'

'She did tell me once that she thought he was Mr Wonderful.'

'He wasn't so wonderful, he was married.'

'Oh, I see.'

Jane stood up. 'I've got to go.' He was so easy to talk to that she knew if she stayed she would end up telling him everything, and that would certainly finish her friendship with Sue.

'Yes, of course. And Jane . . . may I call you Jane?'

She nodded.

'Jane, would you tell Susan that if any time she would like to go out for a drive, I'd be more than happy to take you both out.'

'That's very nice of you. I think once she's got that plaster off we might take you up on your kind offer.'

He opened the door and followed her down the stairs.

When she was outside, Jane gave him a little wave. He was a very nice man.

★ ★ ★

Sue was looking anxiously out of the window. Even though it was Sunday, she could see the kids racing up and down the road on their skates and the carts the boys had made out of orange boxes and pram wheels. She and Jane would never have been allowed to play like that on a Sunday. She remembered when the men came and took up all the tarry blocks that made up the old road, and every night the blocks disappeared into the houses; nobody went cold that winter. When they laid the new concrete surface it seemed as if it went on for ever, and she gave a slight smile as images of her and Jane going up and down the road on their roller skates came to her. In those days they didn't have a care in the world. Now how she envied people going about their everyday lives.

She caught sight of Jane coming down the road and hobbled to the front door and opened it for her friend.

'I've been waiting for you. I saw you go off this morning. Have you got it?'

Jane nodded as Mrs Reed came out of the kitchen.

'Jane, would you like a cup of tea?'

'No thanks. I just thought I'd call in and see if Sue wanted anything.'

'That's very kind of you. Come into the kitchen.'

'Can I talk to Jane on me own first, Mum?' asked Sue.

'Course, love. Come and say hello to me mum before you go, Jane.'

'I will, Mrs Reed.'

The girls went into the front room and Jane gave Sue her precious diary.

'Do you think he read it?'

'No. He seems really nice, and he's very concerned about you. He said that when that plaster's off, he'd like to take us out for a drive.'

'He's not a bad old stick.'

Jane could see she wasn't really wanted. 'Look, I'll go now. Tell your mum that perhaps I can come back later on and talk to your gran.'

'All right.'

She let herself out quietly.

★ ★ ★

Fred was deep in thought. So that bloody singer was married. Was that the reason Susan had been so unhappy lately? He was beginning to put two and two together. She had looked poorly for some time. What if she had been pregnant? Would she have crashed that car on purpose? No, Susan wasn't like that; she was a good girl. But his mind was churning over. He'd have to find out more about this bloke.

★   ★   ★

On Monday afternoon after Jen had left, Fred looked up from his desk to see Ron standing in front of him.

'Would you like a cup of tea?'

'Yes please, Ron.'

'I miss my little Sue making the tea.'

'Yes, so do I.' Fred returned to his papers. He looked up again when the door opened.

'Hello, me old mate, how are you?' Bert Rose was filling the doorway.

Fred stood up. 'Bert, what can I do for you?' He knew he was here to ask for a favour.

'Did you get to see that little girl of yours?'

Fred glanced over at the tiny room where Ron was busy making the tea. 'Yes I did, and thanks for that.'

'Now I fancy a new car. Got one going cheap?'

'It depends on what you call cheap.'

'I'm sure you can do me a good deal.' Bert walked over to the window. 'Shall we take a look outside?'

Fred knew that this was going to cost him.

Any favour Bert Rose did for you had to be paid for. After all, he had spent a great deal of time in prison, and Fred knew it was through people crossing him. Bert didn't like to be made a fool of.

As they opened the door Ron said, 'Mr Hunt, what about your tea?'

'I'll only be a mo.'

Outside, Fred pulled his jacket collar up against the drizzling rain.

'Any idea what you fancy?' he asked Bert.

'This looks a nice clean little motor.' Bert opened the door of a neat blue Morris and took the card from the windscreen. 'Sixty pounds, that's a bit steep.'

'It's a good little car.'

Bert sat in the driver's seat and Fred got in the passenger side.

'So when's sweet Sue coming back to work, then?'

'Dunno. She might never come back.'

'Why's that?'

'She got a terrible scar and she's worried that everybody will look at her.'

'Poor cow. Now what yer gonner let me have this one for?' He ran his gnarled hands round the steering wheel. The wolf tattoo stood out.

'I can't let it go for any less. I ain't making that much on it as it is.'

'Spare me the bleeding hearts and flowers. Tell yer what, I'll give yer fifty.'

'Fifty? I paid that for it and spent a fortune on bringing it up to scratch.'

'That's me offer, take it or leave it. And a little

254

bird told me that fings ain't been that good for the past few weeks.'

'Well, what with the Jarrow marchers and the unemployment, the last thing people want is cars.'

'Stop it, you'll have me in tears next. Na, I reckon the punters miss sweet Sue's lovely smile.'

'Not as much as I do. You drive a hard bargain, Bert.'

'I know. Now take it or leave it.'

'Let me think about it.'

'I'll be back tomorrow. And it 'ad better be good news.'

'I'll see.'

They both got out of the car. Bert walked away, waving as he turned the corner.

Fred went back into the office. Somehow he knew he'd let Bert have the car at his price; after all, you didn't argue with Bert Rose, not if you didn't want your face or your business smashed up. Besides, trade was very slow at the moment and Fred never knew when he would need another favour.

'I'll just pour out your tea, Mr Hunt,' said Ron.

'Thanks.'

'Everything all right?'

'Fine, thanks.'

'He looks a bit of a hard nut.'

'Yes, he is. You don't mess with him, not if you fancy your looks.'

Ron laughed. 'I liked that tattoo. D'you know, I might get meself one of those.'

'I don't think your mum or your sister would approve.'

'I can do what I like. It's my money.'

'Course you can. Now, Ron, could you go and lock all the cars? I'm closing up early tonight.'

'Why's that? Don't you feel well?'

'Just fancy shutting up early, that's all.'

'Here, that bloke ain't upset you, has he?'

Fred smiled. 'No. He's a mate.'

'Well that's all right then. I don't like people I like being upset.'

'Thanks, Ron. Now off you go.' Fred watched him lumber away. In a way he wasn't a bad bloke. He meant well.

29

Fred was sitting eagerly outside Susan's house, waiting to take her and her mother to have Sue's plaster removed. He had been very pleased when Ron told him that Mrs Reed had asked if he wouldn't mind taking them to the hospital. It made him feel useful and close to Susan. He didn't want her to forget him.

'This is very kind of you,' said Mrs Reed as they helped Sue into the car.

'It's my pleasure,' he said, closing the door after they were both settled.

'You don't have to hang about and wait for us. We can get the bus back.'

'I don't mind waiting. Jen is holding the fort.'

'I don't like putting you to any trouble.'

Fred looked at Sue; she hadn't said a word. 'I can assure you it ain't no trouble.'

⋆　⋆　⋆

At long last Sue, without her leg in plaster and with her mother supporting her, emerged from the hospital. They stood on the steps for a moment or two. Sue looked pale and was leaning heavily on her mother's arm.

Fred quickly threw his fag away and rushed up to help her. 'Are you all right?' he asked, taking her other arm.

'It feels ever so funny. It's all thin and wobbly.'

Fred gave her a smile. She was speaking to him. 'It's sure to at first.'

He noted that as usual whenever Sue got into the car, she insisted on sitting with her scar not on the window side. Not a lot was said as they made their way home. When they arrived and Fred had brought the car to a stop outside the house, he helped them both out and said, 'Susan, if you and Jane would like to come out for a ride on Sunday, I'd be more than pleased to take you. I know November's not a good month to go out but I thought you might like a change from your own four walls.'

Before Sue could answer, her mother said, 'That's very nice of you, Mr Hunt. Sue could do with a change of scenery.'

'I could pick you both up before lunch. How would that do?'

Sue shook her head. 'I'm sorry, but I don't want to go to a café.'

'No, don't worry. I'll see about a picnic or something.'

Sue looked at her mother. 'I suppose that'll be all right.' She knew her mother was getting fed up with her moping around the house, and besides, it would be nice to get out for a while.

'Do you want to come in?' Doris asked.

'No thanks. Got to get back. See you Sunday.'

Fred got in his car and drove off. He was overjoyed. He was going to take Susan out. He would have liked to have been alone with her, but he knew that time would come and that this would be the first of many outings. Why was he so besotted with this girl? He had had plenty of girlfriends in the past, and some he had quite liked, but there was something different about Susan.

★ ★ ★

On Sunday when Fred knocked on the Reeds' front door, he was worried that Susan might have changed her mind.

She opened the door; Jane was standing behind her.

'Are you ready, girls?' he asked light-heartedly. He knew he had to keep today uncomplicated.

Susan gave him a weak smile, but Jane was beaming. 'I should say so.'

As they got into the car he could smell their perfume; they had both made an effort for him.

When they'd settled and were on their way Fred said, 'I thought we'd go to Brighton.'

'You're not taking us to a café or anything?' asked Sue, sitting forward, her voice full of fear.

'No, not if you don't want me to.'

She relaxed. 'That's all right then.'

'We can sit in the car along the front, and if you like I can get some fish and chips.' He laughed. 'A bit different to the tea room we went to.'

Sue knew he was trying his best to please her.

Jane giggled. 'That'll be nice. You're very kind, Mr Hunt.'

Sue wanted to ask *why* he was being so kind.

He turned and smiled at them both. 'As I told you before, I enjoy driving and it's always nice to have company.'

Sue noted that he hadn't said good-looking company. Was she going to spend the rest of her life agonising over every word people uttered? Would she only go out in the dark where no one could see her?

When they reached the sea front, Sue looked out of the window. It was blowing a gale and the sea was churning and angry-looking. Everybody was walking along with their heads bent against the wind. She suddenly felt very sad and sorry for herself. Although she knew there were very many people worse off than her. She wanted to jump out of the car and throw herself into the sea. She touched her cheek.

'You're very quiet,' said Jane after Fred had left the car. 'Are you all right?'

'Yes, I'm fine.'

'Well try and cheer up.'

'I told you, I'm all right.'

'My God, it's a bit rough out there,' said Fred as he scrambled back in. 'Three cod and chips. I've put salt and vinegar on them, it that all right?'

'That's fine, Mr Hunt,' said Jane. 'My mum would have a fit if she saw me. Sundays is for praying, not doing naughty things.'

Fred laughed. 'So is eating fish and chips out of newspaper naughty, then?'

'In me mum's eyes it is.' Jane laughed too. 'Me mum's a bit religious.'

'More than a bit, I'd say, with all those statues and pictures of Jesus around the place,' said Sue.

'Well, a lot then,' said Jane. 'It was after me dad died.'

'Ron's not religious, is he?' asked Fred.

'No. He reckons she's daft, and when the vicar comes round he hides away. Talk about an odd family. Me mum's always at church and me brother's a bit nutty.'

'You leave Ron alone,' said Fred. 'He's a damn good worker.'

'Mum will always be grateful to you for giving him a chance.'

'And I'll always be pleased that Susan told me about him.'

Sue sat quietly listening to this conversation. That was all in the past and she didn't want to join in.

They sat for a while looking at the weather and the people. The car was beginning to steam up and Fred rubbed the inside of the windscreen with a cloth. Then he turned round to the girls. 'What say we start to make tracks before it gets dark? We could stop at a pub on the way home. Don't worry, Susan.' He noted her anxiety. 'I can always bring the drinks out.'

'It's getting a bit cold,' she said, pulling her coat round her.

'There's a travelling rug in the back, I'll get it for you.' Fred leapt out of the car and returned with a tartan rug. 'Here, wrap this round your legs, that should help to keep you both warm. Susan, I was going to ask you if you would like to drive home.'

'What?'

'You've driven my car before.'

'I know. But that was before . . . ' Her voice trailed off.

'You mustn't be afraid. You know what they say about getting back on a horse and all that?'

'When am I going to be driving again?'

'When you come back to work.'

'I've told you, I ain't coming back. Is this what this outing is all about? You hoped it would change me mind?'

'No. It's just that I thought you'd like a change from your four walls. I'm sorry if I spoke out of turn.'

Jane gave her friend a filthy look. How could she be so ungrateful?

It was dark when they set off home, and there wasn't a lot of conversation. When they turned into Lily Road, Fred said, 'I'm sorry if I upset you, Susan. I wouldn't do that for the world.'

'That's all right.' She got out of the car without even saying thank you.

As Fred drove away Jane grabbed her friend's arm. 'I think you've been a right pig today. He's taken us out and I've enjoyed myself, but you, you only seem hell bent on upsetting people. What's done is done and nobody can make it better, so try and think of someone else for a change before you open your mouth.'

Sue stood dumbfounded. Under the street-lamp she could see that her best friend was very angry. 'I'm sorry,' she mumbled. But Jane wasn't listening. She'd left and gone into her own house.

★　★　★

262

'Did you have a nice time?' asked her mother when Sue walked into the kitchen.

'It was all right.'

Granny Potts looked at her. 'Where did you go, love?'

'To Brighton.'

'I bet it was cold there.'

'Dunno. I didn't get out of the car. I'm just going to the lav.' She walked through the kitchen and out into the yard. She knew she was being unreasonable, but what could she do, she was so unhappy. She knew, though, that if she carried on like this, she wouldn't have anyone to talk to.

'Hello, my little Sue. Did you have a nice time this afternoon?'

Sue quickly turned her head away from Ron. So far she had managed to keep out of his sight.

'I ain't gonner hurt you.'

'I know that.' She turned and went back inside.

'Little Sue!'

She could hear Ron calling her as she stood behind the door. She buried her head in the kitchen towel and cried bitter, angry tears.

30

When Fred turned in to the forecourt he was surprised to see in his headlights Bert sitting in the car he'd bought. 'Bloody hell,' he said under his breath. 'I hope he ain't got trouble with it.' He got out of his own car. It was very quiet, the only noise the hissing from the streetlamp. By its light Fred could just about make out Bert with his head back and his eyes closed. He banged on the window, making Bert jump.

'Seeing a lot of you just lately. What you after now?'

Bert's eyes sprang open and he quickly wound the window down. 'Bloody hell, you frightened the living daylights out of me.'

'Well,' said Fred. He definitely wasn't pleased to see Bert. There was something about him that always made him feel uneasy.

'Can I come in for a tick?'

'All right.' Reluctantly Fred led the way up to his flat. Upstairs he took off his hat and coat. 'You'd better sit down and tell me what this is all about.'

'Got a drink?' Bert seemed deflated and wasn't his usual bombastic self.

Fred took a bottle of whisky from the sideboard and poured some of the liquid into two glasses. Bert downed his in one mouthful.

'Thanks. I needed that.'

'So, what's the trouble? D'you want me to

supply you with another alibi?'

'No, well, yes, in a way. You see it's me boy.'

'What's he been up to now?'

'He's been beaten up real bad, Fred.' Bert stopped and looked into his empty glass. 'Real bad.'

'I would have thought that went with the game you're in.'

'Yer, it does, but you see, I know who did it and they shouldn't have, not to me boy.'

'So why don't you go and sort 'em out?'

'They'd know it was me.'

'That figures. What you afraid of, then?'

'Don't want another spell in clink, not while me boy needs looking after.'

Fred looked at this hard man. For all his misgivings, he had to admire Bert for the love he had for his son. 'So where do I come in?'

'I've got a gang going after them, but I need you to come out with me and be seen be others. You know, be me alibi.'

'When's this big rumble going to take place?'

'Thursday night about ten.'

'So what d'you want me to do?'

'Come with me for a drink.'

'Why me?'

'You're a respected member of society.'

'Not if I'm seen with you I'm not.'

'Please, Fred.'

'Where're you thinking of going?'

'There's a dance on at the town hall.'

'What? You wonner take me to a dance?'

'That way we can chat up a couple of birds

and we'll get their address so they can verify we was there.'

'No way. I'm too old for that sort of thing.'

'Course you're not.'

'Besides, I ain't getting involved with any of your dodgy dealings.' The last thing Fred wanted was to go to a dance with Bert. 'Why can't we just go to the pub?'

'The coppers won't believe that; they'll know it was a setup. Anyway, what if there ain't many people in the bar? No, I can't take a chance like that.'

'You seem to have thought of everything.'

'Yer. Nobody's gonner get away with hurting me boy.' He clenched his jaw. 'You should see what they've done to the poor little bugger. Got another drink?'

Fred refilled their glasses and thought about what Bert had said. Did he want to get involved?

Bert finished his drink and stood up. He patted Fred on the shoulder. 'You're a good 'un, Fred. Always liked you, even when you was a snotty-nosed little kid at school.' He put on his coat and, running his fingers round the brim of his grey trilby, said, 'I'll owe you big time for this.' He opened the door. 'See you Thursday about eight.' Then he put on his hat and left.

Fred sat stunned. What had he let himself in for? A dance at the local town hall with Bert Rose. He didn't even remember saying he'd go.

He went into the kitchenette to make himself a cup of tea. As he sat drinking it he thought about Bert Rose and when they were at school. Although Fred had tried to be the hard man,

Bert had somehow managed to cut him down to size, but he was always there when Fred was involved in any scrapes, looking after him in his own way.

As he thought about his childhood, memories of his father came back. Fred knew he could have finished up the same way as Bert, but although his father was a hard man and didn't mind using his leather belt on him at times, between him and his mother they'd managed to give him a good start in life, for which he would always be grateful. He sat back. It'd been a funny sort of a day one way and another. He started to think about ways to take Susan out again.

★   ★   ★

Sue had dried her eyes and was busy making some cocoa when her mother came into the scullery.

'Thought you'd fallen down the hole, you've been so long.'

'Thought I'd put the kettle on for a cup of cocoa. Do you and Dad and Gran want one?'

'Sue, is everything all right?'

Sue turned and smiled at her mother. 'Yes, of course.'

'You didn't seem very happy when you first came in.'

'No, I know. But I'm all right now, I promise.' The kettle started to whistle and Sue went and kissed her mother's cheek. 'Now go and ask who wants cocoa.'

Doris went back into the kitchen, bewildered.

What had suddenly happened to her daughter? Had she realised how much she had been upsetting everybody? Had Jane given her a good talking-to? Whatever it was, Doris wasn't going to question it just now.

'Sue's making cocoa,' she said. 'Do you both want one?'

'Please,' they said together.

'Is she all right?' asked her father.

'She's fine. I think that ride out did her the world of good.'

'I hope so,' said Granny Potts. 'Been a bit worried about her.'

'We all have, Mum. I'll give her a hand bringing 'em in.'

Doris returned to the scullery. Sue was still smiling. Had her daughter at long last come to terms with the situation? Could they now talk together? Doris would love to sit and discuss the baby with her, but knew she had to bide her time and not rush things.

★   ★   ★

The next few days flew past, and all too soon it was Thursday. Fred didn't want to go with Bert, but how could he get out of it? And *should* he get out of it? After all, Bert was a very useful person to have on your side.

'You going out tonight, Mr Hunt?' asked Ron when he noticed his boss had had a hair cut.

Fred laughed. 'Yes I am, as a matter of fact. I'm going out with Mr Rose.'

Ron smiled. 'I like him. He looks a hard nut,

but I bet he's really nice when you get to know him.'

'He's not bad.'

Ron put the tea he'd been making on Fred's desk. 'Going anywhere nice?'

'Only out for a drink.' He wasn't going to tell Ron that he was going to a dance; Ron might tell Susan, and all his dreams could be dashed if she thought he did that sort of thing, as most blokes went there looking for females. 'What did your mother and sister say about your tattoo?'

Ron looked at the back of his hand. Clenching it, he could make the wolf's head move. 'Jane thought I was a bloody idiot, and Mum reckons it's the work of the devil. But I don't care, I like it.' He laughed.

Fred licked the envelope he'd been addressing. 'Would you give this letter to Susan for me?'

'Course I will. D'you think she'll come back to work here?'

'I don't know. But I want to stay in touch.'

'She won't talk to me. She runs and hides every time I see her go to the lav. Does she really look that ugly?'

'No. You don't notice it after a while.'

'I wish she'd let me talk to her.'

'She will. Now finish up outside then you can be off. Don't expect anybody will be coming in now. It looks a bit like snow.' Fred looked out at the leaden sky.

'I'll see you tomorrow, then.'

'Yes.' Fred began clearing his desk. He was grateful that Jen came in for a few hours a day; at least she kept the paperwork down. But he

269

would be more than pleased if he could persuade Susan to come back.

★ ★ ★

Ron knocked on Sue's door. He could have put the letter through the letterbox, but he was hoping she would answer then perhaps he could talk to her. Tell her of his undying love for her.

'Hello, Ron,' said Granny Potts. 'What can we do for you?'

'Can I talk to my little Sue?'

'No, sorry, but she don't want to talk to anyone.'

'But I've got a letter here from Mr Hunt.'

Granny Potts held out her hand. 'That's nice. I'll give it to her.'

'Can't I give it to her?'

'No, sorry, Ron. Perhaps when she feels like talking you can come in.'

His sad face lit up. 'Thanks. I'd like that. I won't get in the way, honest.'

'I'll go and give this to her, so bye for now.' She closed the door. She felt very sorry for the poor boy; he was certainly one of life's misfits. Granny Potts was worried about her granddaughter; could she finish up a misfit too?

'Ron's brought you this letter from your boss. Have you seen that daft thing on the back of his hand?'

'You mean his tattoo? Jane told me about it. Seems Mrs Brent went mad and nearly had a heart attack. Said it was devil-worshipping.'

'What did he have it done for?'

270

'I think it's because one of Mr Hunt's friends has got one, and he's a bit of a hard nut. Jane said Ron thinks it will make him look hard too.'

'Silly bugger. Here's your letter.' Granny Potts handed it to her. 'He's got lovely handwriting.'

Sue put the book she was reading to one side. 'He ain't my boss any more.'

Granny didn't answer her; she didn't see the point.

My dear Susan,

Thought I'd get Ron to drop this in to you rather than post it. You see, apparently there's a very good show on in town and I was wondering if you and Jane would be so kind as to accompany me. Before you refuse, I will be getting a box, so we shall be completely on our own, and as I know the manager I shall make sure we go in the back way. Please say yes. I do enjoy taking you both out.

Yours very sincerely,
Fred Hunt

A grin spread slowly across Sue's face.

'You look pleased. So you ain't got the sack, then?'

'No. Here, read it.' She passed the letter to her gran.

'He certainly thinks of everything, don't he?'

Sue nodded. Yes, he did.

31

When Fred walked into the noisy dance hall, he stood for a moment or two just looking around. What was he doing here? He must have been mad to let Bert talk him into this. They all seemed to be so very young, and racing across the floor to a quickstep.

Bert pushed him forward.

'Let's get to the bar. What you drinking?'

'A beer.'

Bert elbowed his way to the bar and called for two beers. When he'd been served, they made their way to a table at the very edge of the dance floor.

'We'll sit here so we can be seen. We'll give a few girls the eye.'

Fred laughed. 'D'you know, I can't believe I'm doing this.'

'Well you are. So sit back and enjoy yourself.'

When the dance finished, a couple of girls came and sat at the table next to them.

'All right, girls?' asked Bert. 'Enjoying yourselves?'

They giggled.

The bandleader announced that the next dance would be a foxtrot.

'D'you fancy this?' Bert asked one of the girls.

'OK.' She stood up and Bert took her in his arms and whirled her away. Fred was very impressed with his dancing.

'You're very quiet,' said her mate as she came and sat beside him. 'Do you dance?'

'A bit.'

'Come on then, let's show 'em how it's done.'

As they danced round, Fred found out that her name was Nancy, and that she lived nearby.

'Not seen you here before,' she said dreamily.

'No, I don't make a habit of it.'

'Don't you think this band's great?'

'It's all right.'

'It's the singer that makes it. All the girls are in love with Cy Taylor.'

Cy Taylor: somehow that name seemed to ring a bell. Fred looked over at the man holding the mike, who appeared to be singing to every girl in the room. Was it him? Was he the one Susan had been in love with? Fred had to admit he was very good looking in a film-star sort of way. He was singing 'I Only Have Eyes For You', and Fred could see that most of the girls in the room were gazing at him longingly.

'Is he here very often?'

'No, just now and again. Why, do you like him?'

'Na, he's not my type. I prefer someone like Al Bowlly.'

'You're very old fashioned, then.'

'Yer, suppose I am. This Cy, you mad about him as well?'

'Na. You see, I know all about him.'

'Do you?'

'Yer, his wife lives near me sister. His name ain't really Cy, it's Cyril.' She laughed. 'Can't have a moniker like that and stand in front

273

of a band, can you?'

'No, I suppose not.' So he really was married. No wonder Susan was so upset.

'What's your name?' asked Nancy as the dance finished and they made their way back to the table.

'Plain old Fred, I'm afraid.'

'That's a bit old fashioned too. Let's see. If you wanted to, you could always call yourself, say, Ferdinand, and as you're dark it's got a nice Spanish ring to it.'

Fred laughed with her.

'You two look as if you're getting on all right,' said Bert, sitting back down at the table with them. 'By the way, Fred, this is Rita.'

Nancy giggled. 'I'm gonner call him Ferdinand. It's more romantic.'

Bert laughed and Fred cringed.

For the rest of the evening Bert danced with Rita while Fred danced with Nancy. But most of the time Fred was looking at Cy Taylor. He had to find out if he was the one who had upset Susan and ruined her life.

It was gone eleven when the band left the stand and Bert suggested they take the girls home.

'We only live round the corner,' said Rita.

'Fred's got a big posh car,' said Bert.

'A car? You've got a car? Well, that's different. Come on, Nance, let's get our coats. I bet it's bloody freezing out there.'

Inside the car Bert had his arm round Rita. 'D'you know, you two have made our evening, ain't they, Fred?'

Fred only nodded.

'Have we? Have we really?' asked Nancy.

'I reckon we should do this again,' said Bert.

Fred glared at him through the rear-view mirror, but he chose to ignore it.

'Give me your address, and when we're free we'll get together. That all right with you, Fred?'

Fred nodded, and Nancy snuggled up to him.

When they arrived at the girls' door, Bert and Fred helped them out of the car.

'Proper gents, ain't yer?' said Nancy.

'We try,' said Bert.

The girls grabbed them and kissed them good night. Fred was taken by surprise and thought he was going to be ill when Nancy forced her tongue into his mouth, almost choking him. She certainly knew her way around. He hadn't met anyone so forward before.

As they drove away, Bert turned to Fred. 'Thanks, mate, that was a very successful evening.'

'Don't you dare ask me to do anything like that again.'

'Oh come off it. You looked like you was enjoying it.'

'I'll tell you something, Bert. If I ever want a favour done, you owe me big time now.'

Bert punched his arm playfully. 'I'll never forget what you've done tonight. Let's hope those blokes who did that to me boy finished up in hospital.'

When they arrived outside the block of flats where Bert lived, he said, 'Come on up and see me boy.'

Fred knew he couldn't refuse, and followed Bert up the concrete stairs. The smell of urine filled his nostrils. 'How can you live in a dump like this?'

'It's not that bad. We blend in with the area. 'Sides, the neighbours don't ask too many questions when the old bill come sniffing around after any trouble.' He opened his front door. 'It's all right, son. It's only me and Fred.'

In the living room Fred was shocked at the sight of Bert's son. His arm was in plaster and his face was covered with bruises; he had two black eyes and the cut under his chin had been stitched up with ugly black stitches.

'Hello, Fred. Thanks for giving Dad an alibi for tonight.' He gave Fred a very lopsided grin. 'I'd get up and shake yer hand, but me ribs hurt something rotten.'

'That's all right, son.'

'Whisky, Fred?' said Bert.

'No, thanks all the same, but I'm not gonner hang about. I'll see you sometime. Look after yourselves, both of you.'

As Fred drove away, he could understand how Bert felt. He knew that he would do the same thing to anybody who hurt someone he loved.

★   ★   ★

When the next day the papers told of a fight between two gangs, Fred wasn't surprised. It went on to say that many of them had been badly injured and that the police were worried there could be some reprisals. Was this the lot

276

who'd done Bert's son? At least Bert had a good alibi.

At the beginning of the week Fred had sent a note to Sue asking if she and her friend would like to go to the theatre the following Friday, and was pleased when she accepted the very next day.

Promptly at six on Friday he collected the two girls. They went up the back stairs to the box and Fred gave them a large box of chocolates.

'This is the best birthday present you've ever had,' said Jane to Sue.

'Is it your birthday?' asked Fred as he pulled a chair out for her.

'It was last week.'

'I didn't know. I should have taken you out last week.'

Sue smiled. 'Tonight more than makes up for it. Thank you.'

'It's my pleasure.'

'I feel like a queen,' said Jane as she looked over the edge at the people arriving below. 'Have a look, Sue.'

'No. I can't.'

'Don't be daft, they can't see you.'

'I know.'

The lights went down and the orchestra struck up. The show was all Fred had expected, with singers, dancers and speciality acts, and he could see that the girls were really enjoying themselves.

When the lights went up for the interval, Sue quickly sat back. Jane was excited as she sat looking this way and that.

'Mr Hunt, this is ever so nice of you,' she said,

licking her fingers after she'd popped another chocolate into her mouth.

'It's my pleasure.'

'I ain't ever been so close to the stage before. Those girls wear a lot of make-up.'

'They have to look as if they've got perfect skin. I've seen some of 'em without all that stuff, and believe me, it ain't always a pretty sight.'

'Here, Sue, why don't you find out what make-up they use? It might hide . . . ' She stopped suddenly when she saw the look Sue was giving her.

Fred suddenly had a thought, but he knew he had to be diplomatic. 'Susan, I don't mean to sound, I don't know, out of place. But I know some of the girls, and if you like, I could always ask them what they use.'

'Thanks all the same, but I don't want you to put yourself out.'

'I can assure you it wouldn't be putting me out. Shall I go and ask for you?'

'If you like.'

Fred left the box and Jane quickly turned on her friend. 'What is it with you? I thought you was enjoying yourself?'

'I am. It's just that I don't want him to keep trying to do things for me.'

'Why?'

'I dunno, it makes me feel as if I'm obliged to go back and work for him.'

'Is that all that's worrying you? I tell you, if I had a boss like that, I'd be a bit more than grateful. Besides, would it be so bad going back to work for him?'

'How can I, looking like this?'

'Honest, Sue, it's not so red and sore-looking as it was when you first come home. What if you did wear some of this stage make-up? That could be the answer; well, I reckon it's the best idea yet.'

'We'll see.'

'There's no pleasing you, is there?'

★   ★   ★

As Fred went downstairs backstage, he bumped into the theatre manager.

''Allo, Fred. What you doing down here? Everything upstairs OK?'

'It's fine, Tom, and thanks for getting me the box at such short notice.'

'No trouble. So what *are* you doing down here, you dirty sod? Come to see how much tits and arse you can feast your eyes on?'

'Na. I've got me own girl. I'll leave that to you.'

'Now you know I ain't into girls.'

Fred laughed. 'I've come to see Lilly. I want to find out about the make-up they use.'

Tom laughed. 'Oh, you are a one. You'll be coming to our club next.'

'I don't think so.'

Tom banged on the dressing-room door and there were shouts of 'Bugger off!' and even riper language.

'It's me, Tom.'

A tall, leggy blonde wearing a dressing gown

that just about met over her ample bosom opened the door. 'Well at least we know you're harmless, Tom. What d'yer want?'

'My mate Fred here wants to have a word with Lilly.'

'Lilly,' screamed the blonde at the top of her voice, 'there's a bloke here to see you.'

Lilly came to the door; she too was wearing a revealing figure-hugging dressing gown. 'Fred. Fred Hunt. Long time no see. What you doing here?'

Fred took her arm and led her outside.

Lilly giggled. 'Here, you've not come to take me away from all this, have you?'

'Na.'

'That's just as well. I've got another week here before we move on to Brighton.'

'Lilly, a friend of mine had a bad accident and, well, she's got quite a nasty scar, and I was wondering if stage make-up would help to hide it?'

'Oh Fred. What a nice thought. Always said you was a nice bloke. Hang on, I'll go and get some for you.' She disappeared into the dressing room, which was full of laughter and shouting, and came back a few moments later holding a tube of make-up. 'Here, take this for the poor cow with my compliments.'

'Lilly, you're a star.' Fred kissed her cheek.

'I wish. Now go on with you, I've got work to do.'

Fred could hear the orchestra starting up as he made his way back up the stairs. He smiled. Could this be the answer to getting

280

Susan back to work? He pushed open the door just as the curtain rose. 'All right, girls?' he whispered.

'Yes thanks,' said Jane.

32

On Saturday evening Jane hurried next door to Sue's.

'She's in her bedroom,' said Mrs Reed when she opened the front door. 'I don't know what she's doing up there, but you can go on up.'

'Have you tried it yet?' asked Jane as soon as she walked in. She was eager for her friend to start living again.

'It's a bit thick.' Sue was holding the tube and Jane could see that she had squeezed some of the make-up on to her fingers.

'D'you want me to put it on for you?'

'No. I think I'd better try and do it.'

Jane sat on the bed while Sue carefully applied the thick make-up in front of her dressing-table mirror. 'Well, what d'you think? Don't make me look like a tart, does it?' She was peering into the mirror, studying her face from all angles. 'It'll look better when all this puckering goes down.' She gently ran her fingers over her face.

'Let me look. You've got a bit of a line here.' Jane pointed to her friend's chin. 'I think you've put too much on.'

Sue applied some cold cream and carefully wiped her face with a wad of cotton wool. 'It might take a bit of getting used to.'

'I expect it will.' Jane grinned. 'It's great to see you taking an interest in yourself, and I reckon it's gonner work.'

Once again Sue carefully squeezed a little of the make-up on to her fingers and covered her scar. 'Well, what d'you think now?'

Jane jumped up and hugged her friend. 'It really hides it. Come on, let's go and show your mum and dad.'

Sue pushed open the kitchen door. 'Mum, Dad.'

Her dad looked up from the newspaper he was reading. 'Sue. What's wrong?'

She went up to him and peered in his face. 'Do I look all right?'

'What you done?'

Doris came in from the scullery wiping her hands on the bottom of her pinny. 'What's going . . . ?' She stopped when Sue came up to her. 'I can't believe it. What have you done?'

'It's make-up like the girls on the stage wear. Mr Hunt got it for me last night.'

'Well it certainly makes a difference. Your scar hardly shows. What d'you reckon, Charlie?'

Her dad stood up and, holding her by the shoulders, said softly, 'D'you know, I reckon that bloke is one in a million.'

Granny Potts, who was sitting in front of the fire, and had been silent up to now, said, suddenly, 'Why is this bloke so concerned about Sue?'

'I dunno,' said her daughter. 'He's just a nice man who thinks a lot of her, that's all.'

'You've changed your tune.'

'Yes, I know, but he's been good to Sue and to us, taking us to the hospital and all that.'

'But why? What's he after?'

283

'Oh Mum. Must you always look for a reason?'

'Well I reckon he's either got something to hide, or he's after her.'

'Gran. Who'd want me now?'

'You're still a pretty little thing.'

Sue looked sad.

'Remember, girl. Looks ain't everything. It's what's on the inside that matters.'

'Did you tell your mum and dad about the show, the big box of chocolates and everything?' said Jane, hoping to lighten the atmosphere.

Sue nodded.

'It sounds as if you had a good time, both of you.'

'We certainly did, Mr Reed.'

Sue gave her mother a little smile.

'It's nice to see you happy and . . . ' Doris didn't like to say 'trying to enjoy life again'. She knew she had to take this as the first step in her daughter's recovery. 'So when d'you feel like going out then, love?'

Sue sat down. 'I don't know.'

'Well you certainly don't have to worry now.'

'Why? D'you want to get rid of me?' Sue was beginning to lose her confidence. 'I'll do it in me own time.'

'All right. I only asked.' Her mother went back into the scullery. She knew she had to tread very carefully where her daughter was concerned.

★   ★   ★

For the rest of the week Sue gradually got used to her makeup, and by Friday night she had to

284

admit to Jane that she was feeling better about herself.

'So how about coming to the pictures Sunday night?'

'I dunno.'

'We can go when it's dark and you can sit on whichever side of the bus you want.'

Sue was very tempted.

'Honestly, Sue, someone would have to come up real close to see your scar.'

'Do you think so?'

'Let's give it a go.'

'Oh all right, then. I'll have to ask me dad for some money, though.'

'I reckon they'll be more than glad to pay for you.' Jane hugged her friend. 'I'm so pleased you've started living again, and it's all down to your Mr Hunt.'

Sue smiled. 'I'll have to thank him sometime.' She was beginning to realise what a kind and thoughtful man he was. After all, he had seen her from the beginning and never made any comment. Could she risk going back to work? With Christmas coming up she needed the money; she couldn't expect her mum and dad to look after her for ever.

★ ★ ★

'Guess what?' said Ron on Monday morning when he went into the office.

Fred looked up. 'What is it?'

'My little Sue went to the pictures last night with me sister.'

'She did?'

'Yer, and me sister said it was all 'cos you got her some sort of make-up.'

Fred was trying hard to suppress his joy. 'Did she look all right?'

'Dunno. They went before I saw her.'

Fred knew she must have felt confident to go out. 'Thanks, Ron.' He carried on with his work; he didn't want Ron to see how pleased he was. Now she had started going out, how long would it be before she came back to work? For Fred it couldn't come soon enough.

⋆   ⋆   ⋆

At four o'clock on Friday, Fred was getting ready to close up. It had been miserable all day, with the low clouds making it dark and depressing. Suddenly the office door opened and Ron came rushing in.

'Mr Hunt, Mr Hunt! Look who's here.' He stepped to one side, and to Fred's joy Susan walked in. He hurried round his desk and took her in his arms. 'Sorry,' he said when he realised what he had done. He let go of her.

She smiled. 'That's all right.'

Ron was hovering round her. 'You don't look that bad,' he said, peering into her face.

'That's all down to Mr Hunt. I only came to thank you.'

'You look very well.'

Sue glanced away. 'I don't mind going out in the dark.'

'Sit down for a bit. D'you fancy a cup of tea?'

'No thanks. I only popped in for a moment.'

'You can't lock yourself away for ever, you know.'

'I know.' She sat at her desk and looked around. 'I see Jen's been keeping things under control.'

'Yes, she has, but I'm a bit worried about the next few weeks, when the children are on Christmas holiday. You wouldn't fancy coming back, would you?'

'Oh go on, little Sue. It would be smashing having you around again.'

Fred glared at Ron.

'I don't know.'

'We're not too busy at the moment. It's mostly old customers, and they're always asking after you.'

'That's nice of them, but I don't know,' repeated Sue. Although she knew she had to work, as she desperately needed the money for Christmas.

'Think about it over the weekend, and if you want to, you can come back on Monday. Jen don't work Mondays, and I'll tell Harry that you'll be coming back; that'll please both of them.'

Sue began to panic. 'I don't know.'

'It would be really nice to have you back. Please think about it.'

'I will. Thank you, Mr Hunt.' She stood up and walked to the door. 'Good night.'

'Good night, Susan.'

As she walked away past all the cars, she realised how much she had missed going to work. It was only three weeks to Christmas and so far there weren't any decorations up in the office. Some of the shops had started to put theirs up, and as she made her way home, she began to think about last year and that wonderful bottle of scent Mr Hunt had given her. She felt tears filling her eyes. Such a lot had happened since then. She knew her life would never be the same, and that the first step towards living again could be going back to work on Monday.

★　★　★

'You're going back to work?' Her mother was trying to hide her joy. 'Are you sure that's what you want?'

Sue nodded.

'You know you don't have to worry about money?'

'But I want to pay me way, and Christmas is coming up.'

'I know. Oh Sue, I'm so proud of you.' Doris held her daughter close.

Her father was just as pleased with the news, and that evening Sue went in to tell Jane.

Ron opened the front door. 'Little Sue.' She let him hold her for just a second.

'Sue. Do come in. How lovely to see you,' said Mrs Brent, coming into the passage. 'I'm just off to church. Jane's in the kitchen.'

Jane was sitting at the table with a book propped up against a milk bottle. She was having her dinner. She quickly swallowed and jumped up. 'Sue.'

Ron had followed her in and was grinning fit to bust. 'Ain't it good to see little Sue again?'

'Yes,' said Jane, still standing.

'Sit down and finish your dinner.'

Jane did as she was told.

'I've come to tell you I'm going back to work on Monday.'

Jane jumped up again and threw her arms round her friend's neck. 'I'm so pleased,' she said, brushing a tear from her cheek.

'Mr Hunt will be ever so pleased about that,' said Ron. 'So will I. I'll have someone to walk home with and I'll protect you. Nobody will ever hurt you.'

'Thanks, Ron. Will you tell Mr Hunt that I'll be coming back on Monday?'

'Course I will.'

When she left Jane, Sue still wasn't sure she had done the right thing. What if people just came to gawp at her? Was she beginning to get paranoid about her looks?

33

On Monday morning, after very carefully applying the stage make-up, Sue walked to work. Ron loped along beside her; he was such an ungainly man. Half of her was pleased to be going back, but the other half was afraid. She kept her head down; she didn't want to look up in case people stared at her. Had she done the right thing? Fear grabbed her and she was very tempted to turn and run back home.

Ron was grinning fit to bust. 'It's really smashing having you coming to work again. Mr Hunt is ever so pleased.' He went to take her arm.

'Don't do that.'

'Sorry.'

'I just hope I ain't forgot how to type.'

'Course you ain't.'

'I'm surprised Mr Hunt has kept you on so long. I would have thought that things were a bit quiet at this time of year.'

'I do a few odd jobs for Mr Field round the garage now.'

'I didn't think you two got on?'

'We do now. I just do as I'm told. I clean some of the grease off things.'

'Oh, I see.'

'It's a bit messy, and Mum has a moan about the state I sometimes come home in, but she's pleased I'm out from under her feet. I like

290

working for Mr Hunt.'

'He is a nice man.'

'I don't get those headaches now I'm working.'

'That's good.'

Sue pushed open the office door. In a way she didn't feel as if she had ever been away. She was back where she had been so happy.

Fred stood up. 'Susan. Thanks for coming back.' He resisted the temptation to take her in his arms. 'Jen said she'll pop in later and go over things with you.'

'All right.'

'Shall I make a cup of tea, Mr Hunt?' asked Ron.

'No thanks. Harry wants you round there.'

'OK.' Off he went without a word.

'He likes working for you.'

'I know. He's not a bad lad. And how about you? Are you happy to be here?'

Sue smiled and nodded. 'I really have missed coming to work.'

'And I've missed having you around.'

Soon everything fell into place. Jen came and told her what she'd done while Sue was away. She didn't even give her a second glance. At first Sue wouldn't look at her, but after a while she found she was chatting away to her, completely forgetting how she looked.

Later that morning Harry Field came in.

'Sue, it's lovely to see you back again. I'd give you a hug, but I'd only make you all dirty.'

Once again nothing was said. Had Mr Hunt told them not to mention the accident?

'It's lovely to be back.'

291

They didn't have any customers who came into the office; Fred talked to them all out front. For the rest of the day Sue just carried on working as though she had never been away.

When it was time to go she stood up. 'Mr Hunt. Thank you so much.'

'What for?'

'For letting me come back here to work.'

He laughed. 'No, it's me who should be thanking you. I really have missed you, and I am so glad you wanted to come back.'

Ron poked his head round the door. 'Ready, little Sue?'

'I'll just get me hat.' She took her beret from the drawer.

'I'll look after her, Mr Hunt.'

'I'm sure you will, Ron. I'm sure you will. Good night, Susan, and thank you.'

'Good night. See you tomorrow.'

As she closed the door, Fred put the papers that he'd been filling in to one side and went to the window. He watched her walk across the road. Today had been wonderful with her sitting opposite him. He knew he couldn't keep his feelings locked away for ever, but he didn't want to frighten her. He had to wait till her confidence returned before he declared his love for her.

★　★　★

At the end of the week the news was all about the King's relationship with Mrs Simpson. Sue was looking at the paper when Fred walked into the office.

'That's certainly put the cat amongst the pigeons. And she's been married a couple of times before,' he said scornfully.

'It must be really wonderful to be loved like that,' said Sue as she gazed at the newspaper.

'Just as long as he ain't throwing his life away. If they get married and she then goes off with someone else, where will he be then?'

'Don't they say it's better to have loved and lost than never to have loved . . . ' Sue's voice drifted off. She had loved and lost and it had been very painful.

Fred looked up and noted the troubled look on her face. 'What is it, Susan?'

'Nothing.' She smiled. 'Just wishful thinking, I suppose.'

Fred kept his thoughts to himself.

That night everybody was glued to the wireless as the King spoke to the nation and told them that he had abdicated.

'Silly bugger,' said Charlie Reed. 'Should have thought of his duty to the country before he started playing around with this American tart.'

'But he's in love,' said Sue.

'I give this marriage a couple of years, then I suppose he'll come back with his tail between his legs,' said Granny Potts, peering over her glasses as she looked up from mending a hole in her son-in-law's trousers.

All evening the talk was about Edward and Mrs Simpson.

★ ★ ★

On Monday morning Fred came into the office with a Christmas tree. 'Don't seem a year ago you was busy decorating this place.'

'No.' Sue didn't want to think about this past year.

'I'll just get the decorations.' He disappeared into the store cupboard. 'Would you and Jane like to come to see a pantomime after Christmas?' he said as he put a cardboard box on her desk.

'That would be very nice. Thank you. Are you going to your mother's for Christmas?'

'Yes. Not got a lot else to do.'

'I'll give you a Christmas card for them.'

'You don't have to do that.'

'But I want to.'

'You know you would always be welcome there if any time you fancy a day out.'

'I couldn't. Not now.'

'They do know all about it, you know.'

'I guessed you would have told them.'

'You didn't mind, did you?'

She shook her head. 'Better get on with this,' she said, taking the tinsel and baubles from the box.

★   ★   ★

That evening Sue went next door to see Jane and after they had discussed the saga of Edward and Mrs Simpson in great depth, Sue said, 'Jane, Mr Hunt wants to take us to see a pantomime after Christmas. D'you fancy it?'

'I should say so. I like going out with him;

well, not really going out.' She giggled. 'You know what I mean.'

'I'll only go if we have a box again.'

'I expect we will. He's very thoughtful.'

Sue nodded. 'Yes, he is. Jane, are you going out on Christmas Eve?'

'Shouldn't think so. I'm usually too tired after working all day. Don't forget, we don't finish till late. Why?'

'Just wondered, that's all.'

'If you want to know if you-know-who will be at the town hall, well yes, he will be.'

'Have you seen the posters?'

Jane nodded. 'I wasn't going to say anything.'

'I guessed he would be. I wonder if he'll bring his wife?' It was said with a lot of anger.

Jane didn't know how to answer. 'Remember, Sue, I'll always be around.'

'I know.'

'D'you fancy going to the pictures one night?'

'Yes, what about tomorrow?'

'If you like.'

'We'll be able to see the King and Mrs Simpson on the newsreels.'

'He must really love her,' said Jane wistfully.

'Yes, he must.'

★   ★   ★

On Saturday morning Bert Rose came into the office. Sue quickly put her head down.

'Hallo, love,' he said cheerfully. 'Great to see you back. I tell yer, old Fred here really missed yer.'

Sue was reluctant to look up.

'Brought you a bottle of Scotland's finest,' he said, putting a bottle on Fred's desk.

'What's this in aid of?' Fred was worried that Bert had something else lined up for him.

'Nothing. Just a Christmas present and a big thank you.'

'Thank you?' repeated Fred. 'What for?'

'Our night out. The police couldn't break me alibi thanks to you and the girls.'

Fred wanted to die. The last thing he wanted was for Susan to know he'd been out with a girl.

'You should've seen him, Sue. Talk about Fred Astaire.'

Sue didn't want to ask questions.

'There's another dance at the town hall on Christmas Eve. D'yer fancy coming? It's that same band.'

Sue sat listening quietly. Fred had been to a dance at the town hall, with Jeff Owen's band playing. He must have seen Cy Taylor.

'The girls are going. Thought it'd make a change for yer.'

'No thanks.' Fred looked across at Sue, who was busy writing. 'That was just a one-off to help you out.'

'Please yerself. Anyway, merry Christmas.'

'Merry Christmas,' said Fred and Sue together as Bert left.

Sue was surprised that she felt a little jealous hearing that he had been to a dance with someone else. Why should she? He was free to do what he liked. She looked up. He was handsome in a rugged way, and he had been so

296

good to her while she was in hospital.

'I went to the dance with Bert because his son had been beaten up and a gang was going to sort things out for him and he wanted an alibi.' It came out in a rush.

'What you do, Mr Hunt, is your business.'

'I know. But I want you to know that I don't make a habit of going out with him and picking up girls.'

'What did you think of the singer?'

'Looked like a bit of a pansy to me, but Nancy, that's the girl I danced with, told me he was married.'

Sue's head shot up. 'How does she know?'

'It seems her sister lives near his wife.'

Sue sat back, dumbfounded.

Fred looked at her. 'I know I shouldn't be asking such personal questions, but did you go out with him?'

Sue nodded and tears filled her eyes.

'Susan, Susan. What is it?' He came round to her side and held her hand.

Sue touched her face. 'This is all his fault.'

'What? Why?'

'Mr Hunt, I am so ashamed.' She buried her head in her hands and wept.

Ron had pushed open the office door. When he saw his little Sue crying, he backed silently out of sight, but left the door slightly open so that he could hear what was being said.

34

Fred looked around anxiously. He wanted to hold her tight. 'Susan, would you like to come up to the flat?'

'No, I'll be all right.'

'Are you sure?'

She nodded and wiped her eyes.

'Do you want to talk about it?'

Again she only nodded.

'I am here for you, you know?'

Sue blew her nose. 'I've kept this bottled up for so long, I must tell someone what happened.'

'Are you sure you want to talk to me? What about Jane or your mum?'

'Jane knows, and she thinks I was a silly cow. I think me mum does as well, but she's never said and we ain't talked about it. You see, I spent an afternoon with Cy Taylor in a hotel and then I found out I was having his baby. When I told him, he told me he was married and didn't want to know. When I had the accident, I was thinking of the shame and of ways to get rid of the baby, but I didn't want it to happen like that and now I've been punished. I shall carry the guilt and this scar till I die.' It was all said in a rush as tears ran down her face. She wanted sympathy. She wanted a shoulder to cry on.

Ron was still listening at the door. He clenched his fists. He wanted to kill this bloke.

Who was he? His little Sue was going to have this bloke's baby.

Fred held her close as he tried to suppress his anger. He wanted to kiss away the hurt she was feeling. 'Do your mum and dad know about the baby?'

She nodded.

'And who the father was?'

She shook her head. 'I think me dad would kill him if he knew.'

'Can't blame him for that.' He felt her give a heartfelt sob and gently stroked her hair. 'And you've never said anything?'

Sue shook her head again. 'They don't know whose it was.' She pulled away from him. 'I shouldn't be telling you all this.'

'Why not?'

'You're me boss.'

He wanted to tell her he wanted to be more, but didn't feel this was the right time.

Ron moved away. His head was suddenly invaded by the demons that used to fill his thoughts before he found contentment working for Mr Hunt. He had to find out more about this bloke. Jane must know who he was.

Fred too was wondering about that singer. He could see why Susan had been attracted to him; after all, he was a good-looking sod. But to lead her on and then walk away from her when she needed him; what sort of bloke was he?

'I'd better get on,' said Sue, interrupting his thoughts.

'Are you sure? You can go home if you like.'

She gave him a weak smile. 'Thank you, but

I'm feeling a lot better now.' She was beginning to see Fred Hunt in a different light. She had felt comfortable in his arms. But was she just being a silly romantic again? After all, he was years older than she was.

'Would you like a cup of tea?' he asked.

'I'll make it.' Sue went into the small cupboard-like room.

Fred sat at his desk. Bert had said that band was coming to the town hall again on Christmas Eve. Would the singer be there? All sorts of thoughts were going through his mind. This was something he would have to think about and plan very carefully.

Ron walked round the cars. He was angry. How could this bloke have done this to his little Sue? He would find out from Jane who he was, then he would find him and . . . He grinned. Heaven help him.

Ron was very quiet as they walked home.

'Is something bothering you?' Sue asked.

'Na. How long will we get off for Christmas?'

'Dunno. Just the Friday and Sat'day, I suppose. Why? You got a date or something?'

'Na. I'm ever so pleased Mr Hunt's still gonner keep me on.'

Sue gave a little smile. 'He's a very kind man.'

'Yes, he is.'

★   ★   ★

'What you doing here?' asked Bert that evening when he opened the front door to Fred. 'I was just going for a drink. Fancy coming along?'

'No thanks. I want to have a word with you.'

'Come in. Bloody hell, it must be important for you to come round here. Here, I ain't put me foot in it be telling young Susan that you've been out dancing with some tart, have I?'

'Course not. Hello, son,' Fred said to Bert's boy. 'How you feeling now?'

'I'm fine now, and thanks.'

'What for?'

'Giving Dad an alibi.'

'Well we've helped each other out in the past.'

'So, what can I do for you?' Bert asked.

Fred looked uneasily at Bert's son.

'It's all right. You can talk. I'll go in the kitchen. Fancy a cuppa, Fred?'

'Yes please.' He waited till the boy had left the room and shut the door. 'I need some advice.'

Bert laughed. 'What about? Here, you ain't got a tart up the duff, have you?'

'No. It's Susan. I shouldn't really be telling you this.' He took a cigarette from a packet that was lying on the table and lit it.

'Go on. What's she done? She ain't been helping herself to money?'

'No. Nothing like that. She's a . . . ' He was going to say 'good girl', but in some people's eyes she certainly wouldn't be called that.

'Come on, spit it out.'

Fred pointed his cigarette at Bert. 'Now remember that what I'm telling you is strictly between you and me.'

Bert sat back. 'I'm listening.'

Fred went through what Sue had told him. When he'd finished, he too sat back.

'So,' said Bert, 'it was that singer. Well let's face it, he is a good-looking bloke. It was a bit of hard luck her getting up the duff and having that accident, but why are you so concerned?'

Fred leant forward and angrily stubbed his cigarette out in the ashtray. He didn't look up as he said, 'I know this might sound daft, but I'm in love with this girl and I'm gonner ask her to marry me. I want that bastard to pay for what he's done.'

'Bloody hell. Now hold on. Remember, it takes two, and she went with him willingly. So what chance do you reckon you stand? After all, he's a bloody sight better looking than you, and a lot younger.'

Bert's son came back into the room with a tray of tea.

'Thanks, son,' said Bert.

'I'll go to me room for a while.'

'OK.' When the boy had left, Bert asked Fred, 'So what d'you intend to do?'

'Make him suffer like she has. Scar him for life.'

Bert gave a bit of a laugh. 'And where do I come in?'

'I'll need an alibi.'

'What you gonner do?'

'Jump him when he goes home.'

Bert looked at Fred. 'I know you used to be handy with yer fists, but I reckon you could be out o'sorts now. He might not be such a pushover.'

'He didn't look that strong.'

'Don't go by looks. Besides, he might have a

few mates with him.'

'I'll have to take that gamble.'

'You sure?'

'Yes, I am.'

'Look, we've got a few days before we go to that dance. Let me think about what to do.'

'Thanks, mate.'

'Do you really intend to ask Susan to marry you?'

Fred nodded.

'What if she turns you down?'

He shrugged. 'I'll take that chance.'

'Yer mum ain't gonner like it.'

'That's not my problem. All I know is that I want to look after her for the rest of her life.'

'This is not just out of sympathy, is it?'

'No. This has been on my mind long before the accident, but I didn't have the guts to ask her.'

'And you want to now? I know she's been badly scarred, but will she thank you?'

Fred stood up. 'Dunno. That's another chance I'll have to take. See you Christmas Eve.'

Bert patted him on the back. 'The best of luck, mate. And if she says yes, can I be your best man?'

Fred laughed. 'I should say so.'

As he walked down the stairs, his thoughts were full of getting even with this little shit. After he'd finished with him he wouldn't want to stand up there on the stage crooning to all those young, vulnerable females. He'd want to hide away like Susan did.

35

Christmas Eve was cold and windy. The only people out and about were those doing their last-minute shopping, and buying a car was the last thing on anyone's mind, so Fred let Sue and Ron go at lunchtime. He also wanted time to think about what he was going to do tonight.

'Have a nice Christmas,' he said as Sue put on her beret.

'Are you driving down to your mother's today?' she asked.

'Yes. I hope to go this afternoon before the weather turns nasty.'

'That's a good idea. Wish them a merry Christmas from me.'

'I will.' She was about to go out of the door when he said, 'Susan, I have a present for you.'

'You shouldn't have. I ain't got you nothing.' Her mother had done Sue's Christmas shopping this year; even though she was gradually getting her confidence back, she still wasn't prepared to go shopping herself. She had got Jane to buy her mother's present: a lovely warm beige scarf and gloves.

'And I don't expect anything.' He handed her a small box.

She smiled. 'This looks exciting.'

'I hope it is.'

'Can I open it now?'

'No. Leave it till Christmas morning.'

'Thank you.' She put the packet in her handbag. She hoped it was scent again, but it looked a bit small for that.

Fred watched Sue walk across the forecourt with Ron trailing behind. He so desperately wanted to tell her he loved her and wanted to marry her, but he had to bide his time. He had to be sure she was aware of his feelings, so that she had time to think it over. He was hoping that his Christmas present would help. But first he had to think about tonight.

★　★　★

Ron was deep in thought as they walked home. He too was thinking about tonight. He had promised his mother that he would go to church with her. He liked going on Christmas Eve; he enjoyed singing the carols, and the mince pie after. And sometimes the vicar gave him a small present. Last year it had been a bookmark. Ron was very proud of it; it had pretty pictures of flowers all round the edge, and in the middle was Jesus.

'You going out tonight?' he asked Sue.

'No.'

'You and Jane used to go out.'

'I know.'

'You used to go dancing.'

'Who would want to dance with me now?'

'I would. I don't care what you look like, you will always be beautiful to me.'

'That's very kind of you Ron, but Jane doesn't finish till late, and anyway, I've given up

305

thinking about dancing.'

'That's a shame.'

'Yes, it is.'

'Mr Hunt gave me two weeks' wages.'

'He gave me a present, so don't you go scaring me like you did last year when you made me drop my bottle of scent.' That sentence brought back a flood of memories, some good, but a lot bad.

'That was 'cos you wouldn't let me walk with you.'

'Well you used to act a bit weird.'

'I'm better now. And that's thanks to Mr Hunt. All me demons have flown away.' He laughed, and Sue smiled.

Ron certainly had changed during this past year.

★　★　★

Fred was busy getting himself ready to go to the town hall. He was picking Bert up at seven, and then they were going to get Nancy and Rita. Fred wasn't happy about that, but Bert had got it all arranged and told him he could sort the singer out during the interval. That way he could drive down to his mother's after he'd done the deed. Bert said he'd see the girls home; he'd grinned and said he reckoned he was on a promise. Fred was very nervous. It was years since he'd done anything like this, but his love for Susan spurred him on.

★　★　★

306

Ron looked up at Jesus on the cross as he stood singing his heart out. He smiled at his mother. He wasn't going to wait till the end even if it did mean he would be missing his mince pie. When his little Sue had come to see Jane last Sunday, he'd overheard her telling his sister what she had told Mr Hunt, and he'd known then that this singer who had caused all her misery would be at the town hall tonight. Ron smiled. Well, he wouldn't be singing any more, not after he'd finished with him.

★ ★ ★

Sue and the family were in the cosy front room. The folding table had been opened up and they were playing cards.

'Lovely fire you've got there,' said Granny Potts as she pulled her shawl round her shoulders.

'That chimney sweep did a good job, much cleaner than that last bloke,' said Doris, leaning forward and giving the coals a prod with the poker, causing the flames to shoot up.

'I like this room, we should come in here more often,' said her mother.

'I've got enough to do without cleaning out another grate every day.'

'Fancy a drop of port, love?' Sue's father asked her.

'She's only nineteen, Charlie, you shouldn't encourage her to drink,' said his wife with a grin.

'Don't worry, it'll only be an eggcupful.'

Sue smiled. They were doing their best to

make Christmas jolly.

'So what d'you reckon is in that little box yer boss bought you?' asked Granny Potts, looking at the wrapped presents under the tree.

'I think it might be scent,' said Sue.

'Bloody small bottle if you ask me. Thought he would have got you something a bit bigger.'

'You know what they say, Mum, good things come in small packages.'

'I know. Go on, love, open it.'

'No, I promised I wouldn't open it till Christmas morning, and I ain't gonner break me promise.' As much as Sue was dying to see what he'd bought her, she was prepared to wait.

★   ★   ★

When the band struck up with a waltz, Nancy grabbed Fred and whisked him on to the dance floor.

'Didn't think I'd ever see you again,' she said as she nuzzled up close to him.

'Have ter get out now and again,' he said, trying to pull away.

'I was hoping you and me could have gone out together.'

'Sorry about that.'

'I ain't that bad, am I?'

'No, course not.'

'I was surprised when Bert came and said that you and him wanted to bring us here again.'

Fred wanted to tell her they were here for a reason, but he said nothing as he watched Cy Taylor singing and giving the girls a wink as they waltzed past. He just wanted to smash his face in.

When the interval came, Nancy was talking away but Fred wasn't listening. He was thinking about going outside.

'I'm just going for a piddle,' said Bert. 'You get the drinks in,' he said to Fred.

Fred went to the bar. He was very nervous. He wanted to go out and see to this Taylor bloke, but he knew he had to follow Bert's instructions; he had told him he knew what he was doing.

The bar was crowded and it took a while to get the drinks. By the time Fred got back to their table, the band had come back on to the stage. Bert was laughing and talking with Rita. Fred was angry. He had missed his chance; now he would have to wait till the end. What was Bert thinking about?

★   ★   ★

Ron made his way towards the town hall. It was dark and cold. He had said goodbye to his mum before the end of the service and told her he was going home as he had a headache. He knew it would be a while before she left the church.

★   ★   ★

Jeff Owen was looking anxiously to the side of the stage. He grabbed the mike and said, 'Now take your partners for a foxtrot,' and the band struck up with, 'The Way You Look Tonight'.

'Where's Cy?' asked Nancy. 'He always sings this.'

Fred looked around and Bert gave him a wink as he whisked Rita on to her feet. What had happened to the bloke? Bert hadn't been gone long enough to do him any damage.

★ ★ ★

Ron got to the town hall and went round the back into the alley, with its smelly, overflowing dustbins. It was very dark and dingy as the light over the door was out. A dustbin had been tipped over and its contents spilled everywhere. A cat scurried away into the darkness. As Ron made his way along the alleyway he tripped over something lying on the ground.

'Help me.' It was a person.

As Ron bent down, the moon came from behind the clouds and he could see more clearly. 'What happened?' he asked, taking the bloke's head in his hands. He could feel it was sticky with blood.

'A couple of bully boys set about me. They've cut my face.'

'Hang on, mate, I'll go and get help. What's your name?'

'Cy. I sing with Jeff Owens' band. Cy Taylor.'

Ron straightened up and jumped back. 'You. You're the bloke upset my little Sue.'

'What you talking about? Go and get help.'

'No.'

'What?'

'You heard.' Ron kicked him in the ribs and

Cy let out a scream. He kicked him again, shouting, 'My little Sue was gonner have your baby and she crashed her car and now she's got this ugly scar and it's all your fault.'

Cy didn't reply.

Ron was suddenly filled with fear. What had he done? He backed away and stared at the lifeless body. At the corner he started to run, his boots echoing on the ground. He passed pubs that were full of noise; people were drinking and singing, some had spilled out into the street. His head was full of voices, his demons pounding inside his temples.

''Ere, watch it, mate,' said a bloke he almost knocked over.

Ron was talking to himself. 'What have I done? What have I done?'

★   ★   ★

Cy still hadn't turned up. After a couple of songs, Jeff went to the sax player and whispered something, and the sax player left the stage. It was only a minute or two before he came rushing back and beckoned urgently to Jeff, who also left the stage. When he returned, he stopped the music and asked, 'Is there a doctor in the house?'

Some people laughed, and one bloke called out, 'You'll be in need of one if you don't carry on playing.'

'There's been an accident.'

The chatter amongst the dancers grew louder.

'It must be poor old Cy,' said Nancy. 'I wonder what's wrong with him?'

311

'Dunno,' said Bert. 'Might be he's got plastered.'

Fred laughed, but it was forced. What had happened to Cy?

After a while the rumour started buzzing around that the singer had been beaten up. Fred looked at Bert, who said, 'I wonder who's done that?'

'D'you know, I reckon it could be the husband of one of his girlfriends, or even his own wife.' Nancy's eyes were shining. 'Serves him bloody well right. It's about time someone took him down a peg or two.'

Fred pulled Bert to one side. 'What's happened?' he hissed.

Bert shrugged. 'Don't ask me.'

'He ain't dead, is he?'

'Buggered if I know. Look why don't you go off now? I'll take the girls home.'

'That all right?'

'Go on, make yourself scarce.'

Fred left quickly before Nancy could grab him back.

36

As Fred drove to his mother's, he thought about what had happened tonight.

So Cy Taylor had been attacked. How bad was he? There was talk that he had been murdered. Fred knew it couldn't have been Bert, as he was with him most of the time, but was it one of his henchmen? He gave a slight smile. For all Bert's faults, he was indeed a true friend. But had he gone too far? Fred knew this would worry him until he found out more and whether Bert was responsible.

Fred's thoughts went to Susan. What if his present and letter offended her? He should have spoken to her face to face, but he couldn't bear the thought of her being embarrassed. This way she had a few days to consider his offer. He only prayed she would say yes.

Soon he left the lights of London behind and was driving through the dark country lanes to his mother's. He knew he could be sure of a warm welcome there, even if it could be a bit overbearing at times. He smiled. Who knows, this time next year I could be going somewhere with my wife.

★　★　★

Jane was in the kitchen when Ron burst in. His eyes were wild and staring.

'Bloody 'ell, Ron, you frightened the life out of me,' said Jane. 'What's wrong? You look like you've seen a ghost.'

'Leave me alone! Leave me alone!'

'All right. I was just going to bed anyway.' She stood at the kitchen door. 'Ron, if you're in any trouble, you will tell me, won't you?'

'Yes. It was all those pictures of Jesus staring at me.'

Jane tutted and tossed her head. There were times when her mother and her religion had a lot to answer for.

Ron was still in the scullery, frantically washing his hands, when his mother returned home.

'Where's Jane?' she asked.

'Gone ter bed.'

'How's your head now?'

'I'm all right.'

'What's that? Is that blood on your sleeve? How did that get there? You bin fighting?'

'No, I had a nose bleed, but I'm all right now.'

'Good. I'm going into the front room to say a few prayers, then I'm off to bed. Do you want to come and pray with me?'

'No thanks. I've done more than me share this year.'

She patted his shoulder. 'You should pray for that kind Mr Hunt. He has made a man of you and I'm so proud.'

She wouldn't say that if she knew what he'd done tonight. Yes, it was all down to Mr Hunt that his demons had disappeared, but tonight they had come back with a vengeance.

* ★ ★

On Christmas morning Sue was awake early. She crept downstairs; she was going to make her parents and Granny Potts a cup of tea. It would be a nice change for her mother to be waited on. As she passed the front-room door, she found herself wondering what sort of present her boss had bought her.

In the scullery she put on the kettle and laid out the crocks. When she'd made the tea she took it upstairs.

'Merry Christmas,' she said, pushing open her parents' bedroom door.

Bleary-eyed, her mother struggled to sit up. 'Sue. What is it? Are you all right?'

'Yes. I've brought you both a cuppa.'

Doris smiled. 'That's lovely. Merry Christmas, love. Charlie, sit up. Sue's brought us a cuppa.'

Grunts came from under the eiderdown.

Sue grinned. 'I'll just take this in to Gran.'

'I'm awake,' said her gran when she tapped on her door.

'Merry Christmas, and here's a nice cup of tea.'

'Thanks, love. I'll be down as soon as I can get these old bones moving again.'

Sue smiled as she left the room and walked down the stairs. She did love them, and despite everything she was happy.

As she passed the front-room door again her curiosity got the better of her and she went in and picked up the parcel from Fred. After all, it was Christmas day. When she took the paper off

315

it she sat down on the sofa quickly. It was a black ring box. Her heart raced. What was he doing buying her a ring? She opened it, and inside she found not a ring but a tiny pearl on a fine gold chain. The note that came with the box read:

My dear Susan,
I hope you like this little gift.
I have never been able to tell you how I feel about you, so please forgive me if this offends you.
I have the ring, and if at some time you feel you could be part of my life, I would be ecstatic.
I know there is an age difference, but don't worry about that as I know I can make you happy.
If you do feel offended, please continue working for me and I will never mention this again.
Fred Hunt

Sue sat staring at the necklace and the note. She couldn't believe that he wanted to marry her. What could she say? What would her mum and dad say? Her mind was in turmoil. She took out the necklace; it was beautiful. He loved her. She knew she was very fond of him and he was very kind, but was that enough to make a good marriage? She quickly put the note and the present in her dressing-gown pocket. She would wait till after today before she even thought about this.

'So where's that present from your boss gone?'

316

asked Granny Potts when she came into the front room.

'Why are you so worried about it, Gran?'

Gran pulled her shawl more tightly round her shoulders. 'If you must know, and if I'm not very much mistaken, it looks like a ring box to me. He ain't asked yer to marry him, has he?'

Sue laughed.

'You shouldn't laugh, young lady. If you ask me, he's a very good catch, and beggars can't be choosers.'

Sue stared at her grandmother. She couldn't believe what she had just said. 'Is that what you think?' she whispered. 'That I should take the first person that asks me to marry him as I'm so ugly?'

'No, love, I didn't mean that. What I meant was . . .'

But Sue wasn't listening. 'Well in that case, I'd better marry Ron; he's always asking me.' Tears ran down her face as she quickly left the room.

On her way up the stairs to her bedroom she bumped into her mother.

'What's wrong, love?'

'Ask Gran,' she said, going into her room and slamming the door.

Doris went into the kitchen, where her mother was busy laying the table. 'Mum, what have you just said to Sue?'

'She's a silly little cow. I didn't mean any harm in it. She just took it the wrong way, that's all.'

'Mum, what 'ave you said?' Doris asked again.

'All I said was if that's a ring from her boss she ought to think about marrying him. After all, he's a good catch and I don't reckon she'll get a lot of choice seeing as how she don't go out much.'

'Mum, how could you? Don't you think she's suffered enough?' Doris left her mother busy making breakfast while she went up to see her daughter.

Sue was lying on her bed with her face buried in the covers. Doris sat down and cradled her daughter's head in her lap. 'Oh Sue, don't take any notice of her. You know how she can be; things come out all wrong.'

'But it's true, nobody will want me now.'

'Course they will. You're still lovely in the eyes of anyone who loves you.'

'But I'm not,' she sobbed.

'Come on now. It's Christmas and we should be happy and jolly.'

Sue sat up and wiped her eyes on the bedcover. 'I don't feel very happy or jolly. Mum, you knew I was having a baby, didn't you?'

'Yes, but we don't have to talk about it now.'

'But I want to. You never asked me about it and I wanted to tell you, have done for weeks.'

Doris looked embarrassed. 'Well only if you're sure . . . '

'I'm sure. And I hope you won't hate me.'

She held her daughter tight, and as the tears came again she gently patted her back and smoothed her hair as she'd done when Sue was a child. 'I will never hate you,' she said with a catch in her throat. 'And it's not the end of the world, you know.'

'If I wasn't going to have that baby I would

never have had the accident. You see, I had been trying to think of ways to get rid of it. So don't you see, I've been punished? I will carry this scar for the rest of my life.' She gently touched her cheek. 'And every time I look in the mirror, I'm reminded of the reason why.'

Doris could find no words of comfort. She held Sue close and murmured, 'There, there,' over and over again, as Sue related how she had met Cy Taylor and gone to the hotel with him. As she finished, she broke away and looked at her mother gratefully.

'Thanks for listening and not shouting at me.'

'That's what mothers are for.'

'I feel better now.'

'That's good.'

Sue blew her nose. 'Mum, I want you to see the letter Mr Hunt gave me with my present.'

Doris sat silently reading the note. When she looked up, she said, 'What are you going to tell him?'

'I don't know. You see, I do like him, he's been very kind to me.'

'I know, but kindness alone won't make for a happy marriage.'

'At least he's more reliable than a young bloke who strings you along until you find out he's already married.'

'Sue, you mustn't feel bitter about that.'

Sue ran her hand over her face. 'I will always be bitter.'

Doris stood up. 'What can I say? Whatever you do, we will stand by you. You know that, don't you?'

'I know, and whatever the outcome I shall always be grateful to you and Dad.'

'We don't want your gratitude, just your happiness. Don't rush into anything, will you?'

Sue shook her head. 'At least he's given me time to think about it, and he knows all about me.'

'What d'you mean?'

'I told him everything. I was having a bad day and wanted a shoulder to cry on.'

'And he was there?'

Sue nodded.

'When was this?'

'A few weeks ago. I do like him, Mum.'

'Liking isn't enough.'

'I know. He was very kind when I was in hospital; he even came to see me.'

'He did? I must say, all that time he was very concerned. But is that enough?'

'I don't know.'

'We'll talk about this later. Now come down and wash your face and have some breakfast.'

'Mum, will you tell Dad?'

'When I think the time is right I will. But for now I don't want to spoil anyone's Christmas.'

'Will it spoil it, him knowing?'

'I don't know. I think he'll be upset and I'm not prepared to risk it, not today.'

'But he knows about the baby?'

'Yes, but your gran don't, so we'll leave it at that for now.'

Sue gave her mother a slight smile. 'Thanks, Mum.'

Doris smiled back. 'By the way, that's a lovely necklace.'

'Yes, it is.' Sue let the chain slip through her fingers. 'He's a very thoughtful man.'

'You'd better bring it down and show your dad and gran.'

'Oh, you're down at last,' said Charlie when Doris opened the kitchen door. 'What's going on? Your mother said Sue was upset over something.'

'She's all right now.'

'What was it?'

'I'll tell you later.'

He smiled. 'Well, merry Christmas, love.' He leant forward and kissed her cheek.

'Thanks, and a merry Christmas to you.'

'Right, I've only done a little bit of eggs and bacon this morning as we'll be having a big dinner later on. I've put the bird in the oven while you've been upstairs.' Gran raised her eyes to the ceiling and said softly, 'She all right?'

'She is now.'

37

Fred gave a sigh of relief as he closed his own front door. Christmas was over and tomorrow morning things would be back to normal. But would they? He desperately wanted to see tomorrow's papers. If that singer was dead, then it would be splashed all over the front page. As much as he'd wanted him duffed up, Fred hadn't wanted him killed. He was sure Bert had had a hand in it; who knows, he might tell him the truth one day. All over Christmas it had been on Fred's mind, that and Susan's answer.

This morning after breakfast he'd managed to get his mother on her own and tactfully brought the subject round to Susan.

'What d'you mean, you're very fond of her? She's half your age.'

'No, Mother, I'm only fourteen years older than her.'

'That's a lifetime.'

'Thanks.'

'So, have you asked her to marry you?'

'In a way. I gave her a note with her Christmas present and asked her to think about it.'

'A note. I never thought of you as lily-livered. Your father wouldn't have done such a thing.'

'Susan is different. She's had a very traumatic time.'

'It's not just out of pity that you're doing this, is it?'

'You don't understand, do you? I love her.'

His mother gave him one of her looks. 'Are you sure there's not a bit of guilt mixed in with this love?'

'No.'

'After all, it was your car.'

That was when he got angry and decided to leave. He'd done his duty and spent Christmas with her, and had told her of his intentions; now he was happy to be back home waiting to see what tomorrow would bring.

★ ★ ★

When the paperboy pushed the newspaper through the letterbox, Fred raced down the stairs. He glanced quickly at the front page; nothing about a murder. Walking into the office, he looked out of the window and saw Susan and Ron turn into the street. What would her answer be?

Sue had her head down against the sharp wind and the rain that was stinging her face. She hadn't really wanted to come in to work this morning, even though Christmas had been a very flat affair after the scene with her gran. Most of the time her thoughts had been on her boss. Even when she and Jane were alone and she had told her friend about his proposal, she couldn't get worked up about it. All the time she had been walking to the office she had been going over the conversation she'd had with Jane. Sue had told her she was worried Fred wanted to marry her out of pity.

'Don't talk daft,' had been Jane's reaction to that statement. 'I've seen the way he looks at you and I reckon he's been in love with you for a long time. Do you like him?'

'Yes, I do. But marry him? That's a big step. Besides, me mind's all over the place.'

'If you ask me, he's much better than Cy. He really cares about you, Sue.'

'I know, and I could love him, but not in the same silly way I felt about Cy. This would be a steadier sort of love.'

'So when you get married will you be having a white wedding with bridesmaids?'

Sue laughed at that. 'How could I get married in white?'

'So I'm gonner be done out of being a bridesmaid, then?'

'Looks like it.'

'What about your mum and dad, what will they say?'

'After I told Mum all about Cy, and about Fred's proposal, she more or less said she approved, and I'm sure she'll talk Dad round. But I know Fred'll do the right thing and ask them properly.'

'So you have made up your mind?'

Sue had nodded. 'I think so.'

Jane had thrown her arms round her friend. 'You know I wish you every happiness, don't you? After all, you deserve it.'

'Thanks.'

★ ★ ★

When they arrived at the office, Ron pushed open the door. 'Good morning, Mr Hunt.'

'Good morning, Ron, Susan. Did you both have a nice Christmas?'

'Yes thanks,' said Ron enthusiastically. He had managed to keep what had happened on Christmas Eve at the back of his mind. In fact he wasn't even sure that it *had* happened; it was just like one of his bad dreams.

Sue only mumbled her reply. When she saw Fred she knew what she wanted, but she didn't want to reveal her feelings, not now, not here.

'That's good. Now, Ron, go round to Harry and see if he's got anything for you to do today.'

'All right.' Ron turned and lumbered away.

Sue took her hat and coat off. 'Would you like me to make a cup of tea before we start?'

'I think that would be a very good idea.' Fred picked up the newspaper. 'I see the King and Mrs Simpson could be going to France to live.'

'Are they? I haven't seen any papers,' Sue said from the kitchen cupboard.

Fred turned a page. 'Oh my God.'

'What is it?' Sue put two cups of tea on the desk.

It was at that moment that Ron walked back into the office.

'It says here that a singer, Cyril Taylor, who was appearing with the Jeff Owen Band at the town hall was attacked on Christmas Eve. It seems he told the police he didn't know the two people who did it, and they are asking for information from anyone who saw anything suspicious. I wonder who did it?'

Ron stood and looked at Fred. But Fred's thoughts were on Bert. He knew then that if Bert had been involved he was off the hook, as the singer hadn't recognised his assailants. He went on, 'He is in hospital and his face has been slashed. It says that 'Girls are hanging round the hospital waiting for news of this popular singer.' ' He looked up at Susan to see how she was reacting to this news.

Ron quickly turned and left the office.

'What did Ron want?' asked Fred.

'I don't know.'

Fred tapped the paper. 'Is this bloke your singer?'

'He's not mine. Was that his real name? Cyril?' Sue let a slight smile lift her face.

'Seems like it.'

'I wonder who could have done something like that?'

'Didn't you tell me he was married?'

Sue nodded.

'He might have upset a few husbands.'

'Yes, I suppose so.'

Fred was pleased that there was no reaction. 'Aren't you a bit upset?'

'In a way. But he will be able to pick himself up again and carry on with his career and life.'

'How do you know?'

'His sort always does.'

'And you couldn't?'

'No. Besides, if he has a scar, that will be considered manly.'

Fred walked over to her desk. 'Susan, I think

you're beautiful and I hope my letter didn't offend you.'

She looked away as she felt her heartbeat quicken. 'No. I'm very flattered that you feel that way towards me.'

He smiled. 'Can you give me your answer?'

'Not at the moment.' She wanted to discuss her feelings with him first. It wasn't as though this was a blind mad passion; it was more of a gentle awareness.

'Well I won't hurry you, but Susan, I am very fond of you.' He was wary of saying how much he loved her, in case it frightened her away. 'And I will make you very, very happy.'

'Thank you. I believe you. Now, what do you want me to do today?'

'We could take the decorations down for a start.'

'That's a good idea.'

★   ★   ★

The atmosphere was very tense. Every time Sue looked up, it seemed Fred was smiling at her. She wanted him to hold her; she wanted him to be more than just fond of her. She knew now that she wanted him to love her and knew she had to make the first move, but this was the office.

'Mr Hunt.'

'Please call me Fred.'

She blushed. 'Fred. Would you like to take me for a drive tonight?'

Fred felt his heart soar. 'If you want.' He had

to keep calm even though he wanted to race round the desk and hold her. He couldn't believe that he, tough businessman Fred Hunt, was so besotted over a girl years younger than him, but Susan was different. Not only was she beautiful in his eyes, but she was also intelligent and kind and he truly loved her. 'Did you want to go anywhere in particular?'

'No, just somewhere we won't be disturbed so that we can sit and talk.'

Fred grinned. Was this going to be the night when his future would be settled?

Sue looked across and smiled at him. She knew she could love him. He was everything she'd ever wanted in a man.

★   ★   ★

Ron was pacing up and down outside. He was thinking about what Mr Hunt had been reading out of the paper. That bloke was attacked by two people; was he one of them? Would the police come and take him away? He didn't notice that the rain was soaking him right through. What if someone recognised him? Would the police come after him? Should he go and tell his mum so that she could pray for him? He shook his head. She would be very angry with him. He could hear the voices calling him and making his head hurt. He couldn't think straight. Should he tell Mr Hunt? His boss was very understanding and Ron liked him. What about his little Sue? She would help him. 'Go away,' he shouted, and banged his head with his hands. 'Leave me alone.'

'Who's Ron shouting at?' asked Sue, going to the window. 'I can't see anyone else out there. He'll be soaked through, the silly devil.'

'I'll go and see what's what.'

Fred had to shout above the noise of the rain pounding on the roofs of the cars. 'Ron! Ron! You all right?'

'No. Go away. Me head. Me demons.'

Fred looked at this big man sitting on the ground crying like a baby. He was hatless and his hair was stuck to his head. Fred hurried over to him. 'What's wrong? You fallen over?'

'No, it's in me head. Me head.'

'Let's get you inside. You're soaked.' With a great deal of difficulty Fred managed to get Ron to his feet and help him into the office.

Sue was standing holding the door open. 'What's happened?' she asked as Fred staggered in with Ron leaning heavily on his shoulder.

'Quick, get a chair. Something to do with his head.' Fred sat him down.

'He looks terrible. What could have upset him?' asked Sue.

'I don't know. I'll go up and get a blanket.' Fred hurried from the room.

'Let me help you get that coat off,' said Sue, pulling Ron's arms through the sleeves.

Fred returned almost at once and put a blanket round Ron's shoulders.

Ron's eyes had glazed over. 'Don't hit me.' He held his head.

'I won't hit you,' said Fred.

'I didn't mean to hurt him.'

'Hurt who?' asked Sue.

329

'That singer.'

'What singer?' asked Fred and Sue together.

'Susan, get Ron a cup of tea. Then he'd better tell us what this is all about.'

Sue quickly brought in the tea and sat and listened to what Ron was telling them. She stared at him. She couldn't believe he would even think of doing something like that for her.

Fred also sat and listened, and his thoughts went to Cyril Taylor. How could one bloke bring so much misery and heartache?

When Ron had finished his story he seemed a little calmer. 'What shall I do, Mr Hunt?' he asked.

'Don't you see, Ron, you only fell over him. He was already injured.'

'But I kicked him.'

'You didn't mean it.'

Ron went to speak, but Fred put his finger to his lips. He knew he had to treat him like a child. 'No, Ron. He was lying on the ground and you fell over him.'

'Did I?'

'Yes. Now let me take you home so you can get out of those wet things.'

Ron stood up and grinned at Sue. She smiled back.

'I only fell over him, little Sue.'

'Yes, I know.'

★   ★   ★

As Fred was driving Ron home, he knew he had to tell him of his intentions. 'Ron, you don't have to worry about Susan any more.'

'Why? You ain't putting me away, are you?'

'No. You see, I'm going to be looking after her for the rest of her life.'

Ron turned to face him. 'What d'you mean?'

Fred gripped the steering wheel. Was this the right time to tell him? After all, he was still traumatised. 'I'm gonner marry her.'

38

Ron laughed. 'You gonner marry my little Sue?'

'Yes, Ron.'

'You can't.'

'Why not?'

''Cos *I* am.'

'Ron, now can you honestly offer her a home and security like I can?' Out of the corner of his eye Fred could see Ron shaking his head.

'But I love her.'

'We all love her and we all want to make her happy. But could you make her *really* happy?'

Ron didn't answer. He was silent for the rest of the journey, and even after Fred stopped the car he still just sat there.

'Come on, lad, you're home.' Fred went round the car and opened the door.

Ron looked up at him with tears running down his fat podgy face. 'I shouldn't have fallen over that bloke, should I?'

'You couldn't help it. Don't worry about it. Come on, let's get you inside. I'm getting soaked standing here.'

'But I did it for my little Sue.'

'You didn't do anything, Ron.' Fred had to convince him. He knew he meant well; besides, he wasn't a bad bloke and he didn't want him put away.

As Ron got out of the car, Mrs Brent opened the front door.

'What is it? What's wrong with my boy?'

'Nothing, Mrs Brent. He's got a bit wet and he was . . . '

'Quick, come on in.'

Inside the passage Fred banged the water from his trilby while Ron stood like a naughty boy, the rain that was still running down his face mixed with his tears.

'Now what's upset you?' said his mother, as if she was speaking to a young child.

'It's my little Sue, Mum. She's gonner marry *him*,' he blurted, pointing at Fred. Then he threw his arms round his mother, dwarfing her in his big arms.

Standing on tiptoes and leaning to one side, Mrs Brent smiled at Fred. 'Congratulations.'

'I haven't asked her parents yet.'

'I know they'll be pleased. Now, Ron, take a hold of yourself.' She pushed him away.

'Mrs Brent.' Fred turn his trilby round and round in his hands. 'There's something else.'

'Oh. What's he done?'

Fred looked at Ron, who had his head down.

'Ron, go up and change your clothes.'

Silently he mounted the stairs.

'Come into the kitchen, Mr Hunt.'

In the warm, cosy kitchen, Mrs Brent waved at a chair. 'Please sit down. You know I'll always be grateful to you for taking on my boy. He has been so different since you let him work for you. I pray every day for you.'

Fred was embarrassed. 'Thank you.'

'So what's he done?'

'It's more what he *thinks* he's done.' Fred was

trying hard to think of what to say. He didn't want Ron to get into trouble. He was worried that he would tell his mother the wrong thing. Although he knew Ron was a little simple, he didn't really think he had been intentionally violent. Fred cleared his throat. 'Susan and I were discussing an incident I'd read in this morning's paper, and Ron overheard us. You see, a singer who was appearing at the town hall was beaten up on Christmas Eve.'

Mrs Brent gasped and put her hand to her mouth. 'He didn't . . . '

'No, but Ron did fall over the man in the alleyway, and now he thinks it was him that hurt him.'

'What was he doing there anyway? He was with me till . . . ' Mrs Brent stopped. 'He could have done it,' she said slowly. 'He did leave church a bit early and he did have blood on his hands when he got home.'

'He might have touched him, tried to help him up. The paper said the singer mentioned two men.'

'But why does he think it was his fault this man was injured? And why would he go to the town hall at that time of night?'

'It seems he knew the singer would be there, and I think that in his own way he thought this bloke had hurt Susan.'

'But why would he think that?'

'He must have overheard something and got the wrong end of the stick.' Fred was trying hard not to say too much. 'Anyway, please try to convince him that he did nothing wrong.'

'I will. And thank you, Mr Hunt.'

'I'll see him tomorrow.'

'Mr Hunt, you are a good man and I know you will make Sue a good husband.'

'Thank you.'

At the front door Mrs Brent took his arm. 'I wish you a very happy new year.'

'And the same to you.'

As Fred drove back to the office he felt almost light-headed. He smiled broadly. Whatever happened in 1937, this was going to be his best year ever when he made Susan Reed his wife.

We do hope that you have enjoyed reading this large print book.

Did you know that all of our titles are available for purchase?

We publish a wide range of high quality large print books including:
Romances, Mysteries, Classics
General Fiction
Non Fiction and Westerns

Special interest titles available in large print are:
The Little Oxford Dictionary
Music Book
Song Book
Hymn Book
Service Book

Also available from us courtesy of Oxford University Press:
Young Readers' Dictionary
(large print edition)
Young Readers' Thesaurus
(large print edition)

For further information or a free brochure, please contact us at:
Ulverscroft Large Print Books Ltd.,
The Green, Bradgate Road, Anstey,
Leicester, LE7 7FU, England.
Tel: (00 44) 0116 236 4325
Fax: (00 44) 0116 234 0205